Raincoats &

Wedding Dresses

Caroline Johnston

To Carol
love from
Caroline
x

IC⁴

IC⁴ Publishing

For more information about Caroline Johnston, please access the author's website at: www.carolinejohnston.co.uk

Cover design: Tanya Rochat

Published by IC⁴ Publishing

Titles by Caroline Johnston

Contemporary Christian Fiction

Raincoats & Sunglasses

Snowboots & Sunglasses

Raincoats & Wedding Dresses

Young Adult Christian Fiction

What If?

Why Not?

Dedication

To Innes, Calum, Cameron and Cara

x

PAUL

I shook my head. "No, Mum! You cannot wear a raincoat over your wedding dress! I know Glasgow weather demands such accessories. But with a wedding dress?"

Mum laughed as she slipped on the utilitarian clothing. "Look out the window, Paul! It's wet and misty and I am not letting that Scottish smirr anywhere near this dress. I'm only wearing my raincoat until I get into the hotel. By the time Alex sees me, I'll have discarded it, and my dress will be pristine and free of any damp patches."

My sister, Lauren, smirked as she put her raincoat on over her bridesmaid dress. I couldn't believe I was surrounded by raincoats again! Admittedly, they were protecting the dresses – but still!

I turned round and peered out the window, looking for the wedding car that would take us to the hotel for Mum's wedding. Despite the raincoat frustration, I was thrilled about today's celebration. It was clear from the first time I saw Alex and Mum together that they were in love. It was the little things: the way they looked at each other; they laughed at each other's stories; and whenever they had people over to their house, they worked as a team.

After everything Mum had been through with Dad, I was surprised, and impressed, that she was getting married again. I had never been a fan of marriage. Between Dad walking out on us and my old dating lifestyle, it had never been something I aspired to. Although, I had never seen the attraction of long-term relationships either, and look at me now. For the first time ever, I was dating someone for longer than a month. I used to think long-term was old and boring, but being with Kirsty proved that assumption wrong. Every minute I spend with her is special and when we're not together, a part of me is missing. When we started dating, I was scared the novelty would wear off, but ten months in and I keep falling more and more in love with her. If I had been wrong about long-term relationships, maybe I was wrong about marriage too…

My thoughts were interrupted by the arrival of the Daimler wedding taxi. Lauren and Mum checked their reflections in the mirror one last time, and then we were on our way.

In the car, Mum patted our hands. "I'm so proud of the two of you." She smiled and tried to keep her emotions in check.

Lauren kissed Mum on the cheek. "Well, we are proud of you, too. You and Alex make a wonderful couple."

I sighed at the sound of their sniffs. "Don't you two start crying."

"There's nothing wrong with a few tears," said Mum.

"True. But if you cry, you'll start fussing about your makeup."

Lauren swiped at my arm. "Poor Kirsty. Imagine having to put up with you!" She winked and returned her attention to Mum. For the remainder of the brief journey, Mum updated us on the wedding gifts they had received over the last few days. I didn't get her enthusiasm for the fancy dinner set, but it was nice to know she was getting something that meant a lot to her. I looked out the window. It was a dull, damp, late December day. Even though Christmas was over, Christmas lights still spread their joy, brightening the darkest of days.

The drizzle turned to heavy rain as the taxi pulled up to the hotel. Armed with black golfing umbrellas, the driver and I did our best to protect Mum and Lauren from the freezing rain. Once inside, the boring raincoats were discarded and left at reception, and the bride and bridesmaid smoothed down their dresses. Mum took my arm and with Lauren behind us, we made our way to the function suite where the wedding would take place.

On either side of the makeshift aisle, rows of chairs seated the guests, each chair decorated with a big red bow. We walked down the aisle to the tune of the Bridal Chorus, Mum's gaze fixed on Alex. I smiled at the way they looked at each other, communicating so much without words. As soon as we reached the front, I kissed her on the cheek and sat next to Kirsty. Kirsty squeezed my hand, her eyes sparkling with excitement. "You look very dashing in a kilt," she whispered.

I leaned over and kissed her. "And you look stunning." I tried to concentrate on what Ben, our pastor, was saying, but Kirsty held my attention. She was wearing the new perfume I'd bought her for Christmas. The scent played havoc with my senses. And she looked gorgeous in her maroon dress, perfect for a Christmas wedding. Glancing down, I smiled at the height of her silver heels. With those heels, we'd be the same height. I shook my head. It was too easy to get distracted by Kirsty. Reluctantly, I forced my attention back to the service.

Mum and Alex don't attend church and hadn't wanted a church wedding but were happy at my suggestion of getting Ben to conduct the service. I missed the first thing Ben said. But it must have been funny, because a wave of laughter spread across the room. "We'll be keeping this section short," he continued. "However, I wanted to share one verse from the Bible before Susan and Alex exchange their vows." He picked up his tablet and clicked on the screen. "In the book of Romans, in the New Testament, we read we should *be joyful in hope, patient in affliction, faithful in prayer.*' I know you're probably wondering why I'm sharing this verse rather than one of the more traditional wedding verses. But this verse speaks so much about Jesus' constant presence with us and it also makes me think of qualities that make for a good marriage – joy, hope, patience, faithfulness. And of course, we add love to that mix, too." He looked at my mum, then at Alex, and smiled. "It's an absolute privilege to be standing here with these two people today. To see the joy in their eyes. This pair know what they're getting into and they are radiating joy and hope."

Kirsty smiled and leaned her head on my shoulder. Once again, my attention wandered from Ben to Kirsty. I looked down at our interlocked fingers and ran my thumb over the back of her hand. When I first met Kirsty, I was instantly attracted to her - tall, slim and beautiful. She is stunning. Everyone can see that. Well, everyone except Kirsty. But as we became friends and then more, I witnessed the depths beyond her beauty. She is kind and caring. She lives life passionately, which brings positives and negatives, but never blandness. But the most amazing thing is that I love this woman. I'm not sure I've ever loved anyone before.

As Ben began leading Mum and Alex through their vows, my thoughts drifted back to the Bible verse he shared and its words of hope and promise. Words that affirmed marriage. Patience and faithfulness spoke of the work that it took to protect a marriage. But joy and hope? The words drew me in and made me excited about what my future could hold.

When Ben announced them husband and wife, Alex took Mum in his arms and kissed her. We all cheered, and then it was time to sign the register, after which, the happy couple walked through to the reception room, where trays of drinks were laid out for the guests. Mum had intended to keep the wedding to close family and friends, but the two of them kept adding more people to their guest list, eager to share their happiness with as many people as possible. I looked around the room. There were familiar faces: aunts, uncles, cousins, Mum's friends and colleagues and many unknowns, I assume, from

Alex's side. I was grateful that the increased numbers meant Mum had also invited my flatmate, Matt, and his girlfriend, Kirsty's best friend, Jo.

"Your mum looks so happy," commented Jo, smiling as she watched my mum walking around the room hand-in-hand with Alex chatting with people.

"Yes." I smiled as I looked over at the happy couple. "And she deserves it. It's good to know she's got someone looking after her." As I continued watching Mum and Alex, I again questioned my aversion to marriage. After all, it wasn't marriage that had let Mum down, it was Dad. And Dad had let me and Lauren down, too. It was time to stop blaming marriage.

Which meant it was time to admit the real reason. I had used Dad as an excuse to live a lifestyle that was in contrast to marriage. Granted, Dad was part of the reason. But it was too easy to create a narrative that excused my lifestyle, blaming Dad instead of taking responsibility for my own actions.

Over the last two years, God had been showing me again and again that I could change and that my past didn't define what was ahead of me. Did I believe that? If I did, then it was time to move forward. My thoughts went back to Ben's words. What was it? *'Be joyful in hope, patient in affliction, faithful in prayer.'* I wanted that for my life. I wanted that for my life with Kirsty.

With the formalities over, Mum and Alex morphed into the life and soul of the party. The speeches were hilarious. Rather than sticking with tradition, they tag teamed, taking it in turn to thank their amazing children, then speaking of their joy at the day before coming out with a bunch of corny wedding jokes.

As soon as the tables were cleared from the meal, Mum and Alex were ready to dance. I laughed and cringed in equal measure as I watched them own the dance floor. Kirsty laughed beside me. "I can see where you get your outgoing nature."

"Let's join them," I said, taking her hand. I held Kirsty tightly in my arms, leading her in exaggerated dance moves. By the time we got to the end of the second tune, there was barely space to move on the packed floor. I hadn't realised weddings could be so much fun.

The DJ's selection of tracks was dubious at times, but just as all looked lost, he would go with a traditional floor filler and have us all dancing and partying again. When he announced it was ABBA time, Lauren, Jo and Kirsty ran on to the dancefloor, leaving me and Matt at the table watching them, laughing as they occasionally turned round and made faces at us or did some crazy dance. It wasn't that long since being on a dance floor would have had Kirsty self-conscious and barely able to move. But tonight she was confident. Laughing with Jo and Lauren as they made up dances, not caring what anyone else thought of them. Matt leaned over and voiced my thoughts. "Kirsty's really come out of her shell these last few months." I nodded as I continued to watch her dance. "You're good for each other."

I smiled at my friend. "I couldn't agree more."

By the time the music changed from the party mix to a 1980s ballad, I almost sprinted onto the dance floor, desperate to dance with my beautiful girlfriend. As I held her close, I breathed in the floral scent of her perfume. My fingers caressed the curls of her hair. Closing my eyes, I savoured the moment. I could stay like this forever.

As we continued to sway in unison, a plan formed in my mind. In two days' time we would travel to Lochcala for New Year. Was that enough time to bring my plan to fruition? Lochcala for Hogmanay, it could prove the perfect setting for one of the most important questions of my life.

I closed my eyes and pulled Kirsty closer.

KIRSTY

Paul squeezed my hand. "Don't worry. It'll be fine. We're only there for a few days."

I sighed.

So many things in my life are good. Dating Paul – amazing! A new job in the council's PR department - who knew work could be so good? And a deepening faith. But there is one area in my life that still fills me with stress; my family. As we boarded the bus for Lochcala, the depression of a trip home descended. Paul shot me one of his killer smiles and snuck a quick kiss.

I tried to return the smile. But failed. "I'm sorry. It's just that every time I go home, I need to face the same issues with my family."

"It will be different this time." I loved Paul's optimism. If only I could share it. As the bus pulled out of Buchanan Street bus station, I looked out the window. The grey, damp streets of Glasgow reflected my mood perfectly.

But it wasn't fair to Paul to cast my gloom over him, too. My mind frantically searched for something positive to talk about. "Your mum's wedding was beautiful," I began. "She always looks stunning. Her dress was perfect for her, the way it fitted her slim figure, the cowl neckline. She looked so beautiful."

Paul laughed. "It was a great day, but don't start talking wedding dresses with me. That's a conversation to have with Jo or Lauren." He pulled me in for a hug. "But I do love how much you and Mum get on."

However, my attempt at coming up with something positive backfired, as it made me think about how different Paul's mum is compared to mine. My mum is a few years older, but you would think there was a generation between them. Paul's mum is slim, goes to the gym, has a trendy hairstyle, courtesy of her talented son. She wears the perfect amount of makeup and has a great sense of humour. Whereas, my mum thinks dressing up in some floral dress she bought in the sales ten years ago is the height of sophistication. I'm still getting to know Paul's mum, but already I know I can talk to her about anything and have an actual conversation rather than being made to feel guilty or irrelevant.

I grimaced at Paul. "I'm sorry it doesn't work that way with you and my family." When we visited in the summer, my family had been less than welcoming to him, except for my brother, Craig. James and Andrew had made snide comments about hairdressers. Well, James made the comments, Andrew just laughed. Mum sat in her chair in the corner and said very little, and Dad worked most of the time. I couldn't believe Paul was willing to put himself through it all again.

"Thankfully, Craig is on our side."

I laughed, not that our conversation was even funny. "Yes, already you've sussed out my family. Craig is the one consistent point of thankfulness. And I'm so jealous that you get to escape to his flat while I'm stuck with the rest of them." Working on one of the local fish farms, it made sense for Craig to remain in Lochcala, but at least he had escaped the family home and had bought a wee flat. He was still close to Mum and Dad's house. Lochcala isn't big enough to offer much distance, but he had his own space and could get on with his life without constant supervision and comment. My brother, James, had moved out to live with his girlfriend last year, but that relationship hadn't been able to survive the two of them living together and he was back at Mum and Dad's. And, as for Andrew, he had shown no inclination of moving out, happy to put up with cramped conditions for minimum loss to his salary. Which made this trip even more difficult. The one family member I could rely on was no longer in the family home. My mood wavered. It would be easy to get depressed again.

"What do you want to do while we're there?" I asked Paul. I needed something to look forward to. "Hopefully, Craig will have something lined up for Hogmanay. Then there's dinner with the family on the first, then our escape back to Glasgow on the second."

"Actually, Hogmanay is taken care of. I've been exchanging ideas with Craig."

I glanced over at him. There was a definite glint in his eye at the mention of Hogmanay. What were he and Craig up to?

The bus pulled into Lochcala mid-afternoon. Dusk was already settling around the village, the shop lights reflecting on the still harbour water. It was a beautiful setting, but one I drew little comfort from.

"Mum, we're here," I shouted, as I opened the back door and entered the dark kitchen. With barely an acknowledgement, she got up and put the kettle on the Aga. Heat spread up my face. She was being so rude to Paul. There was no, 'how are you' or 'make yourself comfortable'.

"How was your Christmas?" I asked as we sat down to our stewed tea and biscuits.

"It was fine."

I glanced over at Paul. He smiled his encouragement. "Where's everyone else?" I asked.

"They're all at work. I suppose they'll be home at their usual time."

I gave up and sat back in silence. Ever since I'd finished college, Mum had been telling me to find a boyfriend and get married. And here I am with the perfect boyfriend and she can't even be civil to him. What is her problem? I was tempted to storm out and never come back, but that wouldn't solve anything. *'God, help me,'* I prayed.

The silence was disturbed by Craig's arrival. "Hey, you guys," he greeted as he came over to hug us. "So good to see you both. Hi, Mum." Mum gave the same treatment to Craig as she'd given us.

"Why don't I take you round to my place and let you get settled in, Paul? Do you two want to have dinner at mine tonight?"

"Great idea," I replied and jumped up. "We'll see you later, Mum." We threw on our coats and rushed out into the damp, grey afternoon.

I hugged Craig as we walked away from the house. "Thanks for rescuing us." Although we only got a few feet before we bumped into James.

"You made it then?" His question was more of a sneer than a greeting. He glared at Paul.

I felt my face flush red. I wasn't sure if it was due to embarrassment or anger. We'd only been in Lochcala for an hour and already I wanted to leave, to get away from my family and their rude behaviour. It was one thing to have their nonsense directed at me, but they would not be rude to Paul.

I pushed past James. "Let's just get to your flat, Craig." As we walked away from James, I took some deep breaths, determined to calm myself down.

"Sorry about that," said Craig. "Since he moved back to Mum and Dad's, he's been even more intolerable."

"Oh great. That's all we need." I glanced at Paul. "I'm sorry."

"Will you two stop apologising for your family? It's not your fault." He put his arm round my shoulders and pulled me in close. "I'm not here to see your family. I'm here because I'm with you."

Craig chuckled beside us. "Okay, you two. I don't need to hear the gooey chat."

A few minutes later, we entered Craig's flat. It was a first floor tenement flat. The living room had a beautiful bay window overlooking the street. The kitchen was a small, galley style room. Next to the kitchen was the bathroom. It had the same long, narrow measurements. His bedroom looked out to the communal gardens at the rear, not that we could see anything as darkness had descended. It was small but functional, much like my flat in Glasgow, except that Jennifer had revitalised mine with her amazing design know-how and brought it to life with colour and texture. Craig's flat was a bachelor's pad. Lacking in colour and finishing touches. The magnolia walls needed a coat of paint and pictures. And there was an underlying odour of fish. I guess that's what happens when you work on a fish farm. Although, the best thing about his new flat was the freedom it gave him from the rest of the family.

I threw myself down on the couch and mock-screamed. "How do you deal with them, Craig?"

"I keep under the radar and ignore them as much as possible. And, with all the drama with James and Andrew, it's not that hard to stay invisible." I looked over at him and raised my eyebrows. He laughed at my expression. "And when all that fails, I hide in my flat and play on my Xbox."

Paul rubbed his hands together. "Now you're talking! Let's get a game going."

"No chance," I said, grabbing the controller before Paul could get it. "You guys will be playing this the whole time I'm stuck in the no-fun zone. Come on, Craig, let's see what you've got."

Craig picked up the other controller and opened up a game of football.

I put my hand on my hip and glared at him. "Football, Craig? Really?"

"Hey, you never said what you wanted to play, and this is my favourite game."

"Whatever. I'll still beat you." As soon as Craig started the game, I was fully engaged in the match playing out on his large TV screen. He was right. Gaming distracted me from the trauma of being around the rest of the family. I even scored a couple of goals.

As the game finished, Craig sat his controller down. "When did you get so good at gaming?"

I put my arm round Paul. "Hanging out with this guy and his flat mate."

Craig shook Paul's hand. "Well done, mate. I never imagined this one would be able to score a goal."

"Hey!" I slapped Craig's arm with the back of my hand. "I was always good. I was just lulling you into a false sense of security."

Craig laughed as he made his way through to the kitchen to cook up chicken nuggets and chips for dinner. For a guy in his mid-twenties, he acted like a teenager. After dinner, we went back to playing games and then watched a movie. As the credits rolled up the screen, I leant my head against the back of the couch. "Ugh! Why is our family so difficult? Can I just stay here with you guys?"

"You know you're always welcome here. But unfortunately, you're expected to stay at the homestead." Craig threw a cushion at me. "And besides, this is a guys' only flat for the next few days!"

"You're so mean," I laughed, as I threw the cushion back at him. But inside I was crying. With the slowest of movements, I wrapped myself in my coat, preparing for the walk home. There was only one place in Lochcala that I felt welcomed and I didn't want to leave it.

PAUL

I stretched and wiggled, trying to get rid of all the kinks and knots in my body from sleeping on Craig's very uncomfortable couch. But even though my body was complaining, my mind was alert. This is it! Today is the day I'm going to ask Kirsty to be my wife! I looked at my watch. Sixteen hours until midnight.

Craig padded through to the living room, his hair at odd angles and scratching his stomach. "Morning, mate. Sleep okay?" Before I could reply, he moved on through to the kitchen and I heard the sweet sounds of coffee filtering. While I waited for the coffee, I cleared up my bedding and dumped it in the corner of the room. A few more stretches before his return, and my body was feeling normal.

"What are your plans for today?" I asked him, as he brought through two mugs of coffee. Taking a deep inhale, I relaxed into the couch, all annoyance at last night's discomfort forgiven.

"I'm working for a few hours this morning. But I'll be back in plenty of time to set everything up for tonight. What about you?"

"It depends on Kirsty. I'm not sure if she has any plans."

A knock on the door interrupted our conversation, signalling Kirsty's arrival at the flat. She came straight over and kissed me good morning. "Ugh!" said Craig. "I don't want to see that. At least wait until I'm not in the room."

Kirsty laughed. "Go and get me a coffee, then you won't see the next one." Craig bolted from the living room as Kirsty proceeded to kiss me again, this time lingering for much longer. Only withdrawing at the sound of Craig closing the kitchen door and slapping his feet on the wooden floor of the hallway.

"Right. I'm going to work now. I'll be back early afternoon. Feel free to hide here." Craig disappeared to his room for a few minutes, then grabbed his jacket and left us alone.

Kirsty stood at the window and waved down to Craig. "What do you want to do today?" she asked, as she turned round and gave me her full attention.

"Why don't we go out for a walk and get some fresh air?"

"Good idea. It is dry for the moment, so let's take advantage of it. Then we can grab something nice for lunch and come back here."

We pulled our scarves higher as we exited Craig's flat, protecting ourselves from the chilly breeze blowing off the water. Kirsty shivered as she snuggled into my side. I wasn't complaining. We walked around the harbour, then took the narrow, clambering path to the castle ruin. It was our go-to place in Lochcala.

The ruin stood above the village, commanding a view of the harbour and the sprinkling of small islands and inlets beyond the harbour walls. The tourists loved the short walk to the castle in summer. For the rest of the year, it belonged to the locals. In the middle of winter, the exposed plateau wasn't very hospitable, and we snuggled further into our coats as the wind chill factor hit. Seeking shelter, we walked around the old ruin. After a couple of rounds of the castle, we settled on a fallen rock and looked down over the village. In Glasgow, there was always noise from people and traffic. But in Lochcala the loudest sound was from the boats bobbing about in the harbour or the occasional seagull. I pulled Kirsty in close beside me. "How did last night go?"

"It was okay. James ignored me. And Andrew is so busy between work and focussing on tonight's party, he barely noticed I was there. It's a lot less stressful without the constant teasing."

"Have they always been like that?"

"I guess. It's hard to look back and remember a time they weren't pranking me and teasing me. I didn't mind when I was younger, but as we got older, their remarks got more cutting and personal, mainly from James. And whenever their friends were around, they took even more delight in my misery and the laughter their jibes brought. Plus, as I got older, Mum got weirder in her comments about boyfriends, flicking between discouraging relationships and then telling me I should get married and settle down in Lochcala."

"So where do you prefer? Glasgow or Lochcala?"

"Sitting here, with you right now – Lochcala wins." She finished her sentence with a wink. "Lochcala has a lot going for it. It's so peaceful, and each season brings its own beauty. But I love Glasgow more. There's always something happening in Glasgow. It's alive with people, restaurants and entertainment. And whatever you want is always close. My life here was too small. I needed Glasgow. I needed everyone I met there."

I interrupted her words with a kiss. "And we needed you, too." She flashed a gleaming smile at me before letting out a big sigh. "Hopefully, one day I won't dread coming to Lochcala. It's so beautiful and yet I shy away from it because coming here means dealing with my family. Staying away is easier, but I guess at some point I need to deal with it." She gazed out over the harbour before suddenly turning round and looking at me. "Wow! People really do tell their hairdressers everything, don't they?"

"It's all part of the service." I put my arm around her shoulder and squeezed her to my side. There was so much I wanted to say on the subject, to point out how amazing she is, to refute the things her brothers and Mum say to her. But to win this battle, Kirsty needs to face it herself. She needs to identify the issues and how to resolve them. Only then will she be able to break the cords of her past.

All day I was convinced Kirsty had guessed what I was planning. Craig assured me she was clueless about our scheming, but I wasn't so sure. Every so often, she looked at me with a questioning glance.

By early evening, we were in Kirsty's family home. Hogmanay dinner passed without incident, with James and Andrew leaving as soon as they had scoffed down their servings of steak pie, mashed potatoes and turnip. They made no secret of how they were expecting their evening to end. Craig, Kirsty and myself washed the dishes and cleaned up the small kitchen, then left Mr and Mrs Price to the peace of their own home.

"Where will we go to see in the New Year?" asked Kirsty, as we walked away from the Price family home. "We could check out what's going on at the hotels and celebrate the New Year there."

"I already told you. We've got midnight sorted," said Craig. "I've got a couple of things I need to take care of just now, but I'll be back soon."

"What do you need to do at this time on Hogmanay?"

"Just a few things I promised to take care of for a friend. I'll be back before the Bells and then we'll head out."

As we entered Craig's flat, Kirsty wriggled out of her coat. "Do you know what he's up to?" I shrugged my shoulders. She sighed and went to the kitchen to make coffee.

We settled down to watch one of the Hogmanay shows. Throughout the programme, my eyes darted between the TV and Kirsty. In contrast, Kirsty made a show of not looking at me, keeping her gaze firmly fixed on the screen. She knew Craig and I were up to something and it was annoying her. I almost caved to the pressure and was about to tell her some of my plans when Craig returned. His wink in my direction didn't help the building tension.

Kirsty jumped up from the settee. "What is going on, you two?" She looked at me, then Craig, demanding a response. Craig took the lead. "Nothing for you to be concerned with. Like I said, I had to do something for a friend. It's done now so we can go out."

Kirsty checked her watch. "But it's only half an hour until the Bells. Will we still be able to get in to either of the hotels?"

"Of course we will. I have connections."

His smirk didn't help.

Despite her concerns, Kirsty grabbed her bag and made for the door. "Slow down there," said Craig. "The temperature has dropped. Make sure you're wrapped up."

"But we're only going a short distance," said Kirsty.

"True. But after the Bells, everyone will spill out from the hotel bars on to the street. You don't want to get cold."

Kirsty laughed but followed through on his suggestion and put on her coat and woolly accessories. I wrapped my arm around Kirsty and guided her towards the harbour. Instead of stopping at one of the hotels, Craig and I kept walking.

"Where are we going?" asked Kirsty, pausing by the second hotel.

"Why don't we go up to the castle ruin? It's a clear night. Don't you think it would be romantic to see in the New Year overlooking the village?" I said. "The ruin, the view… it makes this place special. When it comes to hotels, we've got nicer bars in Glasgow, but we don't have this." I waved my arms around at the pretty harbour front before pointing up to the castle.

"It's dark up there. Wouldn't you rather go with the safe, cosy hotel option?"

"Safe and cosy is boring. Let's have a castle adventure."

I'm not sure what persuaded her, but she leaned back into me. While Craig ran ahead of us, I led Kirsty up the single track to the castle, keeping our progress slow to let Craig get everything set up. As we neared the top of the path, I stopped and turned round to face her. "I've got a confession. Craig and I came up here earlier to surprise you with something."

"I knew the two of you were up to something!"

"I'm going to need you to trust me. Close your eyes and let me lead you the final few steps."

An uncertain smile played on her lips as she looked down and let me direct her steps. A slight shiver passed through her and her hands shook in mine. She shuffled behind me, making sure of each foot placement before taking the next. After a few metres of the rough terrain, we were at the top and walking over the damp grass. The silence of the area surrounded us, an occasional breeze brought the sound of laughter and music from the village.

We turned and walked towards the castle. "Almost there," I said. Craig waved over then disappeared round the side of the ruin, giving us privacy but ready to reappear when required. I couldn't have pulled this off without him.

Another few metres and we stopped. "Okay, you can look up."

Kirsty lifted her gaze and gasped. We were standing to the side of the castle, the village and harbour hidden from our view. In front of us, poles held up a canopy of fairy lights, twinkling against the darkness of the sky. Below the lights, picnic rugs were scattered on the ground. A hamper held the rugs in place as the wind played with the edges, threatening to blow them over. And to the side of the rugs was a fire pit, drawing us closer with its warm, dancing flames.

"Paul!" I barely heard her whisper. "This is beautiful."

"Let's see in the New Year on our own, enjoying these midnight views." I reached out my hand and tucked a strand of hair back under her hat. Gazing into her eyes, I took a step closer and pulled her into a kiss. While the cold air blew around us, my heart erupted in heat. Ten months of dating had not diminished my attraction for this amazing woman. I thanked God I could feel this way about one woman.

She hugged my arm as I led her over to the fire pit and blankets. Taking my phone from my pocket, I selected a playlist and set the phone just in front of us. Next, I opened the hamper and took out oat cakes and cheese and a bottle of champagne.

"Wow! I am impressed," she said, as she watched me prepare our midnight snack. Kirsty leaned her head on my shoulder as we enjoyed our snack and the setting.

"I've always loved coming up here," she said, taking a sip of her champagne.

"It is so special, isn't it?" She nodded as I checked my watch again. "Two minutes until midnight."

"Why have you been checking your watch all day?"

"Let me show you," I said, as I took her hands and guided her to her feet. In the flickering light of the fire, I brushed my lips against hers. Getting down on one knee, I took the ring from my pocket and took her left hand in mine. I looked up into eyes that sparkled as brightly as the fairy lights overhead. "Kirsty Price, from the moment I first saw you, you captivated me. The more I get to know you, the more I want to know. You are beautiful, kind, funny and amazing. This past year as your boyfriend has been the best year of my life. Will you marry me and be with me forever?"

Her gloved hands flew up to her face, tears filling her eyes. "YES! YES! YES!" she shouted. I stood up, removed her glove, and placed the ring on her trembling finger. The next kiss was no brief brushing of our lips. It was a kiss of depth and promise. As we pulled apart, she threw her arms around me and hugged me so tightly. "Thank you so much, Paul. I can't believe you would choose me, but I'm so very glad you did. I can't wait to spend a lifetime with you."

As we kissed, I was vaguely aware of the sound of fireworks in the distance announcing the New Year. And from the harbour, sounds of revelling drifted up to our isolated spot. Stepping back, I held her hands and looked down at the diamond sparkling on her finger. I was the happiest man on the planet.

KIRSTY

As we pulled up outside Scott and Jennifer's house, a profusion of white fairy lights welcomed us to their home. Inside, gold and red decorations radiated their winter colour, the faint pine scent from the Christmas tree still lingered in the air.

Jennifer had invited us all over for one last get together before the end of the holidays. Jo and Matt would be here as well as our friends, Lynn and Carol. I couldn't wait to see everyone and share our exciting news.

Hugs were exchanged, and coats and scarves were removed as we proceeded to the kitchen. Gathering round the breakfast bar, we chatted and selected our drinks. Since returning from Lochcala yesterday, I'd been keeping my left hand out of sight – either in my pocket or wrapped up in my gloves. Now it was time to flash my diamond. I waved my left hand over the counter as I reached for a glass. Carol was the first to notice. Her squeal attracted everyone's attention as she grabbed for my left hand. However, in the process, she knocked over a newly opened bottle of wine, spilling its contents over the counter. Apologising profusely to Jennifer, she was torn between dealing with the spilt wine and scrutinising my ring.

"Never mind the wine," laughed Jennifer. "Let's see this ring!"

Scott patted Paul on the back, then cleared up the wine. Jo was at my side in a flash, jumping up and down with squeals of delight. My friends all hugged me and then it was full attention to the ring. "Oh, it's so beautiful," said Jo. "We need to know everything. When did this happen? How did it happen?"

With drinks in hand, we made our way through to the family room. As I described the setting, there were plenty of 'oohs' and 'aahs' from my friends. Carol clasped her hands together. "That sounds so romantic."

"And we've got pictures." Paul mirrored his phone to the TV so everyone could see our engagement photos.

"My brother, Craig, helped set it all up and hid behind the castle until the ring was on my finger. Then he appeared and took these photographs." As we looked through the images, I couldn't stop grinning. Each photograph captured wonderful memories of the night and reminded me how much effort Paul, and Craig had put into creating the perfect setting. It had been a magical evening full of promise and love.

"It all looks so perfect," said Jennifer. "When did you choose the ring?"

"I had no idea any of this was going to happen. Paul picked the ring." As I spoke, I held out my left hand and gazed at my ring. A sparkling solitaire set on a platinum band with delicate rows of tiny diamonds running along the bridge underneath the solitaire. It was simple and intricate all at the same time. I couldn't have picked a more stunning, perfect ring.

"No way!" said Lynn. "I can't believe you picked such a fabulous ring."

Paul grinned. "I wish I could take all the credit, but I dragged Lauren out to help me."

"Well, whoever picked it – it's stunning. And now, with a wedding on the cards, that can only mean one thing," continued Lynn. "Hen weekend! We need a girls' weekend to celebrate the bride-to-be."

"Slow down, Lynn. We've only just got engaged. Honestly, you're as bad as my mum. The first thing she asked about was potential wedding dates."

"And how did your family react?" asked Jennifer.

I looked down at my hands and twirled my ring. "I suppose it went as expected. Craig is happy for us. Mum and Dad were their usual passive selves. Although they are insisting we have the wedding in Lochcala, which we're not overly thrilled about. But," I looked at Paul for reassurance. "On the positive side, they want to pay for the wedding."

Paul smiled. "Glasgow would be easier but I don't care where the wedding is. I'm just looking forward to being married."

Before we could say anything more about wedding locations, our conversation was interrupted by the arrival of our pizza. Jo pulled me into a hug as people wandered to the kitchen. "I am so happy for you. Paul is good for you. And you're good for him. You make a fabulous couple."

I returned Jo's hug, squeezing her as tightly as I could. "Thank you. And thank you for always being there for me." And I meant every word. Jo was a constant in my life. The first person to cheer me on and the one to pick me up when life got too much.

It was only when we returned to the family room I noticed Jennifer was missing. After a few moments, she returned, but rather than carrying a plate full of pizza, she only had a slice of toast. "Are you okay, Jennifer?" I asked.

She looked down at her sparse plate. "I'm okay. Just not feeling one hundred percent. My body is probably rebelling against all the excess food of the holidays." Jennifer's answer didn't reassure me. It wasn't just her lack of appetite that was out of character, she was quieter than usual and she looked tired. But before I could quiz her any further, Lynn took us back to her earlier question. "So, do we get a hen weekend?"

I laughed at her enthusiasm for a weekend away. "It would be nice but I guess first of all, we need to decide the date and location of the actual wedding." I started nibbling on another slice of pizza. "Anyway, I don't want all the conversation taken up by our news. What did everyone else get up to at Hogmanay?"

Lynn and Carol told us all about a party they were at. And Jo and Matt filled us in on their time with Jo's family on Princes Street in Edinburgh. "It was brilliant," said Jo. "The streets were packed and the fireworks over the castle were spectacular."

"And what about you, Jennifer?" asked Carol.

"We had a nice quiet evening here with Ben and Tara and the girls."

"Speaking of the girls, where are they?" asked Paul.

"They are with my mum and dad tonight for a cinema trip and a sleepover. The girls wanted to be here with all of you, but they were also desperate for time with my parents. We've been trying to arrange it for the past week, but tonight was the only night that worked. The holidays go past too quickly."

"Have you had any course work or studying to do over the holidays?" Jo asked. Jennifer shook her head. In the autumn, Jennifer had embarked on a college course in Interior Design.

"And are you still enjoying the course?" continued Jo.

"Loving it. I'm learning so much." Jennifer yawned as soon as she finished speaking.

The conversation flowed for another few hours. Meandering between plans for the year ahead, silly chat and further questions about our wedding. But every time I looked at Jennifer, she was yawning. Dark circles under her eyes confirmed she was tired. Hopefully, it was just end of holiday tiredness and nothing more serious. Taking Paul's hand, I stood up and looked round the group. "Thanks, Scott and Jennifer, for a lovely evening, but I think it's time for the rest of us to go home. We'll see you at church on Sunday."

As the six of us walked out to Jo and Lynn's cars, we decided we weren't ready to admit that the Christmas holidays were almost over and Matt suggested continuing the evening at his flat. When we arrived, Jo disappeared through to Matt's room, returning with a brown box tied in a pink bow. "I had a feeling it wouldn't be long until you guys got engaged. And so, in preparation, I got you a wee pressie."

Sitting down, I ripped into the box and pulled out a white binder with the title 'Kirsty's Wedding Organiser'. I hugged my friend. "No way! This is amazing!" I ran my hand over the embossed cover and lifted it up to sniff. "Don't you love the smell of new stationery?" Jo laughed as I flicked through the sections. There were pages to help organise the budget and guest lists. Scrap book style pages to paste pictures of dresses and accessories. And a ream of pages with more to-do lists. I hugged the binder and let out a high-pitched squeal. "How much fun are we going to have organising this wedding?"

I glanced over at Paul. "And even though we don't have anything booked yet, we have a few questions for you four. Jo, would you do me the honour of being my chief bridesmaid?" She squealed, jumped up, and was hugging me before I knew what was going on. "Yes! Yes! Yes!"

Glancing over her head at Lynn and Carol, I asked my second question. "And would you two please be my bridesmaids?" Following Jo's lead, the two of them jumped up and joined us in a group hug, adding their joy at being part of the wedding party.

Paul looked over at Matt. "Do you want to be my best man?"

Matt, in a dead-pan expression, replied, "Sure."

Jo and I glared at them. "Seriously?" Paul and Matt started laughing and Matt gave the more expected reply of, "I would be honoured, mate." They joined the group hug.

Jumping up and down, celebrating with my friends, it was easy to feel the warmth of love, joy and peace. The only edge to the night was my lingering worry about Jennifer.

JENNIFER

In my right hand, I held my positive test result. In my left hand I held my New Year to-do list. Both things blurred as my eyes filled with tears. In my right hand a life-changing result and in my left hand a to-do list that would no longer be achieved.

I tried to focus through the tears, all the things I had hoped to accomplish this year now dashed. Completing my college certificate? Hopefully. Progressing to my college diploma course? No way. Working on at least two interior design projects? Unlikely. Looking into family holiday options? Fresh tears.

For the last week, I had been feeling increasingly sick and tired. At first I'd put it down to Christmas overeating and the change of routine. But as the horrible sensations increased, I gave my symptoms further consideration. Of course, that entailed a few very scary thoughts until I finally realised my period was a couple of weeks late. This afternoon I'd rushed out to the local chemist to buy a test and as soon as we tucked the girls into bed I had locked myself in our ensuite to find out if I was pregnant.

I needed to tell Scott. But I didn't want to. Telling Scott would make it real. And how would he react? How could I tell him when I had no idea how I felt about it? And yet, how could I not tell him?

I walked slowly downstairs. Test stick in hand. When I saw Scott stretched out on the sofa, catching up on some football match, I paused. He looked so peaceful and content. Between family life, running his own accountancy firm, and volunteering at church, he didn't get much time to just kick back and relax. Was it fair to drop this news on him while he was enjoying a rare moment of calm? I was about to turn round and leave him in his blissful state of unknowing when he looked round to where I stood in the doorway. I guess the tears must have left their mark because he immediately switched off the TV and stood up.

"What's wrong?" The level of concern in his voice brought back the tears. Unable to speak, I handed him the positive pregnancy test. He stared at it, not saying anything about the family changing news I'd just given him.

He frowned as he looked up from the test. "I don't understand. Whose is this?"

I sniffed, attempting to stop the tears and regain my ability to take part in this conversation. "It's ours."

"What? I don't understand. How could this happen?" Scott paced the room, running his hand through his hair. "I never thought we would be looking at pregnancy tests again."

Turning away, I walked over to the window. I didn't know what to say. What did he expect of me? Why did he think I had any answers? I hugged my arms tightly against me, protecting myself from all the questions. A flash of anger rose against Scott. How dare he ask all these questions and not ask how I felt about it! But my anger quickly abated when I turned round and looked at him. He sat on the edge of the sofa, his head in his hands. Being annoyed with each other was pointless. We were thinking the same thing. How had this happened? Why now?

He lifted his head and looked at me. "Should you take another test to see if you get the same result? Could it be a false positive?"

Why hadn't I thought of that? Probably because I was so shocked at the result. "I guess that would be an idea. I'll do it now." Scott was right behind me as I ran upstairs. Grabbing the box, I ripped the test out of its packaging as I retreated to our ensuite.

We hovered over the test, waiting to see what lines would show up this time. Once again, I was staring at a positive result. Both tests said I was pregnant. We looked at each other, neither of us knowing what to say. The last time we had looked at one of these, we had been overjoyed. The previous pregnancies were all planned. But this time. At this stage. Of course, we would be ecstatic by the time we got to cuddle our baby, but right now, we were in shock.

Scott squeezed my hand as I fought back the tears. I didn't want to cry anymore. This was good news, wasn't it? We were silent for several minutes. Scott took my hand and led me downstairs, "Let's have a cuppa. Do you want to talk about it or leave conversation for another time?" I shrugged my shoulders.

I sat at the breakfast bar, while Scott made our drinks. I broke the silence, going into practical mode. "I'll phone the doctors this week. I wonder if the process will be different now. It's been seven years since we were last at this stage and my age might also affect things." Scott nodded, nothing else to add.

Staring at our mugs wasn't encouraging conversation. Neither of us knew how to voice our thoughts. Scott reached over and rubbed my shoulders. "Come on, let's watch a movie and leave our questions until tomorrow." I followed him to the living room where he selected a goofy movie. It lightened my mood but still a cloud hovered over me.

By the time the film finished and we went to bed I was more than ready to crawl under the duvet and hide from my strange mood and my questions. Scott snuggled into me and held me in his arms. But regardless of my exhaustion, I could not get to sleep. The questions wouldn't stop, a thousand thoughts fought for my attention. I tried to hold on to the elusive wisps of joy and excitement, but today the questions won. How had this happened? And how were things going to change? Would I have the energy and strength to complete my college course? Hopefully! But there would be no way I could continue to the next level. We live in a four-bedroom house, which means the girls all have their own rooms, but what would happen when the baby arrives? And what about our car? Thankfully, we have a seven-seater, but does it have enough room for six of us and all the baby paraphernalia?

And then there was the impact on the family dynamic? How would the age gap work? By the time the baby arrives, Chloe will be seven. Is this kid going to grow up with issues, always feeling like the odd one out or some afterthought? And what about Amy? Now that she's in high school, her reaction to our news could be anywhere on the drama scale.

Scott's gentle snoring let me know he had fallen asleep. I gave up trying and as quietly as I could, I slipped out of bed and went downstairs. With a mug of tea and snack in hand, I walked through to our family room and curled up on the big armchair, pulling a blanket over me as I settled down. Searching through the music app on my phone, I looked for inspiration. I stopped at one of Scott Nicol's songs, She's Fearless. If only I could be fearless right now. Putting the song on repeat, I leaned back on the couch, closed my eyes and focused on the words. I wanted to be fearless, but could I be?

Eventually, I paused the music and looked around the room. *'Why God?'* I let my frustration float out, hoping it would find an answer. Why had I started down this career path only for it to stall? I walked over to the bookcase, my hand drifted along spines of books that failed to catch my attention. Instead, my gaze stayed on the row of photo albums. I selected the girls' baby albums. The pictures reminded me of those happy new-baby days. The snuggly little people who were completely reliant on Scott and me for everything. They were days of exhaustion and trying to work out what babies needed, but there was joy in amongst it all too. Going back to the baby stage would be a challenge, but we could do it. I was relieved to feel a glimmer of joy, but doubts and questions still pushed for attention. What did this all mean in terms of my interior design dreams? The dream had gathered momentum over the last year. Enrolling in the college course had been my stake in the ground that I was serious about pursuing this career; that it was my future. But now what?

The next morning, we rushed into church just as the service started. We slipped in the back row and I tried to adjust my focus from the pregnancy to worship. As I sang along to the familiar choruses, peace surrounded me and settled my anxious thoughts.

"What are your hopes and dreams for the year ahead?" asked Tara, as she began her time of preaching. "This is the time of year when we set our goals and resolutions, or maybe we've all moved beyond those already." There was a murmur of laughter round the hall. "It's good to set goals and plans, but what do we do when those plans don't work out? Do we get upset? Do we blame other people? Do we blame ourselves?" I glanced over at Scott. He returned an awkward smile and squeezed my hand. "Let's read from the Gospel of Matthew, chapter twenty-two, verses thirty-four to forty." Tara opened her Bible and read. *"Hearing that Jesus had silenced the Sadducees, the Pharisees got together. One of them, an expert in the law, tested him with this question: 'Teacher, which is the greatest commandment in the Law?' Jesus replied: ''Love the Lord your God with all your heart and with all your soul and with all your mind.' This is the first and greatest commandment. And the second is like it: 'Love your neighbour as yourself.' All the Law and the Prophets hang on these two commandments. '"* Tara sat her Bible on the lectern and walked around the stage. "I love the way Jesus responded to the questions sent to trick him. The absolute truth in his answers is inspiring. When we follow the greatest commandment, our focus is not on what's going on with us but in loving Jesus with all our heart, mind and soul. It's okay to make plans. It's okay to try to determine your path through the coming weeks, months and year. But before we get too wrapped up in our own lives and our own plans, let's keeping loving Jesus as our main purpose."

'Love the Lord your God with all your heart, and with all your soul and with all your mind.' The words played around in my head, bringing comfort. Although they still had to fight against the noise of all the questions, but maybe they offered the anchor I desperately needed.

The words carried me until routine resumed. On Tuesday morning pregnancy exhaustion meant I was even worse at getting up and the girls were late for school. And then there was the increasing nausea that had me worried about my journeys to and from college. By the time I got to Wednesday night, I was tempted to opt out of house group, but I couldn't give up on things already. Although, I waited until the last minute to go and planned to leave as soon as our Bible study was completed. As tonight was the first small group meeting of the year, I knew there would be a lot of catch up chat before we could get started. By delaying my arrival, I was giving Kirsty time to tell Jane and Elsie, two students who joined our group last year, about her engagement. I entered Kirsty's flat to the sounds of talking and laughter. As I walked into the living room, Elsie was pleading with Kirsty. "Oh, come on, please?" I looked over at Jo. "Elsie's trying to persuade Kirsty to let her organise the engagement party." I sat down and poured myself a glass of water. When I looked up, Kirsty was looking at me with a frown on her face. Out of everyone, she was the one who noticed my lack of appetite last week. Fighting against the nausea and the tiredness, I smiled at my friend. Hopefully, it was enough to ease any concerns she had.

"Come on, Kirsty," said Lynn. "Let Elsie organise your party. You know it will be a great night."

"We'll do everything," pleaded Elsie. "Please, Kirsty. Let us throw you an engagement party."

Kirsty shrugged her shoulders. "It's not something we've thought about, but maybe?"

"Yes!" said Elsie, as she jumped up, grabbed her phone and walked through to the kitchen. Within seconds, we could hear her making enquiries with a bar in the centre of town. As an Event Management student, Elsie already had contacts with several bars in Glasgow.

With Elsie distracted with her calls, and the rest of the group chatting about parties, Kirsty came over and sat beside me. "Are you okay, Jennifer? You still don't seem your usual self."

I took a sip of water and smiled at my friend. "Thank you for asking and for looking out for me. But it's okay. I'm fine. Or at least I will be soon."

"Well, that isn't an answer that reassures me."

Elsie's return interrupted our conversation. "That's us all booked. Your engagement party will take place a week on Saturday."

"Is that enough time to let people know?" Kirsty asked.

"No one has plans for January. It'll be perfect."

Kirsty glanced at me and smiled. She jumped up and looked at Elsie. "Don't organise anything else. I need to phone Paul and check this all works for him, too."

With Kirsty back to the party conversation, she was distracted from her concerns over me. I was glad of the change of focus. I didn't want to lie to any of my friends, but nor was I ready to tell anyone my news yet. I hid myself further into the sofa as the girls discussed the party and their excitement about the wedding. Normally I would be in the middle of these conversations, but for tonight I was happy to keep to the outside, protecting my secret. Tara's preach on Sunday had wrapped me in a blanket of reassurance and peace, but since then the questions had come flooding back. How could I find my way back to the place of loving Jesus with all my heart, mind and soul?

KIRSTY

As I boarded the bus for Lochcala, the familiar feelings of dread descended. I tried to push aside the negative emotions. After all, I was going to plan my wedding! I had appointments set with the minister and the two local hotels to discuss dates. If only Paul was coming with me, but Saturdays are his busiest day in the salon.

Thankfully, the bus was quiet, which was the only positive thing about this journey. I settled down to watch my latest box-set binge on my phone, occasionally gazing out the window at the bleak winter scenery. The low-hanging grey January clouds were doing nothing to brighten my mood. There was no snow to liven up the view, only drab, washed-out colours. Come May, the journey would be stunning. I have to admit, when it comes to setting, Lochcala definitely beats Glasgow. Over the last few days, Paul and I had discussed the pros and cons of Lochcala and Glasgow at length, but in the end Lochcala won – mostly because it meant Mum and Dad would pay for the wedding. But in the quietness of my thoughts, I still struggled with the idea and all the negative memories of my family home. Would the wedding be able to chase those memories away?

I arrived in time for lunch. Andrew and James were both there, as well as Mum and Dad. These trips would be more appealing if I could stay at Craig's flat, but Mum would have a fit if I even suggested such a thing. "Have you dumped that hairdresser yet?" said James, as I sat my bag down and took off my coat.

"Hello to you too," I replied, ignoring his comment. I was fed up with his continual jibes at Paul's career. Honestly! How can one family be so prejudiced?

With dread, I sat down at the kitchen table. Maybe if I tried to initiate the conversation, it would be better. "So, what's the latest news in Lochcala?" My question was met with grunts of 'nothing' from James and Andrew. Why did I even try? As I took another bite of my cheese sandwich, I looked round the table. James kept his head propped up with his hand as he wolfed through his lunch. Andrew ignored everyone in favour of his phone. And Mum and Dad quietly ate their sandwiches, all the while gazing at their plates. I looked beyond the table, but the kitchen seemed duller than normal, in the low light of January. I got up and switched on the lights. "Switch the lights off," moaned James. "My head hurts."

I attempted to stand up to my bully of a brother. "No. We need some light in here." Could I push it further? "Plus, I suspect your headache is self-inflicted. So why should the rest of us sit in darkness?" James glared at me. He shot up out of his chair, knocking it over. Stomping over to the light switch he punched off the lights and stormed out of the kitchen and upstairs to his room. I looked around the table, the raised eyebrows and shakes of the head were signs I was familiar with. I wanted to cry. As always, I was the one in the wrong.

After lunch, Mum, Dad and myself walked to the manse for our meeting with the minister. I had met her briefly two years ago when I attended the Christmas morning service. When we were growing up, we had attended church as a family, with me and the boys going to Sunday school. The only thing I could remember about the minister of my youth was that he rarely spoke to anyone below the age of twenty, but our Sunday school teachers were pleasant enough, providing us with crafts and stories. By the time Andrew and James reached high school, they both refused to go to church and by the time I was twelve, I was ready to follow their lead. But that summer, between my primary and high school years, the church employed a trainee youth leader, Gillian. She brought energy, enthusiasm, crazy games, and a love for Jesus and the Bible that I'd never encountered before. Twice a week she would lead games in the church hall or grounds. That was the summer I got to know Jesus. Unfortunately, with Gillian's departure, I lost the person I could talk to about faith. But I continued going to church. With all my teenage insecurities, it offered a safety I struggled to find anywhere else. By the time I moved to Glasgow, my faith had diminished to a flicker, and yet I felt a draw to check out local churches. LifePoint, or ChurchX as it was called then, was the second church I visited, and it was the one that brought me into contact with people who reminded me of Gillian. People who knew Jesus and how to have fun.

"Welcome," said the minister, as she led us into her study. Another difference between this minister and the last was the manse. The interior of the house had been transformed. In contrast to the previous minister's dull, musty study, the manse now boasted a bright airy room. White bookcases ran the length of one wall, housing reference and study books in neat rows. Scented candles fragranced the room with a subtle aroma of citrus. A sleek laptop sat in the middle of her white, modern desk. And paintings, I'm assuming by her children, were mounted on one wall. I liked this cheerful room. It had the look and feel of a room decorated by Jennifer.

The minister brought my attention back to our meeting. "First of all, congratulations on your engagement, Kirsty."

"Thank you," I replied. "I'm sorry my fiancé isn't able to be here, but he's a hairdresser in Glasgow and Saturdays are his busy day."

"Not a problem. And, not to back up stereotypes, but in my experience, the grooms aren't always as excited by these meetings as the brides are. Now, what dates are you thinking about and what would you like?"

"We're hoping for the last Saturday in May. I know that might be a popular date with it being the holiday weekend, but it would be ideal as we'll have lots of guests coming from Glasgow."

"Okay, let me check the schedule." She turned her attention to the laptop on her desk and clicked on her keyboard. As she checked, I looked around the room again. A canvas on her wall caught my attention. *'Blessed are the peacemakers, for they will be called children of God.'* I liked that. Peace was a foreign concept at my family home, but in this room, it felt possible. The minister brought my attention back to the wedding as she looked up from her laptop and smiled. "Good news. That Saturday is clear. Would you like me to book that for you now?"

"Yes, please," I replied. Flutters of excitement danced in my stomach at the thought of an actual date for my wedding. My wedding!

"Can you let us know the cost?" said Mum, who of course pulled it back to practical details.

The minister handed my mum an outline with various options and costs. We could pick which features we wanted and pay accordingly. Seeing the list prompted more questions. "I hope you don't mind me bringing this up. But my fiancé and I attend church in Glasgow and we were wondering if it would be possible for our pastor to say something at the service and potentially have some of our worship team do the music for the wedding. Would that be a possibility?"

"Of course, no problem." She handed me a card. "Here are my contact details. Get in touch with me anytime and give your pastor my details too. I'm happy to lead part or stay away and let your pastor take the whole thing. It's more meaningful to have someone who knows you. I won't be able to embarrass you the way he can." Her wink brought a fit of the giggles. I liked this minister more and more. Who knew I would be getting so excited about my wedding being in my old church?

However, things took a downward turn as we met with the first of the two hotels in Lochcala. They were fully booked with functions for the whole of the holiday weekend. We entered the second hotel, still feeling hopeful they would be able to accommodate us. But they were also booked for the weekend. What could we do? In contrast to my buoyant mood from the church, I now felt deflated. There was nowhere else to try in Lochcala. And this is the disadvantage of a village. There just aren't as many options.

Over cups of stewed tea, Mum, Dad and I tried to think of nearby venues. "Perhaps if we looked at venues in Lochgilphead?"

"But that wouldn't make any sense." I played with the biscuit crumbs on my plate. "We can't expect our Glasgow guests to drive through Lochgilphead to get here for the service, only to drive back down for the reception."

"Well then, you'll need to find another weekend. A time when you can get the church and one of the hotels. You're rushing things anyway. A bit more time won't make any difference," said Mum, as she cleared our mugs from the table.

I didn't want to delay the wedding. I wanted to marry Paul as soon as possible. If only Mum was open to the wedding being in Glasgow. As far as I knew, there were no weddings at LifePoint in May and there would be more options for venues in Glasgow. Lochcala won on setting, but Glasgow won on all other counts. Plus, it would make it a lot easier for ninety percent of our guests.

"Let's sleep on it and decide tomorrow," said Dad, always one to put off a decision for another day. Although, there was merit in his advice, it would stop Mum from pushing ahead with her agenda and it would give me time to talk to Paul.

"Hey, you," I said, as our video chat opened. "How is my favourite fiancé? How was your day?"

"It's been good. The salon was busy today, which we needed after the quiet start to the year. How did things go there?"

"Well, the minister is lovely, and we got the church booked. But, the hotels are both booked the entire weekend. So, Mum suggested checking the hotels in Lochgilphead, but that doesn't seem like a sensible option. She also said we should delay the wedding until we could get an available date for both church and hotel. What are we going to do?"

Paul looked away from the screen. If it wasn't for the quiet tune he was humming, I would have thought our call had frozen. "One of my clients got engaged over the holidays too. And she was telling me today they are going to hire a marquee for their wedding reception. Could that be an option?"

"I can't believe none of us thought of that. You are a genius!"

Paul's easy laughter relaxed the tension in my shoulders. "Well, the marquee isn't really my idea, I'm just passing on someone else's plan. But the bit I am going to take credit for is suggesting we make enquiries about having it on the castle grounds."

"Wow! That's a great idea. How amazing would that be? And so fitting as the follow up to your romantic proposal. And we could have lots of our wedding photos taken there, too. Oh Paul, I love this idea. I'm glad the hotels aren't available."

He checked his phone as we spoke. "There are a few places offering marquee hire in Argyll. Why don't we phone round a few once you get back and see if any are free that weekend? I guess it could be even more unlikely to find a marquee than a hotel for a holiday weekend. But it's worth a try."

"Okay, I'll say to Mum and Dad and see what they think. Thank you so much, Paul. You always make everything better." As we ended our call, I gave a little shake of excitement. Thanks to Paul's suggestion, we were going to have the best wedding… ever!

PAUL

The lawyer's letter lay open on my bed. How many times had I read it? Too many. And it wasn't as if re-reading it would change anything. The contents were clearly presented. I couldn't tell Kirsty about it. She had enough going on dealing with her family and the wedding. The issue with the hotels had been a welcome distraction from the letter. And it felt good to come up with a solution – especially a solution that was so well received. Hopefully, we would find a company who could provide a marquee, otherwise Kirsty's excitement would be short-lived.

The letter glared at me. How could I tell Brian and Trish? They had put so much work into establishing The Smith Salon. I needed to protect them. It was my name above the door. It was my name on the letter from the lawyer, so, it was up to me to find the solution. My thoughts drifted back to our initial discussions when we decided to start our own salon. We had been so excited. We didn't know if we would succeed, but we were determined to try. And our first year of business had been successful, clearing our start-up debt and building our client lists. Trish had worked tirelessly on our marketing and the three of us had taken every opportunity to tell people about the salon and encourage every client to come back again. So much work had gone in to establishing The Smith Salon. But none of that mattered now, not with this letter.

The lawyer's letter had arrived in today's post. An official document informing me we were being given our notice period for our rental unit. Our lease would end on the thirty-first of March. I got up and paced round the living room. I needed to move to be able to think clearly. If it wasn't so late, I would go for a run. I read the letter again, my mind overflowing with thoughts and questions. I didn't want to deal with this, but I had to. This was my business. I was responsible for finding a solution. Thoughts of the wedding forgotten, I turned my attention to my computer and opened up a new search window. We needed a unit that was close to our current location and was of a similar size. I checked the listings for the South Side of Glasgow. There were a few places available, but nothing that grabbed my attention. I went to bed frustrated. For the first time in months, I didn't fall asleep thinking about Kirsty.

After a night of tossing and turning, I needed to get out and run and good friend that I am, I dragged Matt out with me. I mean, he had said he wanted to exercise more this year. Now was his chance. In the early morning chill, we jogged along the quiet streets of Glasgow city centre. I love early morning runs when businesses are closed and the streets are free of shoppers. As we jogged, I told Matt about the lawyer's letter.

"That's rubbish, mate. What are you going to do?"

"I don't know. Last night, I had a quick look online to see what was available, but there was nothing obvious. When we opened The Smith Salon, I expected to be there for a while, I didn't think we'd be looking for premises again this quickly."

"It's not ideal. But at least you've got a year's experience of running your own place and knowing what works for you."

"True. But from my initial search last night, I'm not optimistic about my choices."

"Have you told Brian and Trish?"

"No. I was hoping to find a solution before I told them."

"You need to tell them. This affects them too. And you never know, they might know of available places."

We ran on in silence for a few seconds, thinking through the options. Our run was doing nothing to relieve any of my frustrations. Matt glanced over at me, his eyebrows scrunching up in thought. "Tell you what, why don't we drive around the South Side this afternoon after church and search for 'To Lease' signs?"

"That would be great, but aren't you spending this afternoon with Jo?"

"She's got prep work she needs to do for school, so I'm a free agent." He wiggled his eyebrows as he turned round and jogged backwards.

I laughed at his expression. "Come on then. Race you back to the flat."

Mid-afternoon we drove around the South Side of Glasgow, but I wasn't feeling hopeful, and I knew my mood wasn't helping. If you're happy, you'll see the good. If you're grumpy, you'll see the negative. And right now I was seeing the negative. Run down shop fronts, bags of rubbish at shop doorways, only a smattering of people out and about on a gloomy January afternoon. Frustration was preventing me from seeing any possibilities. There were a few 'To Lease' signs, but none that appealed. Some were too far away from my current salon location and the ones that were closer were either too big or too small. "This is useless. There isn't anything suitable."

"Is there anywhere else you can search for units? Maybe they aren't always advertised with boards outside the building."

"I don't know. I guess I could ask around and see if anyone knows of anywhere. But I've only got a couple of months. It's not enough time to find somewhere and have it ready by April."

"Can you ask if you can have longer in your current place?"

"I don't know." I rubbed my shoulders. This afternoon was doing nothing to ease my frustration.

"Let's go home. We can search online and see if we can find other options."

Back at the flat, Matt threw together a stir-fry, the scent of the aromatic spices causing my stomach to growl. After we scoffed our dinner, we began our online search. I looked at websites I'd trawled through the night before. Nothing was standing out. Again, any available units were either the wrong size or in the wrong location. Although taking the time to try different search terms, I found other websites with more offerings, but the extra choice still didn't provide any new possibilities.

"Here's one just round the corner from The Smith Salon," said Matt, as he pointed to a unit he found in his searches.

"But look at the size of it. It's way too big. The sign suggests it was a convenience store. It's too much space. You get a better ambiance in a smaller unit. Plus, it looks like it would need a lot of work to make it appealing. I don't think we have the time or the money to transform it into a viable salon."

"Yes, but look at the miracle Jennifer performed for your current salon." I nodded. He had a valid point. "And maybe you could find someone to split the space with."

"That sounds more stressful than trying to find a new salon. We would need to come up with a new business model, and how long would that take?"

"I guess," replied Matt. "But maybe it's good to be innovative and think of alternative ideas. What are your next steps?"

"Tomorrow I'll get in touch with my lawyer. Which is another factor – the cost. Not only will there be the refit cost, but it's the other costs too, like lawyer fees and other things I've not even thought of yet."

"Just keep thinking of how quickly you established The Smith Salon. You can cope with this move. Maybe it will even open new doors for you."

"Thanks for your optimism, mate. I'm glad one of us is feeling it." I rubbed my hands over my face. It wasn't like me to be this unsettled. What was going on? There was only one thing to do. "Can we pray about it?"

"Of course." On a cold January night, Matt prayed for joy. I was expecting prayers for the right salon at the right price, but Matt kept his prayer focussed on joy. Then he took out his phone and tapped on his Bible app. A couple of taps later, he held up his phone and read, *"Be joyful in hope, patient in affliction, faithful in prayer."*

I thought over the words. They seemed familiar. Offering a comfort but also a challenge. And I was already struggling with enough challenges. I needed space to think.

By the time I threw myself into bed, my head hurt and I knew sleep would be elusive. My mind wandered back to the verse Matt had read out. Why did it seem so familiar? I tried to remember why it was significant. And then I remembered. It was the verse Ben had read out at Mum and Alex's wedding. That verse had got me through my final doubts about marriage. Could the reminder of hope, joy and patience now guide me through my business worries?

JENNIFER

My body was now yelling at me that I was pregnant. The sickness was increasing daily, and I was already up a cup size, with all the associated discomfort of expanding breasts. In fact, everything was increasing in size from my toes upwards.

The last few weeks had been overtaken by thoughts of the pregnancy and figuring out what would need to change in my life. A visit to the doctor had confirmed that it had likely happened because of changes to my birth control. I should have paid more attention at my last visit! But life had been racing along so quickly between juggling my studies, the housework, school runs, homework, after-school clubs, small group and a hundred other minor tasks that I had been in a rush and hadn't listened when he imparted the crucial pieces of information.

Over the last few weeks, I'd been having a lot of conversations with God. Trying to figure out the changes that were coming my way. Was the pregnancy down to my lack of attention or was there some bigger meaning behind it? A couple of years ago, I started reading a Psalm every morning. Initially, the driving force was my search for joy. But, as I delved into their riches, the Psalms brought more than joy. They brought reality and rawness. No matter what David was going through, he spoke to God about it. And in all my current questioning, there was comfort in those verses. Each morning, I would read a Psalm and talk to God about the pregnancy. Yet despite all my talking, God's response seemed lacking.

Scott and I were still adjusting to the news and most nights it was the last thing we talked about before going to sleep. We hadn't told anyone yet, for one thing, we were figuring it out ourselves and for another we were unsure how people would react. But today we were taking the first tentative steps in sharing our news. First up, Ben and Tara, the easiest people to tell. Not only are they our pastors, they are our closest friends. And as parents of three boys, albeit empty nesters, they are a great source of parental advice.

We had invited them over for the evening, longing to have their love and wisdom. I was sure Tara guessed during dinner. I was quieter than usual and I wondered how obvious it was that I was struggling to eat. Even the smell of the chilli on my plate was overpowering. Thankfully, our girls are more than capable of joining in with dinner table conversation and jokes and they entertained our guests wonderfully. Once the girls were settled for the night, we made our announcement. Tara jumped up and hugged us, excitement filling her response. Ben sat back, watching the scene before him. "And how are you both feeling about it?"

"Honestly, I'm not sure we can give you a simple answer," said Scott.

"When we found out, we were shocked. And I think it's safe to say, we are still in shock. But we're also getting excited about it. We have no idea what's going to happen next. How will the girls respond? What does it mean for my studies?"

"When is the baby due?" asked Tara.

"We need to wait until the scan to get a more accurate date, but we think late August. So hopefully I'll be okay to complete my certificate from college this year, but I'll definitely not be progressing on to the diploma next year. I'm not sure how much I'll enjoy college between now and the end of the academic year. With a growing bump, I'm going to feel even older and more out of place in college." I wiped away a gathering tear. "Everyone's going to make comments about this poor baby being an accident." My hands went down to caress my stomach.

Tara gave me another hug and kept her arm round my shoulders. "This baby is no accident. It's a beautiful surprise! But I can imagine how much of a mind shift is needed and some of the doubts and questions you have. We're here for you both and I'm so excited about the baby cuddles I'll be getting in the autumn."

I leaned in to her hug. "Thank you," I whispered.

"And what are your thoughts, Scott?" asked Ben.

"I'm still trying to think it through. As the dad, you know what it's like, it's an abstract thing for us at this stage. We're not the ones going through any changes. Sometimes it doesn't feel real and then I remember we'll have another child later this year."

"I know you have a lot of questions and doubts. But I'm so excited for you both," said Tara. "I'm already curious as to who this wee person is going to be. I bet the girls will be excited when you tell them."

"I think Emma and Chloe will be, but I can imagine Amy will struggle with the news. It's one thing having a pregnant mum when you're in primary school, but in high school, it's a completely different scenario."

"You never know how kids will respond. They might be excited, angry or indifferent. And those are only the initial emotions. But your girls are blessed with wonderful parents who will help them navigate this exciting news." I laughed at Tara's compliment. "But for now, we shall be on our way. Those pregnancy hormones will be demanding you get your sleep. We'll see you tomorrow."

Love and joy had filled the conversation with Ben and Tara. I smiled as I realised how wrong I had been. I had been miffed at God for not speaking to me in prayer. But an evening with Ben and Tara had communicated so much of God's love and plans for us as a family and reminded me that God can speak to us in so many ways. My hand instinctively went to my stomach. As we waved off Ben and Tara, Scott drew me into a hug. "And how do you feel now that you've told someone?" I breathed in Scott's musky scent, grateful the pregnancy hormones still allowed me some enjoyments, and nestled into his hug.

"Telling Ben and Tara will probably be our easiest conversation, and it was wonderful to have their encouragement. And now that we've told someone, it feels more real. What about you?"

"I'm not sure if I'm in denial or it hasn't sunk in yet. It almost feels as if we're talking about someone else."

I reached up and kissed him on the cheek. "Just as well we have months to adjust."

However, a couple of days later, my uncertainties were back. My college days are Tuesday and Wednesday. And when I woke up on Tuesday morning, I felt sick. I made my way downstairs, hoping a drink of water would settle my stomach. Feeling slightly better, I returned upstairs to wake up the girls. By the time we sat down to our cereal, I suddenly felt queasy and made it to the bathroom just in time. Should I go to college or stay at home? But if this was morning sickness, there would be several weeks of this still to come. I had to push through and get on with my life.

I walked Emma and Chloe to school, then caught the bus into town. Every time the bus turned a corner, the nausea increased. I prayed I would make it to college. I couldn't be sick on the bus. Thankfully, I arrived at college before a bout of sickness took hold. Today was going to be a long day.

The first few hours passed in a bit of blur as I tried to concentrate on what our lecturer was talking about. *'Please God, let me be able to get my Certificate this year.'* With my previous pregnancies, there had been varying levels of morning sickness, but it had always tapered off by the end of the first trimester. But could I expect the same this time round? After all, age was not on my side and it wasn't just the sickness I had to contend with. It was low energy levels too. Especially with the girls, the school run, homework and after-school activities. I was exhausted just thinking about it.

At lunch time, I made my way down to the college café with my classmates. Instead of my usual coffee, I was sipping from my water bottle. "Are you okay, Jennifer?" asked Ann.

"I'm okay. Just feeling a bit run-down. Maybe it's the January blues." I glanced over at her. She didn't seem convinced by my answer. Thankfully, she didn't get the chance to probe any further. The lights in the café blinked off and on and then went dark. At first there was silence, and then the murmur of conversations began as people queried what was going on. We stayed in our seats, expecting the lights to come back on.

A member of staff came into the café, he banged a spoon on a tray to get everyone's attention. "There is a power cut in the area. We don't know how long it will last."

"What should we do?" asked Ann. "Do you think it will come back on, or should we leave?"

"I don't know," I replied, looking around the café. A steady line of students exited the café, making their way to the main doors. "Although, looks like a lot of people are leaving."

"Oh well, who are we to argue?" said Ann, putting on her coat. With a sigh of relief, I returned home and went to bed.

The extra sleep restored some energy and enabled my fuzzy brain to come up with a new plan. Maybe I didn't need to travel to college for my classes. Being at home gave me the opportunity to sleep when I needed to and it removed the need for cramped bus journeys that fuelled my nausea. What if I could do some of my classes online? That could help me get through the next few weeks. If the second trimester brought relief from my symptoms, I would go back to college, but if things persisted, I could continue with a blended form of learning. I emailed my course director, letting her know I was pregnant, and that we hadn't told people yet, and suggested my blended idea.

Within the hour, she replied, agreeing to my suggestion. I did a little happy dance to celebrate my new schedule and went to collect Emma and Chloe from school.

Although one problem was dealt with, the next one appeared. During dinner, Chloe told Scott that I had been sick in the morning. I hadn't realised she'd noticed. Scott glanced over at me. I returned an awkward smile. There would never be a perfect time to tell the girls, but maybe now was as good a time as any. Plus, my new routine was going to raise questions with them.

"Girls, your dad and I have something we need to talk to you about." I had no idea what to say. I looked at Scott.

"What is it?" asked Emma.

"I'm pregnant!" I held my breath as I waited for the reactions.

"You are?" asked Emma.

"What's pregnant?" asked Chloe.

"Ugh. They're going to have a baby," replied Amy. I glanced over at her. It was the reaction I had expected from my high school child, but it was difficult to hear her negativity. I took a deep breath, determined not to give her into trouble for her response. After all, Scott and I hadn't exactly reacted with cheers.

"Yes!" shouted Chloe. "Finally, I won't be the youngest in the family. The baby will be slower and smaller than me."

Emma smiled. "When will the baby be here? Will it be a boy or a girl?"

"The baby is due after the summer holidays," said Scott. "And we don't know if it will be a boy or a girl."

"This is so embarrassing!" shouted Amy, as she stomped off to her room.

"I think it's lovely," said Emma, as she came round beside me and gave me a hug.

"I won't be the youngest anymore," cheered Chloe, as she ran circles round the dining table.

Three girls. Three different reactions. A deluge of emotions.

KIRSTY

I curled up on my settee, ice cream tub in hand. Jo sat across from me, already delving into her dessert.

"So how did your trip to Lochcala go?" she asked, before taking her next spoonful of chocolate ice cream.

"It was okay. Initially, I wasn't happy at the idea of getting married in Lochcala and when we found out both hotels were fully booked for the weekend, I had a secret hope that we'd have to have the wedding in Glasgow. But with Mum pushing us to change the date, Paul's idea of the marquee was inspired. And now, the marquee is booked and we have a fabulous solution that is way better than a boring hotel."

"So where will they put the marquee?" asked Jo, before returning her attention to scooping out the last morsels of ice cream.

"We're hoping we can have it up next to the castle ruin."

"No way! That's amazing. How will they get it up there?"

"There's an access road. You wouldn't notice it unless you were looking for it. The marquee company are going for a recce trip a week on Monday, to make sure the location is suitable. I'm taking the day off work and me and Paul will go up and meet them. I really hope it works out as it makes the idea of a Lochcala wedding quite magical."

"That's so good. And it is beautiful there. Just think how gorgeous your photographs will be."

"And speaking of photographs, that's another thing me and Mum disagree about. She wants some ancient guy up there to do the photos. But they'll be boring, old-fashioned shots. I want someone who can make the most of the setting. Between the church, the marquee, the castle and the views, there is so much scope for amazing pics."

"You absolutely need to get someone who can do the photos justice. What's next on your list of things to book?"

"I'll push a bit more on the photographer. I've seen a couple here that I like the look of, so I'll phone them and ask if they would be willing to travel to Lochcala and then make my suggestions to Mum. I'll let her have her choice of band. As we're going for a ceilidh, it'll be great no matter what band plays, although a younger band would inject extra energy."

"Brilliant. Is there anything else you need to book now?"

"There's the cake, but Mum will sort that out. I know she wants a traditional cake, so I'll leave her to it. I said I would book the caterer. Which I can imagine could be tricky with the setting and numbers, etc."

"Will it be a buffet?"

"I'm not sure. It wouldn't bother me at all. I think Mum might be horrified. But as we've pushed to go with the marquee option, I'd better make the catering my next priority and get it booked."

"You know, if you need any help with food sampling, I'm more than happy to step in." Jo held up her ice cream tub to show me it was empty. "Especially if ice cream is involved." I laughed as Jo sat her empty tub down. "Now, let's move onto the good part. What about dresses? When are we going dress shopping?"

I sighed. "And that's another friction with Mum."

"How could shopping for dresses cause any problems?" Jo arched her eyebrows, the way she does when she's about to say something silly. "Don't tell me she wants you to wear her wedding dress?"

I giggled. "Thankfully, she can't make that suggestion. A benefit to being six inches taller than her, her dress wouldn't fit me."

"Well, that's a relief. So what is the problem?"

"Mum wants it to be just me and her. But I want all of us to go - you, the other bridesmaids and Paul's mum."

Jo sat bolt upright. "And I want to be there too!" She sat quietly for a few seconds and then started jumping up and down. "I've got it! This is easy to get round."

Should I be nervous as to what Jo's suggestion would be?

"Why don't you have a pre-shop with your bridesmaids? That way, you can try on gorgeous dresses with people you trust to tell you what looks good."

I took a big intake of breath. "Oh, I don't know. I'm so tempted by your idea, but it feels dishonest. And how would she react if she found out?"

"How would she find out?"

I shrugged. "If someone accidentally lets it slip."

But there was no dissuading Jo. "It will be fine. We can do this. It's a win-win. You get a fun day out with your friends and then you'll be prepared for shopping with your mum. When's she coming?"

"I think she's planning on coming down in three or four weeks."

"Right. Let's make up a short list of shops you want to go to and we can go check out dresses before your mum comes."

Buoyed by Jo's enthusiasm, I jumped up, ran to my bedroom and grabbed my laptop, wedding planning folder and latest wedding magazines from my bedside table. Sitting next to Jo, I opened up the magazines to pages I had marked and then clicked on the saved links on my computer, taking me to several dresses that had caught my attention. We took our time absorbing the pictures of A-line, ball gown, sheath, mermaid and empire dresses, discussing the merits of sweetheart necklines versus strapless dresses, halter neck or spaghetti straps. And then there were the options of silk, lace or satin. "There are so many options," I said.

"You will be a stunning bride," said Jo, as she made a note of the shops we wanted to visit. "Would you like me to assume maid of honour status and book our appointments?"

"That would be brilliant. I don't have any plans for the next few Saturdays."

"I'll phone during my lunch break tomorrow and see what we can do."

"The thought of going dress shopping with you is way more exciting than trudging round with my mum."

"I'm excited too. Do you want to invite Paul's mum?"

"Best not to. I think that might be a step too far. It's one thing to go with my three best friends. I don't want to push it."

"We're going to have the best day," said Jo, as she hugged me goodbye.

I was excited at the prospect of wedding dress shopping with my best friends, despite the tinge of guilt at going behind Mum's back. As I flicked through the bridal magazines one more time before going to bed, I pushed my worries aside and hoped for dreams full of wedding dresses.

PAUL

If anyone could pull a party together in just a week and a half, it was Elsie. It wasn't something Kirsty or I had thought about, so I was glad someone else had planned and organised it. With all the stress of the salon situation, I needed a party. Hopefully, a place to find the joy in hope Matt had prayed about.

Thanks to the ease of social media, we'd sent out several group invites. Although it was anyone's guess how many people would show up, Kirsty's family had refused to travel to Glasgow 'just for an engagement party'. Their response wasn't a surprise, but I was annoyed on Kirsty's behalf.

The function room quickly filled up. It was a random mixture of people - our closest friends, people we knew through church, Brian and Trish from the salon, Kirsty's colleagues and friends and people I used to hang out with at the gym. I was surprised so many people came out to celebrate. Weirdly, there were a few ex-girlfriends in the mix too. I didn't know why they were here, and I was still trying to figure out who they had come with.

The black walls of the function room were adorned with pink engagement banners, and a photo booth resided in the back corner, complete with a box of props. I guess this is what happens when Elsie organises a party. We didn't have a DJ, but a good range of songs were playing through the bar's sound system.

I was enjoying catching up with some of my old gym friends, even if it involved keeping their comments about Kirsty in check. Every so often I glanced over to her, hoping she was having a good time. I smiled as I watched her carrying on at the photo booth with her small group. She looked stunning, as always, in a black fitted dress and killer heels. I laughed as I watched them put on oversized sunglasses and lean in together for some silly photos. Excusing myself from my friends, I walked over to Kirsty.

"I think we need some photos of just the two of us," I shouted over the music. She beamed back at me and handed me oversized sunglasses and a pink feather boa while she was adorned with a top hat and moustache. We laughed as the photos were taken, Kirsty's small group standing around us cheering us on.

"Time for a kissing photo," shouted Jo, with the others joining in her chant of 'kiss, kiss, kiss'. Who was I to deny their request? The surrounding noise faded as I took off the ridiculously large glasses and gazed into Kirsty's eyes. As our lips met, I was aware of flashing lights. Our lips parted, and we looked out to see a sea of phones pointed in our direction.

We were still surrounded by people taking photographs when some of my old colleagues from ByDesign arrived. I was touched they came to celebrate my good news. They led me over to the bar, wanting to buy me a celebratory drink. As the group told me the latest news from my old salon, Kirsty tapped me on the shoulder and pointed to the door. "Look! I can't believe they came." She grabbed my hand and pulled me over to the door to greet her brothers. We both hugged Craig. Andrew and James held out hands to shake. It was great to welcome Craig. I just wasn't sure why the other two had joined him. Andrew and James sauntered over to the bar while Craig stayed with us.

"I can't believe you came!" shouted Kirsty over the music. "I didn't think you were coming."

"Did you really think I'd miss this? But rather than tell you, I wanted to surprise you. I persuaded my boss to give me extra hours last week in exchange for getting the weekend off. Unfortunately, when I told Mum and Dad I was coming, the other two realised they could get a free ride and a night out in Glasgow."

Kirsty cast a sympathetic smile to Craig. "Are you staying in Glasgow tonight?"

"No. We'll stay for a bit, then go back home."

"Don't be daft. Why don't you come and crash at my flat?"

"There's no way I would inflict the two of them on you for tonight. This is your party. You should be able to enjoy it without worrying about house guests."

I put my hand on Craig's shoulder. "Well, we're glad you could make it. Let me buy you a drink and introduce you to my friends." I prayed that their presence would be an encouragement for Kirsty, but I had my suspicions Andrew and James were only here for selfish reasons. At least I could make sure Craig enjoyed himself.

As the evening progressed, some of our guests, mostly women, decided part of the room would be the dance floor. I glanced over and watched Kirsty as she danced with Jo, Lynn and Carol. Oblivious to the other people in the room, she was at ease with her best friends laughing and carrying on. I thanked God once again that I would soon be marrying this amazing woman. I'll never understand why she is so plagued with insecurities, but I guess she still sees herself through her family's eyes. Could I help her break those misconceptions? If only she could see herself as I see her. At that moment, Elsie shimmied onto the dance floor and placed a 'bride-to-be' sash over Kirsty's head and balanced it on her left shoulder. Then Elsie turned round and sought me out. Dancing up beside me and putting a 'groom-to-be' sash over my head. "Thanks!" I shouted. She nodded and then grabbed my hand and motioned to Jane and Trish as she led me over to the dance floor. The group circled round me and Kirsty as we danced together.

We were interrupted by the lights getting brighter and the buffet being served. Mum and Alex had volunteered to cover the cost of the buffet, for which I was very grateful. During the break, I went back to my old gym friends. When I worked at ByDesign, I spent most evenings working out with these guys. However, when I started up The Smith Salon, I didn't have the cash flow to allow for gym membership and it was funny how quickly these friendships drifted. I was touched they were here now. But as the empty food trays were being cleared away, my joy was cut short when the long talons of Angie, one of my ex's and part of the gym crowd, wrapped around my arm. She moved her arm round my shoulder and pressed against me, leaning in close to be heard over the music. "It makes me so sad to see that sash on you, Paul. Are you sure you're ready to settle down with just one woman?"

My smile vanished at her words. "Angie." I nodded. "Why are you here? This is my engagement party." I tried stressing the purpose of the night, hoping she would have the decency to back off.

"The guys at the gym were talking about it and I said I would tag along with them. I was wondering if the news of your engagement was true since I haven't seen you in ages. Unfortunately, it is. But if you'd like some excitement before the big day, call me." She winked at me and trailed her fingers down my arm before walking back to the bar. With makeup that was thickly applied and clothes that were thinly applied, she drew plenty of attention. Had that really been the type of woman I dated? I didn't like the answer to my question.

I shook my head, trying to dispel the encounter. The scent of her perfume lingered on my shirt and with it a fear that my old life would pull me back. A fear that I was still attracted to women like Angie. I glanced around looking for Kirsty. Our eyes locked for a micro-second before she turned away. It was enough time to see the hurt play over her features. Of course, Kirsty had seen the interaction. And knowing Kirsty, she would jump to all kinds of wrong conclusions. I had to get to her. To reassure her, she was the only woman for me. Angie knew how to pull out all the stops to create the model-like façade, but it was nothing compared to Kirsty's natural beauty. With a surge of relief, I realised I was no longer the guy who fell for the fake.

I locked eyes with Kirsty and strode towards her, only to have James block my way. "Wow. Who was that talking to you?" I frowned as I looked at him, averting my attention from Kirsty to her brother. He looked at me with a drunken sneer. "Guess there's more to you than I gave you credit for."

"What?" The noise of the music covered the sharpness of my question.

"Did you and her..." I looked away, not wanting to hear any crassness from James. "Hey, I'm not judging. But if you're not together, maybe I'll get to know her."

My brain caught up with James' words. I had to check he just said, or at least implied, what I thought he had. "What did you say? Do you honestly think I'd be seeing someone like Angie when I'm engaged to your sister?" My hand balled up into a fist at the knowing smile spreading over his face. I wanted to punch him so much! But there were so many reasons why it would be wrong to punch my future brother-in-law at my engagement party. And yet, it was the one thing I really wanted to do. He was one of the most disrespectful guys I'd ever come across. Thankfully, Matt was by my side before I could act on my impulse. "Anyone ready for another beer?" I nodded, and he guided me towards the bar.

Matt shouted his order to the barman, then turned to face me. "What was that about?"

"I have no idea. I've just had the weirdest few minutes. First, Angie is draping herself all over me. And then James is at my side, basically asking if I'm still seeing her!" The barman handed us our beers, and I took a drink. "Can you believe it?" Matt shook his head. "Thanks for getting me away from him. I need to figure out how to deal with my future brother-in-law." I looked round to see where James was. Unbelievable, he was already at Angie's side. At least I didn't need to worry about Angie. She would soon put him in his place. But what about Kirsty? I scanned the dance floor. She was no longer there. I couldn't see her anywhere.

JENNIFER

'Love the Lord your God with all your heart and with all your soul and with all your mind.' The verse might be my verse for the year, but my word for the moment was 'tired'. And it wasn't just me saying it. Almost everyone I met felt the need to tell me how tired I looked, as if it was something I really wanted to hear. It made me wonder how much longer we could keep the pregnancy a secret.

On Saturday night, we went to Paul and Kirsty's engagement party, but we snuck away early as I was exhausted. Even before we went to the party, all I wanted to do was put on my pjs and lie on the couch, but we had to celebrate our friends' engagement and cheer them on. However, when we got to church on Sunday morning, Jo whispered about tension at the party and that Paul and Kirsty needed our prayers. During worship, I prayed for our friends. As the worship ended, I went out to help lead Kids' church. It took all my energy to stay engaged and keep up with all the little stories the children were telling me. Plus, there was the added challenge of being surrounded by little kids and all their unique smells with my pregnancy nose.

By the time I got to Monday, I crawled back into bed after taking Emma and Chloe to school, smiling at the prospect of a morning nap under my big, fluffy duvet. But come Monday night, my yawns were back, and the timing couldn't be worse. Ben had asked me and Scott to lead Paul and Kirsty through the pre-marriage course. I had been thrilled when he asked, but right now, all I wanted to do was sleep. As we sat around the coffee table, I tried my best to hide the yawns behind my hands or my mug of herbal tea. After all, when you're in the midst of intense conversations, you can't appear disinterested.

The couple sitting across from us now were not the same couple we partied with on Saturday night. There was a tension in the space between them. There was no hand holding or side-ways glances. They sat quietly, staring at their coffee mugs as if they were the most interesting thing in the room. Scott discarded the notes he'd prepared for the discussions, said a prayer and went straight to the one question that needed discussed. "What happened at your engagement party?"

Paul's gaze darted to Kirsty, while she kept her eyes firmly fixed on the coffee mug in front of her. "One of Paul's many exes showed up, trying to get back with him." Kirsty edged further away from Paul, taking a deep breath to control her shaky voice. "And then, of course, my lovely brother, James, tried to get in on the action and made everything worse. We were having a great party and then my family and Paul's past come along and ruin everything."

Paul sighed and leaned back into the settee, slowly shaking his head. "I don't know how often I need to say I'm not interested in Angie."

Tears were flowing down Kirsty's cheeks. "Yes, but it's not just Angie, is it? I know it's petty and silly. But you've been with a lot of women, Paul. And I just don't know what that means for our marriage. Am I enough?"

Silence. My heart ached for my friend as she buried her face in her hands, the sounds of gentle sobs escaping. Paul sidled up to her and put his arm round her shoulder. He said nothing more. Instead, he just sat and held her. I put on a worship playlist, and Scott and I prayed for our friends as they struggled with their questions.

Sometimes we create problems that aren't there. And sometimes we make too much of minor issues. But no matter the starting point, they can seem overwhelming. And in Kirsty's case, any problem she faces is always magnified by her insecurities. We all have our moments of insecurity, but for Kirsty they are disproportionate. I prayed for her to see beyond her self-doubts and understand the depth of love that Paul has for her. And even more importantly, the depth of love Jesus has for her.

Now wasn't the time for further discussion. Tonight was a time to rest and be. Nothing had really happened at the party, but it had exposed the baggage they both carried. It's easy to see Kirsty's fears and insecurities. But even though Paul appears laid-back, he's hinted several times at the worries that lie below the surface.

Paul and Kirsty were still in my thoughts when I turned up for small group on Wednesday night. As we gathered, the conversation centred on the engagement party. Elsie enthused about the party and how much of a success it had been. "I can't believe there were so many people there. You guys are so popular."

"Well, Paul certainly is," replied Kirsty, with just a bit too much sass.

Lynn sat her coffee mug down and looked at Kirsty. "What's going on?"

Kirsty's reply was quiet, and Lynn had to lean in to hear the response. "Didn't you see the woman making a play for Paul?"

Lynn held up her hand. "Let me stop you right there." Everyone stared at Lynn. "Kirsty, for years you have been complaining about boyfriends who were distant, not there for you, or wouldn't commit. Now you have the gorgeous Paul who has put a ring on that finger and you're still finding faults.

Get over it. He picked you. Be thankful for this dreamy man who asked you to marry him. He asked you. Not anyone else. How many times does the guy need to prove himself to you?"

My gaze darted about the room, trying to gauge reactions and wondering who would be next to speak. It would be easy for me to intervene and break the silence, but it seemed important to let someone else step in. Lynn has always been the most outspoken one of the group. Her comments can be almost cutting at times. She'll challenge people where necessary but is also the one who will push for adventures, like last year's ski trip. At first appearance, she can seem a bit prickly. But take the time to get to know her and you'll find a fiercely loyal friend.

Kirsty looked at Lynn. Her mouth dropped open.

Jo stepped in and broke the tension. "Exactly!" Jo smiled over at Kirsty. "Kirsty, we love you. And I think it's safe to say, we all agree with Lynn. Paul is fantastic. He's the best guy you've ever been with, and he's smitten by you."

I smiled. Lynn's response to Kirsty had probably been exactly what she needed. And it wasn't just Kirsty who needed that reminder. Lynn's words were a nudge for me too. It can be so easy to focus on the negative and the problems, and it is good to be realistic, like we read in the Psalms. But David didn't just point out the negative he turned his thoughts to God and praised him and spoke of the places of blessing in his life.

I look around the women gathered in Kirsty's living room and said a prayer of thanks for each of them. Kirsty didn't say much in response to Lynn, but her frown was gone and she engaged with the group again.

Carol refilled our tea and coffee mugs, and I opened up my Bible. "I've got the perfect Bible verse for us to discuss tonight. It's my verse for this year and it points to where we can find our anchor for life. *'Love the Lord your God with all your heart, and with all your soul and with all your mind.'*"

PAUL

When you have a small, independent salon, you can be creative in how you market yourself, which is both stressful and fun. Thankfully, when you have friends like Elsie and Trish, the fun part is easy to find. The two of them were the perfect brainstorming team, dreaming up low-cost ideas for us to try out. For this year, they were planning theme-Saturdays once a month, and today was the first one. Even though we were a week late to celebrate Burns' Day, we decided to still go with the Scottish theme. Trish was wearing a mini-kilt and Brian and I had borrowed kilts for the day. Elsie had sourced bunting with Scottish flags and had put them up around the salon and in the window. We had Scottish music playing – bagpipe, Celtic and pop music. And there were treats of buttery sweet tablet to go with clients' drinks.

As today was our first theme day, Elsie was volunteering with us. She zipped about - answering phones, welcoming clients and taking photos and videos of the day's activities. She had contacted the local newspaper, securing a feature in last week's paper, with a follow up, including pictures, for next week's edition.

Some of our clients were confused about what we were doing. Others were up for the party. And there were also two new clients who had ventured along to find out more. The cold mist dampening the grey Glasgow streets was forgotten in the party vibe in the salon. Throughout the day, clients sang along with songs, enjoyed their tablet and enthused about how much the theme had lifted their spirits. We even had one client who gave us a display of Highland Dancing. Brian and I tried to copy her steps, but they were too complicated for us. And, of course, Elsie caught it on video!

Setting up The Smith Salon had been a step of faith. There had been highs and lows over the last fourteen months, but in general, owning my own salon brought so much more satisfaction than working for an international chain ever had. However, as the last client of the day left, and the bunting was taken down, it was time to speak to Brian and Trish about the future.

After two weeks of phone calls with lawyers and property people, I was no further forward with the lease on the salon and I was still waiting to hear from the building owner if we could get an extension on our exit date. No new properties had come on to the market and there were no signs of anything new in the pipeline. I'd hoped to have something lined up before I burdened Brian and Trish with the news, but that just hadn't happened. "What's wrong?" asked Trish, as we gathered around our workstations.

Maybe I hadn't done such a good job of hiding my anxiousness over the week. Or maybe Trish's question was nothing more than a conversation opener. "I'm afraid it's not good news." Brian and Trish exchanged worried looks. "I got a letter a few weeks ago informing me that our lease is being terminated at the end of March."

Brian pushed himself upright, no longer leaning against his workstation. "Why?"

"I don't know. The owner hasn't given any information yet, but our lawyer thinks he might be getting ready to sell the building."

"So, does that mean a new owner would give us the option to continue with our lease?"

"That could be a possibility. But our problem with that is time. Would we need to close between the change of ownership? And how long would it take before a new owner could be found and confirm that we can stay? It's a risk. But, also, there's not a lot of choice in other units in the area just now."

We all looked down at the floor, no one sure what to say next. Brian and Trish needed time to take in the news. It wasn't often I saw this pair speechless.

"Why don't we come in early for our Tuesday morning business meeting and we can brainstorm ideas? It will give us a couple of days to think about it."

"I guess so." Brian sounded less than enthusiastic.

Trish attempted a smile. "We need to sort something out, so that would be good." I appreciated Trish trying to rally round and move us forward. She was the one who had done most of the groundwork for our current salon. Hopefully, she would be able to take us forward in this next move too.

Now that I had told Brian and Trish, I needed to tell Kirsty. Tonight's date night would be full of heavy conversation. So much had happened during the past week between the engagement party and our first marriage class, and we hadn't been able to see each other since Monday night. A few phone calls were all we'd achieved.

We met at our favourite city centre burger restaurant and claimed a table by the window. I reached over and took Kirsty's hand. On Monday night, her eyes had mirrored her hurt. Tonight, they were back to their usual sparkle. "It's been a busy week," I began, rubbing my thumb over her fingers. "I'm so sorry about Saturday night. Please believe me, Angie means nothing to me."

Kirsty shook her head. "I'm the one who needs to apologise to you. I overreacted. And I know it's something I need to work on. I'm sorry I made it all about your past when it was as much about mine. Between my family and my not-so-lovely exes, I come with baggage too. So it's not you who needs to apologise. It's me." She paused as she took a drink of her juice. "Plus, Lynn pulled me up on my bad attitude at small group."

I let out a breath I didn't realise I'd been holding. "Funny how we're both carrying stuff from our pasts. Maybe it's time for us to pool our resources and fight our baggage together."

She returned my smile. "I like that idea."

"Kirsty, I want to be honest with you, but I also don't want to scare you and cause you any more worry." Was it wise to tell her how I felt? I wasn't sure. This was all new ground to me. But being in a committed relationship meant being honest and clearing up misunderstandings as quickly as possible. I took a deep breath and continued. "After you left on Monday night, I had a good chat with Scott. In so many ways, I've moved on from my old lifestyle, but sometimes I worry that I could slip back into it. And Saturday night poked those fears. I wasn't tempted by Angie; but I was scared of being tempted back to that life. Scott prayed for me and in those prayers I realised I'm no longer tempted by a trail of one-night stands. Angie was merely one last attempt to pull me back, and I wasn't interested." I glanced over at Kirsty. Tears moistened her eyes. Was she upset with me? "I'm sorry, Kirsty. I'm sorry my past came between us. Please believe me, I only want to be with you."

She gave a little shrug. "Like you said, we're both dealing with things from our pasts." She looked into my eyes. "I love you Paul and I love we get to figure this stuff out together." And with that, she leaned over the table and kissed me. As she pulled back, the waiter came over to take our order. I laughed to myself as I wondered if he'd been hanging back, waiting for our intense conversation to end.

We placed our orders and leaned back in our seats, looking out to the dark, misty city centre. Our biggest conversation was done and with it, we both relaxed into our evening. As our burgers arrived, mine with a portion of haggis on top to celebrate our Scottish themed day, I told her about the salon lease being terminated.

"Wait. When did you say you got the letter?"

"Two weeks ago when you were in Lochcala."

"Paul! I can't believe you're only telling me now."

I looked over at her, not sure what she meant. "But I didn't want to give you something else to worry about when you were busy with the wedding planning." I didn't understand why not telling her sooner was an issue.

"We're a couple, you need to tell me these things." She reached over for my hand. "Please include me."

"I'm sorry. I didn't think." I still felt confused. I thought by not telling her about the salon, I was protecting her, whereas from her perspective I was excluding her. I had a lot to learn!

"It's okay." She rewarded me with a warm smile that let me know we were good. "So, what will you do?"

"We're not sure yet. I said to take the next couple of days to mull it over and then we'll see what we can come up with on Tuesday morning."

"It's so good you've got the two of them to help."

"I know. I feel guilty that it's just my name attached to the salon. The success of the salon is down to them as much as me. And once again, I'll be relying on them a lot as we relaunch in a new place."

"They benefit from it too." Kirsty paused as she ate a chip. "I see how much they respect you, Paul. You're a great boss and you've given them a laid-back atmosphere to work in. And I bet they are busier now, at The Smith Salon, than they were at ByDesign. You've helped them build their client lists." She was right. Leaving our old salon had been revitalising for all three of us. Si, the manager at ByDesign created a toxic, competitive atmosphere. A place that was all about numbers and profits and seemed to forget the customers were core. Setting up our own salon gave us the freedom to put clients first and cheer each other on, rather than being rivals.

As we savoured our burgers, Kirsty filled me in on the latest with the wedding plans. She had been busy all day researching and contacting caterers and had narrowed down the options to three potential companies. After our meeting with the marquee company on Monday, she would finalise which caterers we would hire. She was playing the situation well with her mum, putting her administrative skills to good use and coming up with a few options and then letting her mum have the final say. It was a system that seemed to work well so far. But I confess to only partially listening to Kirsty's wedding chat. My mind was still on the salon lease. It had me worried. I'd found so much joy running my own salon, but now a shadow was hanging over me, waiting to steal my joy.

KIRSTY

In the early morning light, I rushed out of my flat, travel mug in hand, desperately in need of more caffeine. Paul was waiting in the shiny, black car he'd hired for our day trip to Lochcala. In a few hours we would meet the marquee company, who would hopefully approve the castle grounds as the location for our wedding reception.

The weather was kind to us for the start of the drive, with glimmers of sunlight shining through the ever present winter clouds. A light mist of rain started as we left the outskirts of Glasgow and by the time we reached Loch Long the rain was torrential. I sighed as I looked out over the Loch. There was beauty in the terrain's wildness and the fierceness of the rain, but we were on a day-trip to plan our wedding. I wanted lovely blue skies and sunshine.

And it wasn't just the weather that was overcast, Paul was quieter than usual. The news about his salon lease had come as a shock. I wasn't sure if I should ask him about it now or leave him to his own thoughts. "Are you okay?" I ventured.

He turned round and smiled. His smile eased my uncertainties and warmed my toes. I reached over and squeezed his arm. "The salon will all work out, Paul." He continued staring at the twisting road, only responding with a sigh. It wasn't like him to be this quiet. I looked out the window, praying for the right words, before turning back to face Paul. "God's got a plan for The Smith Salon that goes beyond fifteen months."

He glanced round at me then returned his gaze to the road. "I'm sure you're right and I want to live in that faith… it's just a struggle right now."

"And that's okay. We're not told it will be easy."

Paul reached over and ran his finger down my cheek. "I'm sorry. I'll try to let it go. After all, this is a wedding planning day. And one that we get to do together. Are you excited?"

I grinned as the conversation moved on to our wedding. "Excited and nervous. I've no idea what is required for a marquee site. Hopefully, the castle grounds will be suitable."

"I'm sure it will all work out perfectly."

We arrived in Lochcala mid-morning. Exiting the car, I quickly zipped up my raincoat and pulled my hood in tight before the wind and rain could get to me. With half an hour until our meeting, we popped in to see Mum. I wasn't sure if it was the best plan to see her now, as I really didn't want her coming with us. Thankfully, she was more than happy to stay warm and dry in her kitchen.

We walked up to the castle, hand in hand. The rain of earlier had calmed down to a rhythmic pitter-patter. As we reached the ruin, the marquee company's 4x4 drove up the access road to the site. Steve and Alan introduced themselves and, after the obligatory small talk, began their assessment of the area. I was on tenter hooks waiting to hear what they would say. We gave them space to do their job. As they walked around, I watched every scratch of the head and questioning look they sent each other. The longer they took, the more nervous I became, especially when Steve started kicking his heel into the ground as some kind of test. They circled the castle, looking up at the ruined walls, checking the amount of fallen stones around the base. At the edges of the grass, they peered over the rock face and took more notes and photos. Even Paul strengthened his grip on my hand.

Eventually, Steve and Alan returned to where we were standing. Alan ran his hand round his neck. "Sorry." My shoulders sank, and I fought against tears that seemed desperate to express themselves. "There are too many problem areas here. It's good we're here on such a wet day as it's showing up potential issues. The ground is very uneven and we wouldn't advise having a marquee so close to a sheer drop. There's nowhere to park the number of cars that would be coming for a wedding. And the space isn't suitable for the porta cabin toilets and I think it would be an issue for catering too."

Thankfully, Paul was there, holding my hand and ready to engage in problem-solving mode. "So, what do you suggest?"

"Do you have a backup plan? Another location that we could look at?" Alan looked between me and Paul as he spoke. I chewed my lip, still fighting the tears. In search of inspiration, I looked out over Lochcala, unable to see anywhere better. "What about the harbour side?" suggested Alan. I looked down to the harbour and sighed.

Paul squeezed my hand. "That could be good. There is plenty of space for parking, the caterers and the toilets. And we could still come up here for photographs." I tried to smile at Paul's response, but I just didn't want to.

"Why don't we go down and take a look," said Alan.

I was glad of the walk to the harbour to get time alone with Paul. He put his arm around my shoulders as we reached the pavement below the castle. "I'm sorry, it's not working out as you hoped. How are you feeling?"

"Sad." Pesky tears trickled down my cheeks and my shoulders slumped under the weight of the disappointment. Paul stopped and turned round to face me. Wiping away the tears, he traced a whisper of kisses where the tears had been. With each kiss, the disappointment lifted a little. What was it I'd said to Paul a few hours earlier? God's got a plan. I wasn't sure whether to laugh or scream that my advice was coming right back at me.

As we approached the harbour, a police car pulled up beside us and Dad lowered his window. "How did your meeting with the marquee guys go?"

"Not good," I replied. "They said they can't put the marquee up there. So we're going to have a look at the harbour. Do you know who we need to talk to if the space is suitable?"

"Hold on," said Dad. "I'll park up and come with you."

Steve and Alan were waiting for us at the harbour by the time the three of us arrived. Even on a quiet Monday afternoon there was life about the place, the constant clanking of metal, the cries of the seagulls and the lapping of water against the old stone walls. The air was sprinkled with salt spray and the colourful shops and cafes broke up the dullness of the grey clouds and sea. Dad quickly got up to speed with Steve and Alan and in no time at all became our spokesperson. I fought a niggle of annoyance that he was taking over, but he knew what he was talking about. Dad walked along the harbour with the men as Paul and I sat on one of the harbour benches waiting to hear their assessment. Again, they walked back and forwards, measuring the area, peering over the harbour walls. If they said no to the harbour where else could we suggest? As my mind explored all the negatives, they came over to where Paul and I sat. "Yes, this will work," said Alan. There was little enthusiasm in his words and it took me a few seconds to register he was telling me good news.

"I'll go and see about getting permission," said Dad, as he walked over to the harbour office. I glanced at Paul, barely daring to smile. While we waited for Dad, Steve explained the timings and technicalities about having the marquee as our reception venue. To be honest, I didn't take in much of what he said, I couldn't relax until I knew how Dad's conversation was going. Ten minutes later Dad returned informing us the marquee was approved. We shook hands with Steve and Alan, our reception location arranged. It wasn't the romance of the castle grounds, but there was beauty all around the harbour. As second choices go, I couldn't complain.

KIRSTY

On Saturday, it was time for the secret visit to the bridal shops. My bridesmaids, Jo, Lynn and Carol, arrived at my flat with a bag of croissants and take-away coffee cups. Lauren, Paul's sister, was also a bridesmaid, but as she lives in London, she could only be with us for the bridesmaid dress shopping. We munched on our morning pastries as we went over our plan for the day. Jo had booked appointments with four wedding shops, three in the city centre and one in the South Side.

We huddled into our raincoats as we ran from my flat to the bus stop. Thankfully, we didn't need to wait too long until the bus arrived to save us from the horizontal sleet. Though not even the miserable February weather could detract from the thrill of searching for *the* dress.

Our giggles as we entered the first shop were cut short by the sales assistant, expressing annoyance at the wet, muddy splashes coming off our coats. I felt a dip in confidence at her crossed arms, but Jo countered the woman's negative reaction by being over-the-top enthusiastic. "Hi, we're the Price group.

This is my friend Kirsty, the bride. She's seen some gorgeous dresses on your website and would like to try them on. Myself, Lynn and Carol are her bridesmaids, so we'll be letting her know what suits her. But I suspect lots of styles will look amazing on Kirsty."

I tried not to laugh as the sales assistant adjusted to Jo's enthusiasm. I wouldn't say she warmed to us, but Jo's remarks seemed to have dealt with her negative first impression. "Do you have a note of the dresses you've seen?" the sales assistant asked, addressing me.

I pulled out my phone and tapped the folder I'd created for this shop. The assistant nodded as I scrolled through the dresses. However, she scowled at the fourth dress on my list. "That is not one of ours." As she said the words, she actually raised her nose as if I had shown her a picture of a dress so beneath the offerings of her shop.

My pale Scottish skin flashed red. Why were my blushes so quick to give me away? I looked at my phone. I had been so careful when I made up the albums. Checking and double checking that I had assigned the correct dresses to the corresponding shop. Once again, Jo stepped into the breach. "This must happen so often," she laughed. "After all, brides must spend hours searching online and looking through magazines. It's an easy mistake to make."

Jo's attempts at lightening the situation weren't as effective this time round. The assistant turned round, keeping her nose well and truly in the air, and walked off in search of the dresses she did stock. While she was gone, Jo, Lynn and Carol nudged each other and giggled. I raised my eyebrow and glared at them, I didn't want to get thrown out before I'd even tried on any dresses!

The assistant returned a few minutes later and invited us to follow her to the changing area. We walked through the shop, overwhelmed by the number of white, ivory and cream dresses hanging along the sides of the store. Just beyond the wedding gowns were rows of colourful bridesmaid dresses. Today was all about my dress, but it would be helpful to get an appreciation of the options for the bridesmaids.

I held my breath as I entered the changing area. It was a beautiful space. Material hung in drapes around the walls, giving it a glamorous feel, and in the middle was a raised platform with several mirrors positioned to enable the wearer to see their dress from as many angles as possible. I swiped away a few tears as the assistant wheeled in a clothes rail with my dresses hanging on it. Jo had been right. I needed to do this with my friends before trying on dresses with my mum.

Jo, Lynn and Carol sat on a couch while I disappeared into a cubicle to try on the first of the dresses. When I saw this dress online, I had been so excited by its fairy-tale appearance. It had an illusion neckline with a fitted bodice, covered in a lace and crystal design. And from the dropped waist, layers of tulle puffed out. I squinted at the mirror, but it was difficult to get a good look at the dress in the cramped changing area. It didn't look quite right. Maybe I needed to see it in the full-length mirrors to get a better appreciation. When I joined my friends, I was met with mixed reactions. Jo raised an eyebrow, considering the dress and what to say. Carol clasped her hands and exclaimed I looked like a Disney princess. But Lynn shut down any discussion when she exclaimed I was not allowed to walk down the aisle in a 'big floofy princess dress'. Her delivery wasn't tactful, but maybe she had a point. Of course, Lynn's remarks meant the shop assistant was even more bristly, and as a result, there was no enjoyment in trying on the other dresses. Neither of which my friends were excited about. We shrugged into our raincoats and shuffled out the door of the bridal shop. "What did you all think?" I asked.

"None of those dresses were *the one*," said Jo. "You looked great in them, but they didn't have the wow factor."

"I agree," said Carol. "But don't worry about it. There's lots more options ahead of us."

I smiled, trying to overcome the disappointment that was niggling at me. "At least I'm doing this with you three instead of my mum. She would probably tell me to go with the first dress I tried on."

"On to the next shop," said Jo, as she held up her umbrella and waved it in the air like a tour guide. I laughed at her antics. "And after this one, we'll have our lunch break to energise us for the rest of the shopping trip. Don't worry, I know we'll find your perfect dress, Kirsty. Plus, you wouldn't want to buy your dress from that shop. That sales assistant was horrible."

Thankfully, the second shop was much more welcoming. There were no disgusted glances at our raincoats here. They even made fun of the Scottish weather. Above a clothes rail, a sign invited customers to 'leave your soggy clothes behind as you enter the warm glow of our shop'. Instrumental music played softly through the shop speakers. "We're going to have a wonderful time bringing you lots of different dresses to try on," said the sales assistant as she led us through to the changing area. "What styles are you interested in?" I pulled out my phone and opened the folder I had created for this shop. With each picture, she confirmed they had the dress. I was impressed with her product knowledge.

"This shop is so much nicer," whispered Carol. "It's amazing how the experience changes with a change of personnel."

"It makes you wonder how much business the other shop gets," said Lynn.

"I suppose it comes down to their choice of dresses too," I said. "If you have your heart set on a particular dress and they stock it, then you'll need to go there."

The sales assistant returned, pushing a rail with my dresses. She was accompanied by another woman, who had a tray with glasses of orange juice and water. My bridesmaids were directed to the seating area while I was ushered into the large changing cubicle to try on the first of the wedding dresses.

I swished out to the changing area, to the 'oohs' and aahs' of my friends. This time, I was starting with a mermaid style dress. From the bateau neckline to my knees, the white satin clung to my body before kicking out round my ankles. A row of beads sat around my waist. "Oh, Kirsty," said Jo, as she clasped her hands to her chest. "You look beautiful." Lynn and Carol also expressed their delight in the dress. "What do you think?" asked Jo.

"I think I like it." I twirled on the pedestal and watched the dress twirl around my ankles. A thousand little crystals catching the light, lifting the sparkle of the dress. I ran my hand over the soft, delicate material.

"Let's talk specifics," said the sales assistant. "Saying you think you like it tells me this isn't the right dress for you. What do you think of the shape, the neckline, the material? Is there anything you particularly like about it, anything you're not so sure about?"

"Oh, I don't know. It's all so much to take in."

Jo stood up and walked around me, examining the dress. "Why don't we take pictures of you in the dresses and then you can compare them later?" She turned round to the sales assistant. "Would that be okay?"

"Of course. Choosing the perfect dress is an important decision. We don't want you to feel rushed. Take as many pictures as you like and consider your options."

"I'll need to come back another time, anyway," I confessed. "My mum wants to be with me to choose my dress, but I wanted to come with my friends first to get their input. Does that sound silly?"

"Not at all. It sounds like a wise way to navigate the emotions of choosing your dress."

I tried on my next three dresses. There was a stunning ball gown with a square neckline, the bodice and bottom of the skirt covered in a beautiful lace motif. Then there was the A-line dress with the halter neckline and yet more beading and sparkles. And finally a straight dress with a high neckline. The staff were doing their utmost to make us feel valued and special and would gently give us advice. Often their suggestions were spot on. After I had tried on my four choices, the sales assistant suggested one different style. When I walked out of the changing cubicle, Jo, Lynn and Carol all stopped their conversation and looked at me with open mouths. It was another mermaid style dress, only this time with a plunging V-neck. It felt far too risqué. "It looks amazing on you," reassured Jo. "But you just look so awkward in it."

"It looks stunning on you," said the assistant. "But if you don't feel comfortable in it, then it's not the dress for you. It's a shame though because with your height and figure, this dress is sensational."

Eventually, we emerged from the bouquet of exquisite gowns. It had been wonderful trying on such beautiful dresses. Though, I was feeling a bit flat after the first two shops. And I was tired and hungry. "Can we sit in for lunch somewhere?" I asked. "I need rest and sustenance."

"Sorry, there's no time," said Jo, as she glanced at her watch again. "That shop took longer than planned. Let's grab sandwiches from this deli and head to the next shop."

But between the horizontal sleet and trying to eat bland sandwiches while holding up hoods or battling with umbrellas, our excitement for the day diminished further. It was probably an indicator that we needed a proper food stop. "Do you think we can cancel the South Side appointment and make this our last shop of the day?"

"You're the bride," said Jo. "It's up to you."

"Do you think the other shop will be annoyed at us for cancelling?"

"Stop worrying about what people think. I'm sure this happens a lot. I'll phone them now." Jo rummaged through her bag and pulled out her phone. As she searched through her contacts for the shop's phone number, I held my umbrella over us. But in my anxiousness about cancelling the appointment, I didn't pay attention to our surroundings. I didn't see the puddle beside the pavement. I didn't see the bus approaching the puddle. But when the bus hit the puddle, I felt the tidal wave of cold, dirty water that engulfed me. My umbrella and raincoat offered little protection. I was soaked from my hair to my toes. Gasping against the shock, I shivered as cold water ran down the inside of my raincoat. The dress shopping wasn't going to plan and now I was soaked in gross water. All I wanted to do was cry.

KIRSTY

"Don't panic," said Jo. "I'm going to cancel the next shop. Then we can go to your flat? You can get dried off and then, if you want to, we could keep our appointment with South Veil Bridal."

Tears threatened to fall, as if I needed any more moisture on me. "Okay," I sniffed, looking round my friends.

"Let's get a taxi rather than the bus," said Carol as she waved at an approaching cab.

Back at my flat, I went for a quick shower and left them to make coffee. A steaming hot shower did wonders to revive my flagging spirits. "Better?" asked Carol as I returned to the living room. I nodded as Jo handed me a mug of coffee. "Brilliant. Now drink your coffee and you'll be ready for your third dress shop of the day."

As we left my flat, I wondered if there would be a standout dress for me today. I was disappointed I hadn't fallen in love with one yet.

Our third shop of the day seemed insignificant from the street. The small front section only allowed for one dress to be on display. My online search had revealed three dresses I wanted to try on, but how many dresses would they even have in stock?

"Welcome to South Veil Bridal," said the woman who opened the door for us. "I'm Samantha and I'll be serving you today." We all introduced ourselves and she led us through the narrow front section of the shop. On one side, glass cabinets displayed bridal jewellery, tiaras and hair slides. The other side showcased a range of veils. As we continued, the shop opened up into a large airy space. We all gasped at the array of dresses before us. Sky lights brought a beautiful natural light and fairy lights and waves of pastel tulle brought a magical and intimate atmosphere. Floor to ceiling posters showed radiant brides in their beautiful dresses. Some pictures were of brides on their own, others included smiling bridesmaids, and others had the bride in the arms of her dashing groom. As with the last shop, instrumental music played through shop speakers, only this time, the music was much more upbeat and modern.

"This is it," I whispered to my friends. "This is the shop where I'm going to find my dress."

As we sat down in the viewing area, another woman appeared with a tray containing glasses and bottles of sparkling water, orange juice or prosecco. A serving plate contained delicious, dainty little pastries for us to nibble on.

"Are you ready to have fun?" asked Samantha once we were all catered for.

"Absolutely," I replied. The exhaustion and disappointment of this morning vanished in this magical setting. As with the previous shops, I showed Samantha the dresses I had seen on their website that had caught my attention. She nodded her head as I flicked through the images. "Yes, we have those in stock. Do you know what type of shoes you'll be wearing on the day?" I shook my head. "Will you be wearing trainers, heels, flats, sandals?"

"Probably heels."

"And will you be wearing a veil?" Again, I nodded my reply.

"Okay, I'll grab you a pair of heels and a veil, too. Why don't you go to the changing room and get yourself ready and I'll bring your dresses." Even the way she described them as 'your dresses' had me excited. I turned round to my friends and gave them a big thumbs up as I dashed over to the changing room.

The first dress was a stunning ivory ball gown. The V-neck bodice was embellished with lace and tiny pearls, and the tulle skirt shimmered in the spotlights of the changing room. As I walked out to my friends, I swished my way on to the platform. "It's beautiful," said Carol. Jo and Lynn partially agreed, but they seemed to be holding back. Samantha voiced their concerns. "It is beautiful. But I know we can get something with more of a Wow! factor for you. Once you've tried on your other two dresses, I'll bring you my suggestion."

I knew this dress wasn't *the one,* but instead of feeling disappointed, I was excited to see what would come next. The satin ball gown and mermaid dresses I tried on subsequently were beautiful, but not as special as the first dress.

"Now it's my turn to choose," said Samantha, with a glint in her eye. In my excitement, I struggled to get the mermaid dress off. I couldn't wait to see Samantha's suggestion. She returned a few minutes later, her arm supporting the mystery dress. She helped me untangle myself from the mermaid dress and then guided me into her choice. There were no mirrors in these changing rooms. The only mirrors were in the viewing area. Samantha explained there was no point having a mirror in a pokey changing room. With bridal dresses, you needed to be out in the open with lots of lights and mirrors around you to see them at their best.

I walked out of the changing room, desperate to see myself in this dress.

"Oh, Kirsty!" said Jo, putting her hands up to her face as she brushed away a tear. "That's your dress. It's perfect."

I stepped up to the platform and looked in the mirror. My breath caught and tears of joy clouded my vision. I had always imagined I would scream and jump up and down when I found my dress, instead the significance of the moment left me speechless, a silent joy dancing deep within.

Samantha was beside me with a tissue. "It's so beautiful," I whispered. I hugged Samantha. "Thank you so much for picking this dress out for me." Jo, Lynn and Carol gathered round me and we hugged. The simple design negated the princess style of the ball gowns and softened the tightness of the mermaid styles. It was simpler yet more stunning than any of the other dresses I had tried on. And when I looked in the mirror, it was love at first sight. An under layer of apricot satin highlighted the gorgeous pattern on the top layer of lace. I checked the reflections in the mirrors to look at the back of the dress. The delicate straps ran down to my lower back, where they connected with the dress. And a mid-length train ran behind me. I loved everything about this dress. Samantha disappeared, giving us time to look at the dress in more detail and discuss it.

"I have my dress!" I ran on the spot, absolute delight flowing through me. My friends once again gathered in a group hug, all in agreement that this was my perfect dress.

Samantha returned just as the others sat back down on their chairs. "This dress was crying out for someone with your height and slender build, Kirsty. It is the perfect pairing."

"It's absolutely stunning. Thank you so much." Again, I twirled and gazed at the reflections surrounding me.

"There is something else I need your help with," I said, looking over at Samantha. "My mum wanted to be the one to come dress shopping with me. But I wanted to come with my friends first. Mum will be here next weekend but she doesn't know I've been looking today. Would it be possible to put this dress aside for me? And then once Mum sees it, we'll buy it."

"No problem. You're not the first bride to make such a request. Do you want to book your appointment for next week and I'll put a note with the dress?"

"Thank you so much. Can we also book in for bridesmaid dresses?"

"Would you like to do that on the same day?"

"No, that will be for the following Saturday. As well as Jo, Lynn and Carol, my fiancé's sister, is also a bridesmaid. But she lives in London and won't be up until then."

Samantha looked through her appointments book and added our dates. "That's perfect. You're booked in for both, and I'll leave a note on the dress."

As we walked out of South Veil Bridal, I looked round at my friends. "Well, I've done it. I've said yes to the dress!"

JENNIFER

It was time to tell our parents about the baby. Scott had suggested inviting the four of them over for Saturday lunch so we could tell them all at the same time. It had seemed like a good idea; until now. Sitting in our living room, the walls showcasing framed photographs of the girls over the years; I shakily uttered words they were not expecting. "So, we've got some news for you." I smiled at Scott as he put his arm round my shoulders. "I'm pregnant!"

Silence.

With a smile fixed in place, I glanced round the room at four shocked faces. Mum didn't say anything, proof she was in shock. Scott's mum was frowning. And the two dads were looking at their shoes. I can't say I blame them. We were shocked when we found out too. But was it so hard to say 'congratulations'?

I needed to guide them. "We were a bit surprised by the news too. But we're excited about extending our family." My comment didn't open a floodgate of jubilation, but it encouraged them to give their congratulations, although none of them did a good job of hiding their questions and concerns.

However, once our awkward lunch ended, Mum and Dad volunteered to take the girls to the cinema. As we waved them off, we walked to the park. The sky was overcast and the chill of the February afternoon caused a shiver, but at least the rain had stopped. We walked past a father who was trying to coax his daughter to get back on her scooter. She ignored his pleas and lay on the ground crying. He threw his arms up in frustration then scooped her under one arm and carried the scooter with his other hand. We smiled as we passed. He nodded back to us and grimaced as he adjusted his hold on the wriggling girl. Over towards the play park, we heard the cries of a mum as she grabbed her errant toddler before he got in front of some joggers. There are so many wonderful parenting moments, but these reminders of the toddler tantrums and challenges weren't helping me. Scott noticed it all too. "Maybe the park wasn't the best place for us today. Let's get a cuppa." I nodded, and we made our way from the park to one of the many nearby cafes.

The café was nice and quiet. I sat on one of the leather settees while Scott ordered our drinks and scones from the counter. In the last few weeks, my drink of choice had gone from coffee to milkshake. The cool, milky drink was proving invaluable at calming my queasy tummy.

"How do you think our parents took the news?" I asked, as I layered jam on my scone.

"I'm not sure. They didn't seem all that enthusiastic."

"I don't want all our announcements to be met with such half-hearted responses. I know it will be a shock for everyone. But I feel bad for this poor wee baby." I leaned back and rubbed my hands over my stomach.

My gaze darted up at Scott's laughter. "Why are you laughing? It's not funny."

"You're right. It's not. But look at you. Just a few announcements in and already you've changed the conversation from how this affects us as a family to protecting our baby. It's because your heart is full of love." He leaned over and kissed me. "See! You're a great mum."

Sometimes negative comments can pull you down. But there are also times when someone's words reach out and lift you up, going beyond your conscious, communicating more than mere words. Scott was right. The reactions from others were helping me process my own thoughts. I didn't want to pretend everything was okay. There would be many changes this year. But I also wanted to celebrate and be prepared for our expanding family. And, as I thought about the girls, a plan formed. "Let's do a games night tonight. We can put out a buffet spread and nibble our way through their favourite foods."

"That sounds like a brilliant idea. What time are your parents bringing them home?"

"I'm not sure. I'll send Mum a text now and tell her to bring the girls home as soon as the movie is finished."

When Mum and Dad dropped the girls off, they presented us with an enormous bunch of flowers and a box of chocolates. "I'm sorry we weren't more excited for you earlier," said Mum. "You took us by surprise."

Scott laughed. "We took ourselves by surprise too!"

"We just wanted to let you know we are excited."

I gave my mum a hug. "Thanks. And thanks for taking the girls to the cinema this afternoon."

After Mum and Dad left, Scott took the girls out to let them pick the food for tonight's buffet. With the house to myself, I snuck upstairs and into bed. Snuggling under my duvet, I selected a praise playlist on my phone, a mixture of favourite songs, new and old. I think I only heard one or two songs before I fell asleep. By the time I woke up, Scott and the girls were home and dinner was almost ready. Revived from my nap, I was ready for a games night with my family.

Chloe started us off with a game of Snap. Then it was Emma's turn with Dobble. We laughed as we played the quick draw games. With Chloe's game, we wanted as many cards as possible and with Emma's game, we wanted the least amount of cards. Amy opted for game challenges on our phones when it was her turn. After which, Chloe declared it was time for Twister.

I grabbed the arrow board. "I'll be the games master for this one. I'm not sure I'll be able to twist into crazy positions."

Chloe pushed a strand of hair away from her face and looked at my stomach. "But you don't have a big tummy like Katie's mum. So you can still play."

I hugged Chloe. "You're right, I don't have a baby bump yet, but I'm feeling yukky at the moment. So I'll just direct the rest of you."

Chloe shrugged and threw off her slippers in preparation for the game. Emma glanced over at me. "Will you feel ill the whole time you're pregnant?"

"I hope not! Usually it's just for the first few months."

After a few rounds of Twister, Amy wanted to watch a movie, her suggestions all seemed to involve singing and dancing high school pupils. She selected one, and we all cuddled on the settee to watch the easy-going movie. I'm not going to lie, a few tears escaped as Amy pushed in to get beside me. Ever since we had told the girls about the baby, she had kept her distance. Hopefully, tonight had helped reassure her. She might think she's beyond snuggles with her mum, but there will be plenty of times in the coming years when this will be her place of safety. As we sat watching the movie, I played with her hair and said a prayer of thanksgiving for the family I have and the family I'm about to have. When we told the girls about the baby, they had bombarded us with a range of questions and emotions. But for tonight, the questions were forgotten as peace and love surrounded us.

PAUL

I collapsed onto the sofa and let out a sigh.

"What's wrong, mate?" asked Matt, as he handed me a cool beer.

"Thanks." I took a drink and leaned my head back. "I'm worried about the salon. No new units have come on to the lease market. Nothing is standing out. And I've still not heard anything from the lawyer about the chance of an extension or if we're definitely out at the end of March."

"Maybe it's time for some brainstorming."

"I tried that with Trish and Brian on Tuesday and we got nowhere. We couldn't think of anything else."

"What's your key criteria for a new place?"

"I'm not sure if I would say location, size or its suitability as a salon."

"So, let's check the available units again. And start with location. We'll list the places that are within a fifteen-minute walk of the current salon and then rate them on plus and minus and suitability. Then we can do the same thing, but by size of unit."

I considered Matt's suggestion. Tuesday's discussion with Brian and Trish had been a disaster as we flailed about, our suggestions and discussions going nowhere. In fact, all we seemed to do was panic each other. But Matt's suggestion had structure and purpose. I needed his analytical outlook for this problem.

"Great idea. But if we're going to do this, we need sustenance," said Matt. "Why don't I make us some pasta and then we'll get started."

Digging in to heaped bowls of spaghetti bolognese, we began Matt's analytical review of the lease listings, marking each property against the various search parameters. After a while, we sat back and Matt reviewed our work. "So there are two main contenders. The big unit round the corner from the current salon or a unit of a similar size a couple of miles away. Which one stands out most for you?"

"I'm not sure. I think this has highlighted location is the thing I'm most drawn to. But the nearest unit is far too big." I clicked on the link for the shop again. Being on a main road and at a bus stop, the location was perfect, even better than the street we were on. What a shame it was too big. I read over the description one more time. A large open plan double shopfront with kitchen, WC and office located to the rear. The property had so much potential. And one day, it would be my ideal salon. Over the past year, The Smith Salon had proven itself and we had increasingly busy schedules, to the extent that I had been considering inviting another stylist or two to join the team, but that would need to be put on hold until we secured a new location and re-established the business. We couldn't expand now.

Matt interrupted my thoughts. "We can't do anything more tonight. Why not give it a few days, then revisit it? Maybe give the lawyer a call on Monday to see if there are any new developments."

As I fell asleep, my thoughts returned to the potential of the large retail unit. If only…

The next day, I sat next to Kirsty in church. She had sent me a text yesterday to let me know she had found *the dress*. And now, she could barely sit still, fidgeting with the cuff of her sweater and crossing and uncrossing her legs. Her excitement was palpable. As the service followed its regular pattern of worship and preaching, my mind wandered, refusing to settle on any one subject. Thoughts of the salon filled my mind, interjected with thoughts of the wedding. I felt a twinge of guilt that the issues with the salon overshadowed my thoughts about our wedding. Kirsty was all excitement, and I was seeing only problems. What was wrong with me? What had happened to my laid-back, take-life-as-it-comes outlook? Initially, leaving the security of the ByDesign salary to set up my own business had been exciting, an adventure. But had stress been creeping in over the last year? Was I getting more absorbed by the business decisions rather than the clients? Was continuing with The Smith Salon the right decision, or did this all show me I should revert to working in someone else's salon? Was that the answer?

As Ben stood up to preach, the words *'Be joyful in hope, patient in affliction, faithful in prayer'* flashed up on the screen behind him. I leaned forward, drawn by the words. Words Matt had prayed for me just a few weeks ago. Words Ben had spoken at my mum's wedding. Was it a trick on my eyesight that 'joyful in hope' seemed to stand out against the rest of the verse? Joyful in hope... that's what I needed. That's what I was missing. I sat back and closed my eyes, letting the words drift round my mind. Feeling their release.

When the service ended, I suggested to Kirsty that we walk back to my flat. Typically, Sunday afternoons will involve hanging out with some of our friends. But for today, I needed time alone with her. As we left church, a mist of fine rain swirled around us. Kirsty quickly adjusted the hood of her jacket, then took my hand. "Are you okay?"

"Getting there." I smiled at her. "I really needed Ben's message this morning." Kirsty squeezed my hand, willing me on. "I've been so distracted with the salon and I've not been there for you for the wedding planning. The salon is taking up all my thoughts."

"Aww, Paul. Please don't worry about that. You know I love organising. Plus, you came up with the idea of hiring a marquee."

I put my arm round her shoulders and hugged her to my side. As I filled her in on last night's rating of units, the light mist of rain transformed into a deluge of hail.

"Ouch!" cried Kirsty, as the hail bounced off her face.

"Come on!" I grabbed her hand and started running towards my flat. In retrospect, running half a mile through a hail storm wasn't the most sensible idea. We entered my empty flat, drenched through. Standing in the hallway, we tried to catch our breath, dripping muddy water all over the floor. We wrestled out of our soaking coats and wet footwear, laughing at our crazy situation.

Kirsty shivered in the chill of her wet clothes, rubbing her arms, trying to heat herself up. "Come here," I said, as I moved towards her, wrapping my arms around her and rubbing her back.

But she pushed me away. "You're all cold and wet."

I laughed. "I think we both are. Come through to my room and grab a sweatshirt and joggers to change into while I put your clothes in the drier." We dripped our way through to my room, leaving a trail of wet footprints.

As she entered, she caught sight of herself in a mirror. "Paul! You should have told me. My makeup! My face!"

I stopped searching through my clothes and walked over to her. Taking my thumbs, I rubbed away the mascara tracks running down her face. And in that moment, something changed. An intense silence sparked between us. I searched her eyes, desperate to know if she felt the intensity too. Her eyes focused on my lips. Leaning in, I kissed her cheeks where moments earlier I'd wiped away the mascara. She let out a gasp and my lips moved to hers. As our kiss deepened, I felt the tremor of her shivers. I pulled back and looked into her eyes. The next few moments were a blur as our tops came off and our desire deepened to an intensity we'd never allowed before. Neither of us able to pull away. This was heading to one conclusion.

The sounds of Matt and Jo entering the flat broke through our crazy actions. We stepped back from one another, gazes lingering for just a moment. Before I could move away, Kirsty brushed her lips against mine and wiped away the signs of her lipstick. I threw on a dry sweatshirt and silently walked from my room. "Hey, guys," I shouted to Jo and Matt as I entered the living room. I had to tone it down. I was being too loud. "We just got here before you, only we walked and got soaked. I've just given Kirsty some dry clothes to change into."

I was sure Matt and Jo could see beyond my words that they knew I'd gone further than I meant to with Kirsty. But they merely nodded their response as they went to the kitchen to put away the food shopping they had brought with them.

For the rest of the afternoon, the four of us played board games and talked about the wedding, salons and teaching. From the outside looking in, it would seem like any normal Sunday afternoon. But inside, my thoughts were churning. I would need to be careful. After all, I had promised Kirsty my old ways were behind me and that I would prove my resolve by waiting until our wedding night until we slept together. But things had progressed too quickly this afternoon. I was floundering in unfamiliar territory, both with the salon and Kirsty. What did that Bible verse say about patience? To be patient in affliction. I almost laughed out loud. Today it felt like an affliction to be patient. I glanced over at Kirsty. She smiled and blushed. As I returned her smile, I realised that the flip side of that affliction would be the joy of our wedding night and knowing I had proven to us both that I had changed.

JENNIFER

I tried not to focus on the fact that at forty-one I was the oldest woman sitting in the waiting room. Instead, I took some deep breaths and closed my eyes. When I was pregnant with the girls, these days were full of emotions. There was the excitement of seeing our baby for the first time, coupled with a tinge of trepidation. Today was even more intense. Holding on to Scott kept me from biting my nails or constantly playing with my hair.

A young couple emerged from the examination room. Huge smiles stretched across their faces as they shared the joy and wonder of the tiny lifeform they'd just seen. Their joy was contagious and my worry was momentarily doused.

'Love the Lord your God with all your heart and with all your soul and with all your mind.' Today was a day for love, not because it was Valentine's Day, but because every day is a day to love God. Would I trust God with whatever showed up on the screen? Would I love him no matter what happened in the next half hour?

"Jennifer Thompson," shouted a midwife. As we stood and walked towards her, she greeted us with a smile. "Good morning. How are you feeling today?"

My laugh was shaky as I replied, "Nervous."

The midwife placed her hand on my arm and gave a reassuring squeeze. Although, I noticed she didn't offer any platitudes. As a midwife, she knows that not every pregnancy goes according to plan. But I appreciated her smile.

We sat at a desk and went through some details, and then it was over to the bed for the scan. First up, the squirt of cold jelly over my stomach. No matter how much you brace against it, you always squirm as the first dollop makes contact with your skin. But as soon as the probe was placed over my uterus, my eyes darted to the screen. As always, I was in awe of professionals who know what they are looking at. All I could see were lines and blurriness on the screen. With a few movements of the probe and clicks on the monitor, the image began to change. Scott squeezed my hand as a tiny little form moved about on the screen. Silent tears streamed down my cheeks as I looked at our baby. Our baby. All the shock and surprise of the pregnancy melted away as I watched the baby moving and floating about inside me. Scott bent down and kissed my wet cheek.

The technician confirmed the baby measured as being twelve weeks, giving us a due date of twenty-ninth of August. In just half an hour, the pregnancy had become a measurable thing. Now we had pictures of our baby and a due date.

Scott glanced at his watch. "Do you want to go for lunch before I go back to work?" I nodded my agreement and Scott drove us to a nearby café.

As we waited to be served our cheese and ham toasties, I looked at the scan images again. Scott leaned over to look at the pictures with me. "How do you feel now you've seen our baby?"

I glanced around as I searched for words to express my feelings. The café was lovely and bright, decorated in light greys and whites. Fairy lights draped along the walls and strings with red love hearts dangled from the ceiling, yet another reminder that it was Valentine's Day. Maybe it was the interior designer in me, but the décor helped me give words to my feelings. "I have so many thoughts and feelings flowing through me. I feel a lightness at seeing our baby and seeing it moving. I feel love for this brand new person. And I feel everything will work out okay." I smiled over at Scott. "What about you?"

Scott scratched his head and laughed. "I think you summed it up really well. With the girls, the scan always made it real. And with this one, I needed that proof more than ever." The server brought over our glasses of juice. "I can't wait to meet our surprise bundle and to figure out how we change and adapt to having four kids. Just think how boring it would be if things actually worked out according to our plans?"

I laughed at Scott's words. "Well, I guess that's one way of looking at it."

After lunch, Scott drove me home before going to the office. In the stillness of the early afternoon, I sat in the family room, trying to decide if I had enough energy to participate in my afternoon classes. Once again, I was thankful for online learning and the flexibility it gave me to catch up on lessons I missed due to medical appointments or sickness. But it didn't mean I could simply skip classes. I had just about built up my resolve to switch on the computer when the doorbell chimed. Tara stood on my doorstep, laden down with a huge lasagne and two milkshakes. This is the definition of a genuine friend.

"How did the scan go?" she asked, as she handed me my milkshake.

"Perfect." I showed her the pictures and we 'oohed' and 'aahed' over the images as we slurped on our tasty milkshakes. Now that I knew I was twelve weeks pregnant, I was even more hopeful that I was nearing the end of the queasiness and would soon enjoy my usual range of food and drinks. But for now, at least, milkshakes were helping.

"Isn't it so exciting watching your baby move about on a screen?" enthused Tara. "It was always the beacon of hope I needed in my pregnancies. With all the discomfort and sickness, it was a great reminder of the reward that was to come."

"Absolutely. Although you should have seen me this morning. You know me, I'll cry at the slightest thing and the tears were streaming down my face as I looked at the scan monitor." Even the thought of it now almost had me crying again. "And I still have so, so many questions. But I'm excited to have another child, and so is Scott."

Tara clapped and laughed. "I really am so excited for you both. Just let me know whenever I can help with anything."

I hugged my friend. "Thank you so much. You've already done loads by providing tonight's dinner. But there is something else I want to thank you for."

"Now I'm intrigued," said Tara. "Is it for knowing that you needed a yummy milkshake?"

I laughed as she took a big noisy sip of her shake. "No. Well, yes, obviously. But back in January, you preached from Matthew. And spoke on the verse, *'Love the Lord your God with all your heart and with all your soul and with all your mind.'* I really needed those words. I needed the perspective that, no matter what is going on, it's about loving God first and above all else. The verse has been a real anchor for me over the last few weeks. So, thank you."

"Don't thank me. God knew what you needed. But I'm thrilled to know it helped you just when you needed it. You've been through a lot of changes over the last couple of years and there's more to come. And you'll handle it all beautifully because you know you're not doing it in your own strength."

That night over Tara's delicious lasagne, we let the girls see the images of their new sibling. Emma smiled at the pictures. Amy seemed a bit more accepting of the situation. And Chloe bent over the image and landed a big kiss on the baby's face. "I love you, tiny baby." I looked away before the girls could see the tears filling my eyes.

KIRSTY

For the next couple of days, I couldn't concentrate. My mind continually replayed the scene in Paul's bedroom. The way he had kissed me. The depth of desire I had for him. It was terrifying and exciting all at the same time. For the last two nights, I had fallen asleep thinking of what had happened. Imagining different conclusions. Was I disappointed that Matt and Jo arrived at the flat when they did, or was I relieved? I honestly didn't know.

Before Paul, I had rarely been tempted to go further. Yes, I had been curious, and a few boyfriends had tried to persuade me to give more. But Paul was different. Maybe it was because I felt secure in our relationship, even with my baggage of insecurities. Or maybe it was just down to the fact the guy is hot and the best boyfriend I've ever had.

My brain was so busy trying to figure out how I felt I was useless at work. I kept putting things in the wrong files, putting the wrong dates on upcoming events, and working way slower than usual as I stared off into space. My colleagues noticed and asked if anything was wrong, but they weren't the ones I needed to talk to. I needed to talk to Paul. Although a nervous flutter danced in my stomach, reminding me I didn't have the best track record when it came to conversations of the heart.

And all of this was colliding with Valentine's Day. What was it with me and Valentine's Day? Last year I had been bunged up with a cold and this year I was completely distracted. When Paul buzzed up to my flat, I shivered with apprehension. But as I opened the door, I fixed a smile in place and welcomed my handsome fiancé. Paul looked amazing, even wrapped up in his coat and hat, and the scent of his aftershave teased my senses. He handed me a beautiful bouquet of red roses. I blushed and hid my face in them, pretending I was leaning in to sniff their delicate perfume. I didn't want to feel awkward with Paul. But when he leaned in to kiss me, I froze.

Paul stepped back and took my hand, leading me into the living room. "We need to talk," he said, as we sat next to each other on the settee. He ran his finger over my engagement ring. "I'm so sorry about Sunday afternoon. For letting things run ahead of us." I tried to return his smile, but I'm not sure my face muscles understood what they were supposed to be doing. Paul continued. "I love you, Kirsty. And I want you to know that I've changed. You're not just *another one,* you're *the one.*"

I threw myself into Paul's arms, delighting in his declaration.

Though when it came to Sunday afternoon, it wasn't all down to Paul, and I had to make that clear to him. "Paul, there were two of us involved. And I'm pretty sure we both wanted the same thing." An awkward laugh passed between us. "I've been so confused since Sunday, going between defending our actions and feeling guilty."

Paul leaned over and kissed my cheek. This time I didn't withdraw. "I love you, Kirsty Price. And I'm sorry we're in this confused place on Valentine's Day of all days. But know that I love you and I don't want to mess things up for us. You're the only one who matters to me."

"I love you too," I said, as I hugged him. "Thank you for making it so easy to talk about things. We'll figure this out."

"Now," said Paul, standing up and holding out his hand to take mine. "Let's go and enjoy our special dinner."

Dinner was okay. The restaurant had gone all out on the Valentines' vibe, each table had a vase with a single red rose, red tea light candles and shiny red confetti scattered around the place settings. There was low mood lighting and soft instrumental music to complete the ambiance. However, with all the attention on the setting, maybe they forgot to focus on the food. My sea bass lacked taste and Paul's burger seemed thinner than usual.

"Happy one-year anniversary," said Paul, as he clinked his glass to mine.

I laughed as I responded to his toast. "Yes, happy anniversary." We both took a sip of our drinks. "I'm still impressed you were brave enough to ask me out when I was all bunged up with a cold and attired in my big fleecy pjs."

"It must be love," he said, and produced the biggest fake sigh. With my laughter still filling the space between us, he sat his glass down and took both my hands in his. "It is love. I've never asked a woman out before while she was in her pyjamas. And I've never dated anyone for more than a month before. I'm in unfamiliar territory with you, Kirsty Price. And I love that I get to experience all this with you."

I squeezed Paul's hands and smiled. "Well, I must confess I have reached the one-year anniversary before. But by that point, we both knew it was over. Especially Glen. He'd already been dating someone else behind my back for a month by then." I pulled a lopsided smile. I didn't want Paul to think I was looking for pity. "But I'm so glad my previous boyfriends were such jerks, because it meant all those past encounters ended and I was free to meet you." I leaned over the table and kissed his warm lips. "Thank you for asking me out. Thank you for asking me to marry you. And thank you for your constant love and support."

Later, as we entered my flat, I felt a spike of worry that the expectations of Valentine's Day might prove too much for us, alone in my flat. But I had a fool proof plan for our evening that involved an apology and a gift. I looked down at my sparkling diamond and smiled. "I love this ring. Although, it has caused me to become very left-handed. At every opportunity, I wave my left hand about, letting the light play with the diamonds. I use my left hand to answer the phone at work, any time I pay for something, putting my hand out to stop the bus. Basically, as much as possible. And last week as I was admiring it, I suddenly realised I owe you an apology."

Paul raised his eyebrows. "Why?" I tried not to laugh at the confused look on his face.

"Because you gave me this beautiful ring and I haven't given you anything." I picked up the big box I had hidden behind the settee and handed it to him. "Here is your engagement gift." Without a moment's hesitation, Paul ripped into the packaging to reveal his brand new games console. A big grin spread over his face as he turned the box round to check the details of his new toy. Paul sat the box down as he said, "Thank you," and pulled me into his arms, brushing his lips against mine. But what started out as a light kiss quickly deepened to more. I didn't want to break away, but we couldn't risk this going further. We both pulled back, eyes locked. Were we checking to see if the other was okay or if there was permission to go further?

I jumped back and picked up Paul's gift. "So, not only is this your engagement gift, but it's also your first house-warming gift. As Matt already has a console, I was thinking you could set this one up here. In fact, why not set it up now and we could play some of the games that came with it." I pointed to the game pictures on the side of the box. "Have you played any of these before? Do you have a favourite? Which one do you think would be easiest for me to play? Out of the games we've played at your flat, I prefer the football and car racing ones."

Paul put the box back down. He took my hands in his and gazed into my eyes. "Take a breath. It's okay. You don't need to talk non-stop to stop me kissing you. I mean, I want to kiss you. But it's fine. We're okay."

My shoulders relaxed as Paul pecked me on the cheek, then set about connecting his new games console. I sat down and watched as he set it up.

By the time Paul kissed me goodnight, I almost floated off to bed. But a shadow of disquiet poked at my peace. My thoughts drifted back over my evening with Paul. Was there something about tonight that unsettled me? No, if anything, Paul's words had chased away so many of my insecurities and fears about our relationship. In just one evening, he had reassured me more than any previous boyfriends ever had over the course of our relationships.

So what was it? Whenever my doubts spike, it usually involves my family. But we've had minimal contact since I was last in Lochcala. Thinking of Lochcala drew my mind back to making wedding arrangements and our meeting at the manse. There was a print on the wall that said something about peacemakers. I had meant to look it up when I got home but I'd forgotten. Picking up my Bible, I flicked to Matthew chapter five and read, *'blessed are the peacemakers, for they will be called children of God'*. I lay back down, letting the words permeate. But the unsettled feeling remained. I sat up in bed and reached for my Bible again, intent on reading the whole of Matthew chapter five. However, I couldn't get past the Beatitudes. I had to keep swiping away my tears to focus on the words. I read the same verses over and over again. All these things – meekness, righteousness, merciful, pure in heart, peacemakers – are attributes my older brothers scoff at, as if they are signs of weakness. And yet, Jesus tells us these are the qualities that will be blessed. Throughout my teenage years, I felt alone and at odds with my family. But Jesus was there, and he saw. He led Gillian to Lochcala to tell me about him. And even though she was only there for a short time, she impacted my life. I hadn't intended to go to church when I moved to Glasgow and yet I was drawn to LifePoint. I might have felt alone, but Jesus had been guiding me.

I switched my light off and lay down. As I fell asleep, the shadows were no longer there. Only the words *'blessed are the peacemakers, for they will be called the children of God'*. Although one question remained. Why had these thoughts surfaced tonight? Was it time to be the peacemaker in my family?

The next evening, Jo arrived first for house group. As soon as I opened the door, she started waving her left hand, brandishing her ring finger to let me see the gorgeous row of diamonds sparkling in their platinum band. We jumped and squealed together. I grabbed her hand for a closer look at her ring. "I'm so happy for you. It's gorgeous. I take it this happened last night?"

"Thank you. And yes, Matt proposed last night. We had dinner, then went for a walk. As we were crossing the footbridge over the Clyde he stopped, got down on one knee and asked me to marry him. And I said 'yes'."

I laughed at Jo's description of the evening. They were a perfect couple.

"So, I've brought celebratory cream cakes for tonight," she said, making her way through to my kitchen to put the cakes in the fridge.

"And what are all the parents saying?" I asked, as I followed her to make tea and coffee.

"Good reactions all round." I could hear the smile in her reply even before I turned round to see my friend smiling and gazing at her ring.

The doorbell rang, signalling the arrival of other members of our small group. By the time everyone arrived, the coffee was made and laid out for people to help themselves. Jo kept her left hand hidden until everyone was there and then held it out for all to see. There were 'oohs' and 'aahs' from everyone as her ring was admired and she was congratulated. With the rest of the group still smitten with the ring, I went to get the cream cakes. "Jo is treating us all to celebratory cakes," I said, sitting the box on my coffee table.

Jennifer cleared her throat. "I've also got some celebratory treats for us." Before we could ask why, Jennifer opened a box that contained cookies in the shape of baby bottles, some decorated with pink icing others blue. "I'm pregnant!" There was a moment of silence. Jo's engagement we had all expected. But this?

I rushed round to my friend and hugged her. "Congratulations! That's lovely news." Everyone else followed my lead and added their congratulations.

"When are you due?" asked Carol.

"I can finally answer that question. I had my scan yesterday, and they have calculated the due date as twenty-ninth of August." She pulled out her phone and opened up her photo album to show us the scan pictures.

"Amazing," said Jo. "What did the girls say about it?"

"We've been through a lot of emotions with them. But I think they're getting used to the idea now and are happy about it, which probably goes for me and Scott too." Jennifer laughed, as we all tucked into cake and cookies.

"What will you do about your studies?" asked Lynn.

"I'll finish my certificate in June and then take a break before I go back to do my diploma. From that point of view, the timing works well."

As the group continued their discussion on Jennifer's pregnancy and Jo's engagement, I sat back and looked round this group of friends. Each person in this room is special, but Jo and Jennifer will always be my go-to friends. This turning out to be an eventful year between weddings and babies!

KIRSTY

A few days later, Mum arrived for her weekend in Glasgow. I fought through the sleet and the crowds of Friday afternoon commuters as I made my way to the bus station. Unfortunately, Mum's bus had arrived a few minutes early and she was standing waiting outside the ticket office. "At last," she said, as I approached. "I'm getting soaked waiting for you. What kept you?"

I made a show of looking at my watch. "Your bus arrived early. Why didn't you wait in the ticket office rather than out here?"

"I didn't want you missing me."

I put all my effort into not rolling my eyes. I counted to ten. And smiled. Once again, I reminded myself, *'Blessed are the peacemakers, for they will be called children of God'.* Being a peacemaker in my family would be a challenge.

Despite the horrible weather, we didn't have to wait too long to get a taxi to my flat. We had enough time to enjoy a cup of tea, of the non-stewed variety, before leaving for Paul's mum's house. As we drank our tea, Mum didn't ask what I had been up to or anything about the wedding. Instead, she told me all about how busy she was with James, Andrew and Dad with their different shift patterns and their social life. I kept glancing at my watch, counting down the minutes until we could be with other people.

As we entered Susan's house, we were greeted with hugs and smiles. "Thanks so much for inviting us over for dinner," I said, as I shuffled out of my raincoat, trying not to drip water over her shaggy hall rug.

"My pleasure. And don't worry about your coats being wet," said Susan as she took our coats. I gazed through to the dining room, the table set for dinner. And in the living room, candles flickered their gentle lights and cast their subtle fragrancies. Soft music played through the downstairs speakers.

Susan reached her hand out to Mum. "It's lovely to meet you, Mrs Price. I'm Susan."

"It's nice to meet you, too."

I cringed. I couldn't believe my mum didn't reciprocate and tell Susan her first name. They were pretty much the same age. But if Susan noticed she gave no indication, instead she ushered us through to her living room. Alex and Paul stood up to welcome us and I snuggled into Paul while he asked Mum about her journey to Glasgow. Once again, she offered nothing more than a curt response. Alex merely shook her hand and said hello. Over a delicious dinner, Susan and Alex steered the conversation, keeping it all light and easy-going. If Mum had engaged with the conversation, even just a little, I could have relaxed. True to form, she remained detached, only offering curt replies to questions directed towards her. I could only hope she wasn't coming across as rude.

"So what are you hoping to achieve this weekend?" asked Susan, looking between me and Mum.

"We've got an appointment at South Veil Bridal tomorrow afternoon to try on dresses. And in the morning Mum wants to shop for Mother of the Bride outfits."

"That sounds like a lovely day."

If only that were true. It would be lovely if Susan came with us, but Mum had refused to include anyone else in our day. I glanced up at Susan and smiled. As she cleared away the plates, she reached over and squeezed my hand and returned my smile.

"Are you hoping to book anything else this weekend?" asked Paul, as we settled down in the living room with our after-dinner coffees.

"I don't know," I replied. "We'll have a look through what's still to be organised and take it from there. We should really get advice from you, Susan. Your wedding was so beautiful and you've probably got lots of tips we could learn from." Mum kept stubbornly quiet beside me. This was the perfect opportunity for her to engage with Susan and Alex. But she refused. I leaned back into the soft settee, trying to hide from my shame.

Susan sent me yet another reassuring smile. "That's so kind of you, Kirsty. But I know you and your mum will put together the perfect wedding."

If only that were true. Tonight only added to the ominous feeling I had for this weekend. There was no sign of peace.

The following morning we were up and out of my flat early to begin our search for Mum's wedding outfit. "Have you thought about what you would like?" I asked as we entered the first shop on her list.

"I don't know. Nothing modern or fancy."

Of course not! Although maybe if I was careful in my approach, I could guide her to something nicer than her usual flowery outfits. I followed behind as she rummaged through the rails of dresses and suits hanging in their protective

113

holders. "This place is too fancy for me," she said, in her embarrassingly loud voice.

"Well, as we're here, why not try on a few outfits? Maybe it will help you decide on styles and colours."

"I suppose so." I tried not to react to her grudging response.

"Look, they've got lots of gorgeous dresses in so many styles and colours. Why don't you try a few different options and see what you like? They also have dresses with jackets."

She replied with a shrug, as she continued to flick through the racks.

I looked away and counted to ten. How often was I going to have to employ this trick today? Eventually, she selected two dresses and made her way to the changing rooms. While she got changed, I updated Jo on the painful progress. Her funny gif replies had me giggling and lightened my mood. Just as well, because when Mum came out of the changing room in the first dress, all my negative thoughts came rushing back. How had she managed to pick the one frumpy outfit in a shop of stylish clothing? At that moment, a sales assistant came over. "How are you getting on, ladies? Would you like to try on a different style?" I wondered if that was shop speak for, 'that doesn't suit you'.

"No, we're fine," said Mum, admiring the outfit in a floor to ceiling mirror. "I think I quite like this one."

I shot a glance at the sales assistant, pleading for her help. "Why don't you try on the next outfit and we'll find some other options for you?" said the assistant.

Mum shrugged and returned to the changing room while I followed the assistant. "Please help. I'm getting married in May and my mum is clueless." The woman smiled and ushered me to a rail of clothes at the opposite side of the shop. "Don't worry, we've been helping brides for years."

We looked through the rail and she suggested styles and colours she thought Mum would suit. Armed with three dresses, we made our way back to the changing room just as Mum emerged. Again, her choice of outfit did nothing for her.

"We thought you might like to try these outfits," said the sales assistant, handing the items to Mum. She glanced down at the dresses with no sign of approval, merely retreating into the changing room with them. Once again, I counted to ten. However, the next time Mum emerged from the changing room, I smiled. "Mum! That really suits you." The dress fitted her beautifully and the blues and purples brightened her face. It was, in my opinion, an old-fashioned outfit, but it suited Mum and was a marked improvement on her choices. She tried on the other two dresses and then put the blue and purple dress on again. It looked like we had a winner. The assistant brought her shoes, a bag and a hat to match. In the complete outfit, she was transformed. "Mum, you look amazing." I was impressed. The sales assistant's smile confirmed that this was the outfit to go for.

"What do you think?" I asked.

"I'm not sure." She searched for the price tags on each of the items. "It is a lot of money."

"Well, you only get to be the Mother of the Bride once. So treat yourself. This outfit works."

"Maybe we could go for a cup of tea and I'll think about it."

I suppressed my frustration. She wasn't saying no, she just needed time to think about it. "So, what are you thinking?" I asked as we finished our teas and shortbread.

"I'm not sure. It's a lot of money."

"Do you like the dress?"

"I do. I like the feel of the material and the fit."

As we sat in the café discussing Mum's outfit for my wedding, I realised Mum needed encouragement. How often does she treat herself? In fact, how often does she even buy anything for herself? It's so easy to get frustrated at my relationship with my parents. But now I was beginning to see Mum in a new light and I realised I could do something positive for her today. "Get the dress, Mum. Treat yourself. You deserve to have something nice. It's okay to spend money."

She almost smiled. "You're right. Let's buy the dress."

Who would have thought shopping for Mum's outfit would lead to a bonding experience? Maybe there could be peace this weekend.

JENNIFER

Is it strange that I love ironing on Saturday mornings? For me, ironing is a time to crank up the music and dance along to my favourite tunes. While the rest of the family slowly wake up, I'm getting another thing ticked off my to-do list. Although, my dancing was having to go at a slower pace, as exerting energy raised my nausea levels too much. Not that it was taking much to make me feel sick at the moment, hopefully it wouldn't be long until I was through this stage.

As I ironed the girls' school uniforms, I prayed for them and for the baby. Since we'd told them about the baby, we'd been getting non-stop questions about where their new sibling was going to sleep. Chloe had asked if the baby could sleep in her room. Not going to happen! The poor baby would never get any sleep. Emma had also volunteered to let the baby share her room. She would be the easiest one to share with a sibling, but just because she is the quietest doesn't mean she should be the one to change. And Amy was adamant she wouldn't share her room with anyone. A sentiment she had been very vocal about this week, to the point where I'd had to talk with her about her attitude.

As I continued ironing, one of my favourite praise songs came on. I sang along, the connection between praise and joy brightening the dull February morning. I might be feeling constantly sick, but I was also feeling more joy about the baby. My thoughts drifted back to my Bible verse for the year. '*Love the Lord your God with all your heart and with all your soul and with all your mind.*' As long as I kept loving God as my top focus, other things diminished in intensity. It didn't mean my questions vanished, but I came at them from a much better perspective.

I gathered up the newly ironed clothes and took them to the various bedrooms. Walking through the house, the sounds of a lazy Saturday spilled out from various rooms. Scott and Emma were lying on the sofa in the family room reading books. Amy was in her room singing along with her favourite songs. And Chloe was chattering away as she had a tea party with her teddy bears. I love our house, a home that has witnessed tears, laughter, arguments, hugs and joy. The downstairs was perfect for family life, with its large kitchen, living room and family room. There were no issues with the downstairs space. However, I was still trying to figure out how to work the sleeping arrangements. I wandered around the bedrooms.

The girls' bedrooms were a good size and big enough to share. If they had to share, they would be fine, but was there another option? I paused at the walk-in cupboard between Chloe and Emma's rooms. Opening the door, I was greeted by a cluttered space. I am meticulous about keeping our house tidy, but this is my dumping ground, the one space that is never tidy. Curious about the potential beyond the clutter, I started pulling out the strange combination of items, intrigued to see how big the cupboard was. Out came sleeping bags, summer jackets, buckets and spades, forgotten cushions and throws. Tubs with colouring pencils and craft supplies. Boxes of old toys and books that should have been taken to charity shops years ago. Right at the back of the cupboard was a box of baby toys. I sat in the hallway and opened the box. Each toy brought their own glow of memory. The teething rings that consoled Amy as the pain of erupting teeth transformed her from a contented baby to a child in constant discomfort. The squeaky elephant that at first made Emma cry before it became her must-have toy. The building blocks that Chloe insisted were throwing toys rather than building toys. Each memory brought tears and smiles. Who knew untidy cupboards could be a family treasure trove?

I sat in the jumble of memories and looked into the now empty cupboard. It was listed as a cupboard in the house schedule, but it could be more. A tall narrow window on the far wall furnished the space with natural light. If we removed the shelves lining the walls, would it provide enough space for a nursery? I felt a flutter of excitement as I considered the interior design challenge in front of me. In fact, it could even form part of my portfolio. I could take plenty of photos of before, during and after and record the whole project. I pushed myself up from the floor, planning to get my tape measure. I almost skipped downstairs at the thought of my maternity time still involving design. But a scream of "Mum!" stopped me in my tracks. Amy!

Running back upstairs, I tried to push aside the feeling of nausea that my sudden burst of activity had caused. I rushed into Amy's bedroom, but she wasn't there. "Amy? Where are you?"

"In the bathroom."

Not knowing what to expect I took a deep breath and tried the bathroom door. It was locked. As Amy unlocked the door, she pulled me into a hug. What was going on?

"I've started bleeding." As she uttered those words, I heard Scott rushing up the stairs, followed by Emma and Chloe. I gently guided Amy further into the bathroom and locked the door behind us.

"We're okay," I shouted out to the rest of the family as I hugged Amy. We'd had the chat about periods last year. And I'd bought her a box of items to prepare her for this transition. But it still came as a surprise. Now the increased emotions of last week made sense. "How are you feeling? Are you sore? Do you have a headache?"

She sniffed. "No, nothing like that. I just got a shock at the sight of blood. My friends have been talking about their periods, so I knew what to expect."

"Tell you what. Why don't I get you a pair of the period pants? You get yourself sorted in here and then I'll take you out for a milkshake." I was rewarded with the biggest smile I'd seen from my daughter in a long time.

We bundled up in our cosy jackets and winter woollies and walked to the local café for our drinks. Nestled in comfy seats, in the warmth of the café, the coolness of my vanilla milkshake quelling my nausea, I realised it was a while since the two of us had last hung out. We needed this time. Especially as she entered the season of hormone adjustment. As she sipped on her chocolate milkshake, Amy filled me in on stories from school. Her favourite subjects, her favourite teachers, the drama of high school life and whom had fallen out with whom.

"Why were you clearing out the hall cupboard?" she asked, as her stories of school ended.

"I was wondering if I could convert it into a bedroom for this one." I rubbed my hand over my stomach.

"Ugh, Mum. Don't get all mooshy with that pregnant woman tummy thing." I laughed at her comment. Although it served as a reminder that she was still struggling with the baby news. And that was okay. She, like many others, needed time to adjust. "But I'm glad you've come up with a solution that means we've still got our own rooms."

"Well, it's not set yet. I need to discuss it with Dad and check the measurements. And then make some calculations to see if it will work."

"Hopefully it will. Plus, it would be a fun project for you to practice your new interior design skills."

I smiled across at her. "Sometimes I forget you notice what's going on in my life." She shrugged and picked up her phone to check-in with her friends.

As we finished our milkshakes, I thought again about loving God with all my heart, soul and mind. Today was a reminder of the constant change in family life. In a few months, we would be at the new baby stage, Amy was dealing with puberty, and in-between were Chloe's energy levels and Emma's quiet depths. Family life would always be changing. Study and work would always be changing. But loving God was my anchor in the midst of it all, the place where I would be re-energised and equipped for all those changes. On a boring February afternoon, something shifted in my outlook.

KIRSTY

We walked into South Veil Bridal like a regular mother and daughter. Chatting and smiling. The success of purchasing Mum's Mother-of-the-Bride outfit had worked some kind of miracle on our relationship. Just imagine if planning my wedding ended up bringing us closer together!

Over lunch, Mum made lots of comments about her new outfit. She noted how delicious her bowl of carrot and coriander soup was. She enthused about the atmosphere in the café. I couldn't believe the difference buying one dress made. By the time we get to the wedding, we'll be the perfect family, laughing and talking like normal families. No more negative jibes. My imagination took flight, picturing the relationship with Mum that I'd never had but always wanted. I could see us now, smiling for the mother and bride photographs. Instead of the boys being her focus, she would ensure she made the most of my special day. And, most importantly, she would keep James and Andrew from making their usual snide remarks.

"Good afternoon, ladies," greeted Samantha, doing a stellar job of pretending we'd never met before.

"Hi, I'm Kirsty, the bride. And this is my mum. It looks like you have lots of gorgeous dresses here."

"And I can tell we won't have any problem finding you your perfect dress. Do you have any styles in mind?"

I took out my phone and went through the charade of showing Samantha the selection of dresses I'd shown her on my first visit. Again, she nodded as she looked at the photos on my phone. "Yes, we have those in stock. I'm not sure we'll have them in your size, but we'll do our best. Take a seat while I find the dresses. Would you like a tea or coffee or cold drink?"

"I would love an orange juice. Mum, what about you?"

"A cup of tea would be appreciated," replied Mum. She seemed disorientated in the shop. As if the sight of so many dresses was too much for her.

"Isn't it beautiful here?" I asked, determined to keep our renewed mother and daughter relationship skipping along.

She didn't answer immediately, continuing to look around. "There are so many dresses. How on earth can you choose? And how did you know what to ask for?"

Her words brought a wave of panic, or maybe that was guilt, until I realised her comments didn't mean she had guessed my secret. Rather, it pointed to her disengagement with the online world and lack of awareness that brides-to-be simply needed to go to a shop's website to peruse dresses. I let the realisation sink in and allowed myself to relax.

Samantha soon returned with the dresses I had asked for. I slipped into the changing room to try on the first dress. Before I tried on any dresses last week, this had been my first choice. It was a beautiful princess-worthy dress. The fitted bodice clung to my torso and the beautiful layers of tulle produced a wonderful swishing effect. I came out of the changing room and stood on the platform. I gazed in the mirrors, admiring the beauty of the dress. Even though I knew a more perfect dress existed, I still loved this one. I wondered what Mum would say. She took a sip of tea as she looked at the dress. "It is pretty. But I need to see you in other dresses to have something to compare it to."

"Okay, on to the next," I said, as I swooshed back to the changing room. It was wonderful getting to wear these beautiful dresses again. Although, I felt a bit guilty. I should have been honest with Mum and told her I'd visited some bridal shops with my friends. I get annoyed at my parents' attitude towards me, but perhaps I hadn't been fair to Mum either. She wanted the dress shopping to be a mother and daughter experience, but maybe she would have been okay with me having an initial look with my friends.

As with my previous visit, the other two dresses didn't appeal to me as much as the first dress, or the dress I was leaving for last. Mum gave her opinion on each dress. I was surprised at how positive she was being about the whole experience.

"Now for my suggestion," said Samantha, ushering me back to the changing room. When we were alone, she whispered, "What do you think of the dresses this time?"

"I'm loving them. I'm so lucky getting to try on these beautiful dresses again. And I'm noticing details about them I missed the first time. I'm feeling nervous about this dress. What if it's not all I remember it being?"

"It's no problem to change your mind. Trying on bridal dresses can feel a bit like a whirl wind and as soon as you are away from all the silk and lace, the dresses all blend into one. Even with photos to look back on."

Samantha's words were the reassurance I needed. She helped me into the last dress. My dress. I squeezed my eyes closed. Desperately hoping I would still love it. Once again, I swished out to the viewing area. I took my place and looked in the mirror. Tears filled my eyes. I still loved the dress. This is the one. The dress I'll wear when I become Mrs Smith. I couldn't wait for Paul to see me in it. I fingered the skirt detail, loving every millimetre of the dress. "I prefer the second dress," said Mum, pushing me back into all my insecurities. The second dress was beautiful. A satin ball gown with a high neckline. Simple and elegant. But my friends had all agreed it was too plain and didn't make the most of my height and figure.

Thankfully, Samantha came to the rescue. "What do you prefer about the other dress?"

"It was classic and modest. The neckline of this dress is too low, and her back is exposed."

I could cry, but not from happy tears. What had I been thinking? Getting so excited about the way things were progressing with Mum. Of course, she would say something to cast a cloud over the day. Why couldn't she see how beautiful this dress was? I bet Paul's mum would love it and encourage me to go for it. If only I'd insisted Susan had accompanied us, or even Jo. Someone who would bring a voice of reason and style to this shopping excursion.

"What do you think, Kirsty?" asked Samantha.

"I love this dress. When I picture the church and the marquee, this is the dress I'm wearing."

"It's important you feel special and comfortable with your choice. It is your day."

I could hug Samantha. This woman knew her job well. She's probably had years of experience navigating bridezillas and difficult mothers.

"I'm still not convinced," replied Mum. "It just seems too exposed at the top."

"Mum! It's not exposed. Everything's covered that needs covered." Despite my frustration at Mum, I almost burst out laughing at my words. What a ridiculous situation.

"I suppose you could always get a shawl or stole to put around your shoulders."

What? Should I agree with her to get my dress, or should I say no? I looked pleading to Samantha. "Well, that could be an option," she said in her soothing voice. "But look at the beautiful details of the dress. You wouldn't want this hidden. This is a very tasteful dress, and it really does suit Kirsty's slender build and height. Our seamstress will ensure it's perfectly fitted. Trust me, Mrs Price, in this dress, Kirsty will be a stunning bride."

Mum stood up and walked round me. What a difference to coming with my friends. They all jumped up and hugged me when they saw me in this dress. That was the experience a bride-to-be wanted, not this negativity. But then the second miracle of the day happened. Mum relented! She looked from my reflection to Samantha. "I suppose you have a point. Perhaps this will be okay." As she spoke, she turned back to me and started tugging the bodice up higher. But I could ignore her embarrassing actions if it all meant the dress would be mine.

Before she could say anything else, I took the lead. After all, it is my wedding and my dress. "We'll take the dress, thanks."

Samantha smiled at me and nodded. "Excellent choice. Let's get all your dates and details noted, and we can book your fittings."

Twenty minutes later, we were getting ready to leave South Veil Bridal. My dress bought, and the date set for my first fitting. Samantha's assistant brought our raincoats over for us. "Lovely to see you again. When I saw you in that dress at your last visit, I knew it was the dress for you."

Mum glared at me. "Your last visit?"

PAUL

I rang Tara and Ben's doorbell, shuffling back and forwards, a multitude of questions wrestling for my attention. Where would my new salon be? Would I even be able to find one before the wedding? How could I comfort Kirsty when I was guilty of only half-listening to her stories about the wedding and the fallout with her mum? And why had Tara asked to see me today?

Tara had pulled me aside at church yesterday and said she wanted to talk to me about something. But she refused to give me any clues, and I had no idea what to expect from this lunch meetup.

The smell of bacon teased my senses as I entered their kitchen. "Lunch will be ready in a few minutes," greeted Ben. Tara motioned for me to sit at their kitchen table and poured me a mug of coffee. My stomach growled as Ben put a plate full of bacon sandwiches on the table. "Wow! This looks and smells amazing. Thanks." I said, as we tucked into our lunch.

"How did Kirsty's dress search go at the weekend?" asked Tara.

"All good. The dress has been bought. Although the day ended with a fallout between Kirsty and her mum, but that's a big story on its own."

"Oh dear. There are always disagreements during wedding planning. But don't worry, it will be forgotten come the big day."

I took another bite of my sandwich, wondering what the purpose of today's meeting was. Small talk was fine, but I was curious why I was here. I'm not sure if Ben picked up on my thoughts, but he turned the conversation to the reason for my invite. "You're probably wondering why Tara invited you over." I nodded.

"I'm sorry I didn't say more yesterday, but it's a rather long story, so I thought it would be better to meet up and talk it all through," said Tara, licking her fingers as she finished her sandwich. "For a while now, we've been thinking about setting up a community café. But we just weren't sure where. On the one hand, it would make sense to have it close to church, but city centre prices are crazy. And then we thought that as we're also close to the South Side of the city, we could expand our search there."

I slowly nodded, not sure why they were telling me. I grabbed another bacon sandwich while Tara continued. "We've seen a unit on Kilmarnock Road that we love, although we felt something was missing." At Tara's mention of Kilmarnock Road, my attention racked up a notch.

"We've been thinking and praying about the cafe for months," continued Ben. "And we couldn't understand why the plan wasn't progressing, even after looking at that unit. But then Jennifer and Tara were talking last week and Jennifer mentioned you need to find new premises. And we realised the unit we've been praying about is round the corner from your current salon."

Tara became even more animated as she continued, her hands waving around as she spoke. "I suddenly realised The Smith Salon was the missing piece. This new venture was never supposed to be just a café. It needs to be a community space." Tara's eyes sparkled and she could barely sit still. "Imagine if we went into this together! The unit could be split between the café and your salon. Even though it's one unit, we could operate it and partition it as two separate entities. How exciting would that be?"

I didn't know what to say. What could I say? I couldn't believe we'd both been looking at the same premises. Was it exciting, or was it a tease? Could this work? Did it make sense to go into business with church? We would have our own space and businesses, to an extent. But they would also be tied together. And what if the café didn't work out? I'd be right back to my current problem. Was there too much uncertainty?

Tara sat across from me, an expectant look on her face, desperately waiting for my 'yes'. But I couldn't agree even if I was totally on board. I needed to talk to Brian and Trish about it too. The smile on Tara's face was diminishing the longer I took to reply.

"What are you thinking?" asked Ben, coming to the rescue. "We realise it's a whole new concept for you to process and it's not fair to expect your answer now. But have a think about it and let us know any questions or concerns you have. The unit has been available for a while, so we've got time to think it over."

I rubbed the back of my neck and cleared my throat, giving myself time to put together the right answer. "Thanks so much. I really appreciate the thought. But honestly, I've no idea how I feel right now. I can't believe we've been looking at the same unit. So I guess that means something. I'm excited by the idea but I also have loads of questions and would need to discuss it with Brian and Trish. As soon as I've spoken to them, I'll get back to you. I'm sorry I can't give you a definite answer yet."

"We understand." Tara tried to raise a smile to cover the disappointment that had flashed across her face. I didn't want to disappoint anyone, but nor did I want to rush off in a new direction. There was an excitement in Ben and Tara's proposition but it also added to the questions I had arrived with.

All afternoon I wrestled with the idea of the salon being attached to the church café. I just couldn't decide if it was a good idea. Pacing round the flat wasn't helping. I needed to get out and run. It was a cloudy, still day, chilly, but perfect for a run. With my music cranked up, I ran to Glasgow Green, pushing myself faster and faster to combat the frustration. Once at the park, I sat down on a bench. There were plenty to choose from on an overcast February afternoon. Taking my phone out of my arm holder, I opened my Bible app. I looked up the verse in Romans, *'Be joyful in hope, patient in affliction, faithful in prayer.'* Had I been faithful in prayer? No, I hadn't been. It was time I prayed more about the salon situation and asked God what he thought. Instead of listening to music on my return run, I prayed.

By the time Kirsty arrived at my flat in the evening, I was feeling more peaceful about the salon. I still wasn't sure going in with the church café was the right decision, but there was a spark of joy and excitement at the prospect. Which all meant I could give Kirsty my full attention. It was time I engaged with the wedding planning.

Kirsty flopped down onto my sofa. "Still not heard anything from your mum?" I asked, handing her a glass of juice.

"Nope! She's not answered the phone or replied to any text messages." She took a sip of her drink and sighed.

"Have you asked Craig about it?"

"Nope. I don't want to pull him in to my drama. I'll leave it another few days and try again."

'Be joyful in hope.' I wasn't the only one who needed some joy and hope. It was time for me to step up and help Kirsty with the wedding planning. "What else is still to be done?"

"I think we've got most things organised."

It was the least enthusiastic I'd seen her about the wedding. I ran my hands through my hair and looked up to the ceiling, as if inspiration was about to pop out from the lampshade. Kirsty picked up the TV remote, flicked on the TV and surfed through the channels. An advert caught my attention. I took the remote from her hand and switched off the TV. She looked up at me and was about to say something when I shouted. "Honeymoon!" Kirsty stared at me, open mouthed. "We need to decide where to go on our honeymoon," I continued.

I grabbed my laptop. "Have you had any thoughts about where you would like to go to celebrate becoming Mr & Mrs Smith?"

Kirsty giggled as she sat up and looked at the screen. "Somewhere warm and sunny with a beach," she suggested.

"That should be easy at the end of May." I typed honeymoon destinations into the internet search bar. "And I forgot to tell you. Mum said she'll give us money towards our honeymoon."

"Brilliant. I'd love to go somewhere romantic and couply."

I gazed at my laptop. "There are pages of result! We need to narrow this down."

"Maybe search by continent. How about we start with Europe? Maybe one of the Greek islands?" said Kirsty. "I've never been before, but I've heard they are amazing."

I typed in 'honeymoon destinations Greece'. Images of white-washed buildings set against radiant blue water filled the screen. "I think you've hit on a winner with your first suggestion, Mrs Smith-to-be." I clicked on a resort on the island of Crete. The beautiful white hotel was a complex of bungalow-like accommodation. Each room had a secluded terrace that opened on to the hotel pools. Palm trees planted in large planters adorned the pool areas. It was a honeymoon paradise. "What do you think?" I whispered, trying not to let my thoughts get too carried away.

Kirsty gazed at the screen. "It's beautiful. I can't believe this could be our first holiday destination as a married couple." She leaned in and kissed me. As soon as her lips were on mine, I wanted more. The kiss progressed into a passionate hunger. Were we both imagining being on a private terrace as a married couple? Moving my laptop onto the settee beside me, I ran my hands through Kirsty's hair, massaging the base of her skull. She relaxed into my touch and ran her hands under my jumper. The longing that was interrupted a week ago was back with increased passion. Neither of us willing or able to pull away. Both of us edging over the boundaries we'd set.

This time we didn't hear Jo and Matt come in to the flat. Neither of them said anything. Matt merely cleared his throat. Kirsty's eyes opened wide in horror as she realised we were no longer alone. She tried to button up her shirt as she ran to the bathroom. What had I done?

KIRSTY

Tears of shame were streaming down my face. I wanted to stay hidden in the bathroom until everyone left the flat. But a gentle tapping at the door let me know that would not happen. Maybe if I stayed quiet, whoever was there would give up and go away. There was a pause. And then Jo's soft voice drifted to me. "Kirsty, let me in. I know you're upset and embarrassed, but I'm not going anywhere. Please let me in." I sniffed and rubbed some tissues under my eyes and nose and unlocked the door but didn't open it. Jo slowly opened the door and stepped into the bathroom. She didn't say anything. Instead, she wrapped her arms around me. Safe in the arms of my best friend, my tears returned. After a few minutes, we sat on the edge of the bath and she handed me more tissues. I leant my head on her arm. "Am I overreacting, Jo?"

Jo reached her hand up and stroked my hair. "Maybe just a bit." I could hear the smile in her voice. The smile of one who has walked me through years of over reactions. "Let's go back to the others. The four of us need to talk."

Jo took my hand and led me through to the living room. I lowered my head and let my hair hide my face, not because my face was blotchy and mascara streaked from the tears, but because it gave me a veil to hide behind. Slinking into the armchair, I pulled my legs up in front of me and wrapped my arms around them. I chanced a glance at Paul. He was watching me and sent me an awkward smile. Matt came through from the kitchen carrying a pot of coffee. The welcoming aroma doing its best to untangle my defences. But I kept my gaze on my hands.

Jo brought my cup over to me and perched on the arm of my chair. I let out a sigh as I accepted my coffee. Wrapping my hands around my mug, I glanced around the room. My face flushed red as I spoke. "I'm sorry you guys saw that."

I heard Paul's intake of breath as he prepared to speak. But Jo cut him off. "No apologies are necessary." She rubbed my arm. "And don't think you are the only couple struggling with pre-marriage boundaries."

My mouth fell open, but I didn't know what to say. Jo smiled. "Yes, Kirsty. We're struggling too. It's all so difficult and confusing. The world looks at us and judges us as weird for saying we'll wait until we're married to have sex. After all, compared to some of the stuff that goes on, what is the big deal about sleeping with your fiancé? But then, on the flip side, there are people who would judge us if we 'go too far' before we get married. And then there are still others who hope we go all the way to ease their consciences. It feels like no matter what choice we make; people are judging us. Even though it's no one else's business." Jo paused and took a sip of coffee. I rarely saw her get this emotional about a subject. "I guess all we can do is work out what we believe is right. Matt and I have talked about it and we want to wait until we're married to have sex. But what is permissible between now and then?" Jo let out a sigh. "At the end of the day, these are private matters between a couple and not something to be shared with just anyone. But we thought that as you guys are probably in a similar position, we could have a kind of accountability pact. You know, help each other keep the boundaries we've set."

"That sounds like a great idea," said Paul, as he walked over to me and pulled me into a hug. I nestled into his arms, enjoying the security and the familiar scent of his aftershave.

Matt gave a nervous laugh. "And don't think we're doing this for your benefit. On the night we got engaged, we were in a similar position to you guys." Uncharacteristically, he blushed. "Pardon the pun!" Seeing Matt's blush broke some of my own feelings of shame and doubt and started me giggling. And in the midst of my giggles, I whispered a prayer of thanks for our best friends.

By the next weekend, I had recovered from the traumatic shopping trip with Mum and my evening of embarrassment. And now it was time for another major shopping trip. Lauren had flown up from London to join us for bridesmaid dress shopping. She breezed into my flat, hugging everyone and congratulating Jo on her engagement, lifting her hand to examine the sparkling jewel. "So much excitement!" She gave Jo an extra hug. I watched in awe as Lauren chatted and laughed with the others. I would be shy and quiet coming into an established friendship grouping. But Lauren had no such hang ups. But then, neither does Paul.

"Will I get to see your dress?" asked Lauren, as we arrived at South Veil Bridal.

"Hopefully, I'd love to see it again too." Today was about finding bridesmaid dresses, but I was secretly hoping I would get the chance to wear my dress too.

"Will you be looking at wedding dresses today, Jo?" asked Lauren.

"No. This is Kirsty's day. I'll start looking at dresses in the next week or two."

Samantha greeted us all as we shrugged out of our wet raincoats. I hoped the rain and floods of winter would mean a dry May and perfect conditions for a marquee wedding. But dry weather was never guaranteed in the West of Scotland. "It's lovely to see you all again," said Samantha, as she led us through to the bridesmaid dresses. "Have you seen any styles you would like to try?"

Even though I was excited about today's shopping trip, I was also nervous about getting these four friends to agree to a style. I looked round my bridesmaids and shrugged. "No. And we don't even know if it's best to have all the bridesmaids in the same style and colour or do some mix'n'match. What do you think?"

Samantha considered each of the bridesmaids. "The 'mix-n-match' approach works well when you have a range of heights and colouring."

"You mean small people like me versus tall women like Lauren," said Jo.

Samantha didn't hesitate at Jo's comment. "It is about the positives in each bridesmaid and what suits them."

Jo nodded along with Samantha's response. "I like that. I think maybe we should go for the different styles. What do you think, Kirsty?"

"I want the four of you to be happy and feel comfortable on the day."

"Well, it's your day," said Carol. "So you get to say what you want." Carol will always look for the fairest solution she can find. Although at this rate, we would never make any decision. I gave an imploring look to Samantha. "I guess I'm still not sure. If we learned anything from the wedding dress search, we know it's not always our initial choice we go with. And we know you have impeccable taste."

"Okay," said Samantha, taking her cue. "Here's what I suggest. Let's start with the style. I'll get the four of you to try on five or six styles, then you'll each pick your favourite dress and we'll see what that looks like."

"That sounds like a great idea," said Lauren. "I'm so excited about trying on lots of pretty dresses."

Samantha laughed at Lauren's enthusiasm before returning her attention to me. "Style is our first consideration, but it would be good to think about colours too. Have you had any thoughts on colours?"

"Paul will be wearing a kilt. He's hoping to get the Smith tartan, which is mainly blues and greens. So maybe blue or green." I beamed at the thought of Paul in a kilt.

Samantha grinned. "I love the kilt weddings. They give a great range of colour options. I'll select blue or green dresses where we have them. You can either have all the dresses the same colour or complimentary blues and greens."

"So many options." I sighed. "I'm glad we've got you to guide us through all the choices." As my friends tried on their dresses, I sat back and relaxed, sipping my refreshing orange juice and flicking through wedding magazines. I couldn't wait to find out what this dress search would bring.

For the next hour, I marvelled at the beautiful dresses modelled by my wonderful bridesmaids. As they tried on full-length dresses, mid-length dresses, sweetheart necklines, strapless dresses, dresses in chiffon, dresses with lace detail, dresses with embellishments, one thing became clear. This would not be a simple task. We discussed the pros and cons of each dress as they modelled them. Lauren, with her slender height, suited all the dresses she appeared in. But seemed to prefer the fit and V-neckline of one of the dresses. Jo's preference was for a strapless dress with a cute sweetheart neckline. The dress came with a lace jacket with cap sleeves. Lynn preferred a dress with an illusion neckline and ruched bodice. While Carol's favourite was another V-neck dress, but unlike the smooth fit of Lauren's favourite, this one had a criss-crossed bodice that had a subtle slimming effect on Carol. I sat back and listened to the conversation. How were we ever going to decide?

"Okay," said Samantha, "Now it's time for each of you to put on your favourite dress."

Each of my friends retreated to the changing rooms. While they were occupied, I spoke to Samantha. "What do you think? Does this mean we should go for the 'mix-n-match' approach?"

"Based on the conversations, I think that will work best for your bridesmaids. When they all come out, you'll see what I mean."

"Should I do or say anything?"

"Why don't you direct them to the colour scheme you would like for your day? Have you had any more thoughts regarding colour?"

"I like your idea of different colours. Maybe Lauren and Jo in blues and Lynn and Carol in greens?"

"Yes. I think that would work really well. Lauren and Jo's choices are both in blues. I don't have the other dresses in greens, but we can see what is available later." Samantha walked to the changing area to check on my friends.

I sat on my hands to avoid the temptation of nibbling my fingernails while I waited. A few minutes later, Samantha returned with my bridesmaids. I gasped at the sight of them. "Yes!" I jumped up and hugged them all. "I love these designs together."

Jo twirled round in her dress. "Me too. Why don't you try on your dress, Kirsty, and we can see how it all looks together?"

I grinned at Samantha. "Can I?"

"Of course," she laughed.

Fifteen minutes later, I stood in the middle of my bridesmaids. Samantha took some photos for us with my phone. "What do you think about the colours?" she asked. Jo and Lauren loved the colours of their dresses. Jo's was a beautiful deep sapphire and Lauren's was a slightly darker marine blue. "I really love the slight difference in the blues," replied Jo.

"Me too," agreed Lauren.

Samantha turned to Lynn and Carol. "Kirsty and I were talking about the dress colours, and we thought it would be lovely to have your dresses in shades of green. What do you think?"

I dipped my head to hide my smile. I could hug Samantha. She knew what I wanted and was willing to be the one to make it happen. Lynn is a wonderful friend, but if she has her mind made up on something, it's impossible to get her to change it. I was intrigued to see how Samantha would navigate this one.

"Of course," Carol replied. "Whatever Kirsty wants, it's her big day." Carol looked over at me and beamed.

Lynn frowned slightly. "I'm just trying to imagine what this dress will look like in a dark shade."

Samantha, again, stepped in to my rescue. "Just because it's green, it doesn't mean we need to go for a dark shade." She produced a binder with colour samples to show the range of shades available.

Lynn considered the colour options before her. "I like that one," she said, as she pointed to muted-sage. Carol was looking on and selected a gorgeous, deep emerald. Samantha nodded her approval. "These styles and colours will work really well together."

Last week I left this shop on the brink of tears. Today I was leaving with the biggest smile on my face. It was the retail therapy I needed to get my wedding mojo back on track. I was excited again!

PAUL

After a few hours in the salon, it was time for kilt shopping. As Matt drove to the kilt outfitters, I looked out the window and sighed at yet another day of grey skies and sleet. Would this winter never end? I couldn't wait for the first hints of spring. A season that would bring brighter days and the wedding. During the week, Kirsty and I had a good chat about what had happened at the weekend and the boundaries we wanted to stick to. It would be easy to justify going further physically, and sometimes I wondered if it really was that big a deal. And yet, I knew there was a significance for me, for us, in waiting until our wedding night before we slept together. I couldn't explain it to anyone, not even myself, but I knew it was important. Maybe it was the proof I needed that I had changed.

Matt parked his car and we ran to the shop, hoping to stay dry. But even those few metres had us shaking the sleet off our coats and hair.

The smell of leather drew our attention to the display of ghillie brogues to our left. Rows of the traditional kilt shoes gleamed in the bright lights of the shop. There was an array of jackets, shirts, tartans, and every accessory that could be paired with a kilt. A man of about our age, in a kilt and polo shirt, walked up to us. "Good afternoon. How can I help you?"

Matt took the lead. "Hi, we're Matt and Paul. I booked an appointment for us?" The salesman nodded. "It's wedding year for us – we're both getting married and we're each other's best man."

"Excellent," replied the salesman. "Do you know what tartan you want? Is it for hire or buy?"

"We're not sure if we want to hire our kilts or buy them. Paul's looking for the Modern Smith and I'm looking for the Cunningham Dress Purple."

"Okay, let's go through to the office and I can talk you through the various options. Neither of those tartans are ones we normally carry for our hire range. But I'm sure we can sort something out."

We followed Gordon, the salesman, to the office at the back of the shop, passing kilted mannequins and life-size posters on our way. For Mum's wedding, I'd hired my kilt from an old-fashioned, stuffy shop in the city centre. In contrast, this out-of-town unit was bright and airy, much more to my liking. Over glasses of chilled water, Gordon pointed to the prices displayed on his computer screen and explained our options.

"You can either buy or hire the complete outfit, although hiring could be a challenge with the tartans you are looking for. You could also buy your kilts and hire the rest of the outfit. Or you could buy your kilts and see what is available to buy from our ex-hire range. Items in our ex-hire range still look good as new, so it's a popular option for a lot of our customers. And as you have at least two weddings this year, it might be an idea to buy your kilts." Gordon stood up. "I'll leave you to look through our price lists."

"What do you think?" I asked.

"I think I like the idea of buying the kilt and seeing what's available as ex-hire for the rest."

I nodded, clicking through some of the options again. "That sounds like a good idea. But do you know what style of jacket you want?"

Matt looked over to the posters, the telltale crease on his forehead letting me know he was thinking. "I want to try on different options and see what I like best."

"That also sounds like a good idea," I replied, as I followed his gaze round the shop to the mannequins and posters showing the different kilt outfits.

Gordon returned to us when he noticed us looking around. "Have you made your decision?" We updated him on our thoughts. After getting us measured, he led us to the changing rooms and brought us kilts. Unfortunately, they didn't have the tartans we wanted, but they gave us kilts in the same general colour scheme. Our changing rooms quickly filled up as we were given Prince Charlie, Tweed and Jacobite jackets and waistcoats, shirts, bow ties, ruche ties, socks, flashes, belts, buckles and sporrans. There are a lot of parts when it comes to kilts!

From the other side of the changing room, I could hear Matt huffing and puffing. "You alright there, mate?"

"Just trying to remember what goes where." I laughed at his frustration.

"Do you require any assistance??" Gordon asked.

"I think I've got it," replied Matt.

After our battle with buckles, bow ties, jackets and calf-length laces, we stepped out of the changing rooms. "Very smart," commented Gordon. I felt a surge of excitement. For the next half hour, we tried on various combinations with our kilts, from the formal Prince Charlie to the more casual Jacobite apparel. With each change, Matt and I discussed the pros and cons.

"Do you know what combinations you want to go for?" asked Gordon, as we exited the changing rooms back in our jeans and t-shirts.

I glanced into the changing room at the kilts, jackets and accessories I'd just tried on. "I think so, yes. Can we see what you have in your ex-hire range?"

"I'll see what we have in stock," said Gordon, moving towards his desk. "Do you have a preference for the jacket?"

"I like the grey tweed jacket and waistcoat. What are you thinking of Matt?"

"I'm thinking the same. I'll order a Cunningham tartan kilt and if you have stock, I'll also go for the tweed jacket and waistcoat."

"Okay, let's get everything ordered for you." As we sat back down with Gordon, we ordered our kilts. Then we went through the list of jackets, waistcoats, shirts, ruche ties, socks, shoes, flashes, belts, buckles, kilt pins, sgian dubhs and sporrans. Thankfully, we could order the more expensive items from their ex-hire range.

With Kirsty and Jo out for dinner with their friends, we opted for an evening of takeaway and gaming. As we manoeuvred our characters through the game, Matt glanced over to me. "So, what are your latest thoughts about the salon?"

"I don't know. It was a relief to get a month's extension on the termination of our lease but I'm confused. Ben and Tara's offer is going round and round my head. And I can't work out why I'm not jumping at it."

"Did you talk to Brian and Trish about it?"

Before I answered him, I clicked my controller, finishing the task on the screen. "Not yet."

"Why not?"

After pausing the game, I sat my controller on the table. "I guess I'm still feeling uncertain about everything and trying to get my own thoughts clear before I talk to them."

Matt wandered through to the kitchen and came back with cans of Irn-Bru. "What is it about Ben and Tara's offer that has you confused?"

"I don't know. I'm not sure if it's because this whole thing is making me feel the business is going backwards rather than forwards. Or that it's taking the business in a route I hadn't envisaged. Hair salons are difficult enough, but cafes have an even higher failure rate. What if the café is a complete flop? I'll be back to this again." I took a drink of juice. "If only I knew what the right decision was. How many times can the salon move before I lose my client base?" I leaned forwards and held my head in my hands.

"It's tough having to move so soon after setting up," replied Matt. "But you guys have great connections with many of your clients. And the unit on Kilmarnock Road is close to where you are now. So I can't imagine that putting anyone off. And being on a busy road will raise your profile and the local awareness of the salon."

Speaking to Matt always helped to clear my head. "That's all true." I sighed. "I think I'm just struggling with the thought of what if I need to move again."

"What are the options, though? You're going to have to move now, regardless. When you took on your current location, you expected it to last longer than fifteen months. But in that time, the three of you have increased your client base. Going in with the café can only increase that and if you do need to move again, it will be frustrating, but you'll be in an even stronger position." Matt finished his drink and sat his can on the table. "Why don't we pray about it?"

I nodded. Reminded once again of the importance of prayer. The last time we had prayed together, Matt had quoted the verse in Romans. '*Be joyful in hope, patient in affliction, faithful in prayer.*' It was everything I needed to navigate this uncertainty. Matt had helped me think through the next steps. Now it was time to pray. I closed my eyes and prayed for God's guidance.

PAUL

As March nudged February from the calendar, little touches of spring brought their much needed hope. Joy and hope were constantly on my mind as I tried to work out the future of The Smith Salon. For the past week, I had been talking through the options with Matt and Kirsty and praying I would make the right decision. Now it was time to make that decision.

A quiet morning at the salon gave me the opportunity to look over the numbers again. With Scott's financial expertise guiding us through our first year of business, we had managed our turnover to the penny. It had been hard work, and not where I wanted to concentrate my efforts. But as a result, we had paid off our set-up costs. However, with a salon move, there would be more costs to contend with. I prayed against the discouragement and prayed for joy in hope.

At the end of the day, the three of us sat down to talk. Trish fidgeted with her jar of hair clips, constantly glancing over at me, then averting her gaze. I put my hand over hers. "Talk to me, Trish. What's on your mind?"

"We've only got two months left at The Smith Salon. I'm really hoping you're about to tell us you've got something lined up."

I'd never seen Trish so nervous and unsure of herself. When we'd started The Smith Salon, she'd been integral to planning and finding our current location. I felt a gut wrench as I realised how unfair I'd been to these two colleagues. "I'm sorry, guys. I should have included you more. Honestly, I was trying to spare you the worry, but now I realise I've probably added to it. Sorry."

They both offered reassuring platitudes, but I knew I had messed up. It wasn't like either of them to keep quiet. Had I become the unapproachable salon owner? It was time to rectify the situation and bring joy back to our team dynamics.

"There is one option that has presented itself. And, again, I'm sorry I'm only telling you about it now. Ben and Tara, the pastors at my church, are thinking of opening a community coffee shop. They've been looking at the unit on Kilmarnock Road. Remember, it was one of the properties I told you about before?" Neither of them responded, waiting to hear what this meant for them. "We discounted it because it's too big. And Ben and Tara hesitated with it because it's also too big for them. So they suggested we lease it together and split it into the two businesses. What do you think?"

Silence.

"Please be honest. I know it's quite the mind shift."

After a moment, Trish sat up. "Yes. I walk past it on my way to the salon. It's right at a bus stop. It's an interesting thought." She leaned back in her seat and looked at Brian. He took his cue. "As you say, it's a completely different plan. But maybe... Do you still have the pictures?"

I nodded and lifted my phone from the table. Scrolling through my photos, I stopped at the images I'd taken from the online listing. Brian took my phone and studied the pictures. "It's hard to tell from this because it just shows one big area cluttered with shelves."

Trish jumped back into the conversation. "I can see how a hair salon and coffee shop could work out. I'm just trying to think of the positives and negatives."

"Like noise levels," said Brian. "It can get pretty noisy in the salon when all the hairdryers are going. And coffee machines are noisy."

"Those are valid points," I replied. "Another negative is different opening times when we are using the same front door. Although I guess that will be addressed when the unit is split into the two businesses. And the solution to that might also help with the noise."

"I think there could be potential for cross-selling," said Trish. "So it could bring us new clients. And that's always a good thing."

Brian nodded in agreement. "I guess we would all prefer to be in our own space. But with nothing else available, it seems like the best option." Brian took out his phone and pulled up the plans of the unit. "Has anyone been to view it yet? Seeing it in real life might answer the question of whether it is viable."

"Ben and Tara went to see it and thought it could work. But I haven't seen it yet. I was thinking of checking it out on Monday. Do you want to come with me?"

They both nodded. "Absolutely," said Trish. "I'm curious to see it and how it could work."

By the time we brought our meeting to a close, Brian and Trish were excited about the opportunities of joining with the coffee shop. There was joy in our shared hope.

On Monday morning, an agent from the commercial property agency ushered us in to the retail unit on Kilmarnock Road. We stepped over the pile of junk mail at the door and had a walk around. The premises were cluttered with retail shelving, and a musty dampness hung in the air. The shadows of buses passed the window every few minutes and there was a constant backdrop of noise from the busy road and pavement. I tried to push my imagination past the clutter to the potential around me, my thoughts skipping between the possibilities of new beginnings and the depression of having to start again.

I glanced over to Brian and Trish, this viewing wasn't just about me, it was also crucial to hear their thoughts. I needed them to be honest. I watched their facial expressions as they took it all in. Trish was getting more animated. Rushing from one end to the other, and then disappearing as she went to examine the staff area to the rear. In contrast, Brian walked around more slowly. Taking in the details, sometimes nodding, sometimes frowning. It was difficult to read his thoughts.

"I think it's got potential," said Trish, bounding back through to us.

"Do you think so?" I replied. "I need you to be honest with me, Trish. Don't just say what you think I want to hear."

"As if," she laughed. Grabbing our hands, she led us back to the front door. "Imagine the scene. People come in and go to the café, waiting until it's time for their appointment. And people who pop in for a cuppa realise there is an amazing salon right next door. They peek through and then make an appointment. Two businesses supporting each other."

Before we could completely picture the scene, she was dragging us over to the area, she claimed for the salon. "Jennifer will come and transform this bland space into another beautiful salon. Full of calming colours and a welcoming environment for our clients. We'll have the sinks at the back, which probably works best for the plumbing. And then we'll have our stations along these two walls." As she spoke, she pointed to where the workstations would be positioned. "And there might even be space for an additional workplace." Brian and I stood quietly, picturing the scene Trish had described. "I'm excited about this. I think it could work."

Trish's joy was infectious. I gave her a hug and laughed. "You're right! And you've helped me think about how it could work. I hadn't even thought about the layout and how it lends itself to four workstations, rather than just three." I turned round to Brian. "What do you think?"

"I think I can see it, but I'm a step or two behind you two. I can't quite visualise it."

"That's okay. It's a lot to take in. And don't feel you need to agree with everything that's being said. We need to be able to share our doubts and questions with each other. I'm sorry I didn't do that until now. But let's process this together."

Brian inspected the unit again. In its current state, it wasn't presenting itself in the best light, but hopefully Trish's enthusiasm and vision would filter through to him.

"I wonder how long it would take to transform this place?" said Trish, interrupting our thoughts. "Some items from our current salon can be brought here. But we'll need a budget for décor, joinery and plumbing."

We needed to make a choice. I looked at Brian and Trish. Trish's face shone with her enthusiasm as she pictured a future here. Brian still carried a slight frown, and that was okay, he needed time. "Why don't we all sleep on it and then talk about it tomorrow at our Tuesday morning business meeting? Bring your questions, your ideas, your hopes and doubts."

The agent locked up, and we went our separate ways. Without even thinking, I ended up in Queen's Park. On a cloudy Monday morning, the park was quiet, save for a few dog walkers and joggers. The hint of leaf buds on the trees and patches of crocus reminded me of the hope and new life of spring. I hadn't wanted a new start for the salon, but factors beyond my control had forced it upon us. But maybe this new start would be good for The Smith Salon. The salon had been doing well, but maybe somewhere in my subconscious, I knew something was missing. Or was I just imagining that now? As I thought back to Trish's enthusiasm for the café-salon plan, I smiled. It was a good idea. We had nothing to lose and everything to gain. Trish saw it immediately, I was seeing it now too, and I was confident that Brian would be on board by the morning. I quickened my pace through the park. There was a lot to do. We would need to book trades people. Clients would need to be informed. And on top of all that, I had a salon to run, and it was only eleven weeks until my wedding. Did I have enough capacity to juggle it all? A joyful glimmer of hope told me I did.

JENNIFER

"Past, present or future. Where is your focus?" Scott threw out the question to Paul and Kirsty as they sat across from us at their second pre-marriage meeting. Kirsty immediately picked up her coffee mug and hid behind it. In contrast, Paul sat up and grinned. "I'm all about now. Especially tonight." Paul hadn't been able to sit still since he had arrived at our house. His legs were shaking, and he kept running his hands through his hair. "I met up with Brian and Trish this morning and we viewed the unit on Kilmarnock Road. Trish is really excited about it. Brian hasn't said much, but I know he'll go for it. Since I received that letter about the salon, my mind's been full of questions. Panicking about my future." He looked round to Kirsty. "And I'm sorry. Because I know I haven't been there for you with the wedding planning."

"Stop apologising, Paul. I understand, honestly."

He returned his attention to me and Scott. "Anyway, I'm excited a decision has pretty much been made." He picked up the plate of biscuits and offered it round everyone, unable to sit still. "I guess I've always been a 'live life in the moment guy', which hasn't always led to the best decisions. Owning my own business means I need to consider the future, but I'm not sure what that looks like." He quickly scoffed another biscuit before continuing. "And then there's me and Kirsty." He sent her a wink as he brought her in to the conversation. "I'm assuming this is something we'll talk about further. But so far, I've viewed our relationship as just in the present. Obviously, by getting engaged, we're committing to the future, but I get so distracted by the day-to-day, I'm also not sure what relationship planning looks like."

I took a sip of my herbal tea, exhausted by Paul's energy. Kirsty was still nursing her mug of coffee, happy for the focus to be on Paul, but it was important for her to be part of tonight's discussions. "What about you, Kirsty?" I asked.

She gave a nervous laugh. "Don't expect as long an answer from me." I smiled, encouraging her to continue. "I feel silly saying this, but I guess I'm more of a future thinker. Or more accurately, dreamer and worrier. In the past, I've let my imagination soar to unrealistic dreams of my future. Although, the joy of the engagement and wedding planning makes living in the present easier. I want to keep that mind-set, rather than constantly dreaming of what is coming. But I must confess, I still have moments of dreaming of the future and where we'll live, and so on."

I glanced at Scott, hoping he had words of wisdom to draw this together. He cleared his throat as he prepared to speak. "Just to clarify, this isn't a trick question. There is no right or wrong answer. Sometimes we're in a season where we spend more time thinking about our past, other times we'll be completely caught up in the present, and still other times the future will hold our attention. We're complex people, and our past, present and future constantly direct us. There are Bible passages that tell us it's good to remember our past. There are passages where we're told to consider the present and not worry about the future. And there are passages of reassurance that God knows what is ahead. The important thing to know is that God is in the past, present and future." Scott took a sip of coffee as he considered his next words. "Paul, you've identified yourself as living more in the present. Kirsty, you've said your thoughts focus on the future. But you've both also said that can change depending on the circumstances. These meetings are to help you talk about these things and how you'll process life together. You don't need to have the same answers, but you need to be able to discuss issues and appreciate where the other person is coming from."

Paul poured himself a glass of water, then glanced over at me and Scott. "So, can I ask where you two land on the same question?"

Scott laughed. "Good one. When I was younger, I lived life in the present. But once I started working, I definitely switched to being a planner and thinking about my career progression. What would you say, Jennifer?"

Now it was my turn to hide behind my mug. "I don't know. The past couple of years have been crazy. Some days it's all about the present and running around after the girls and other days my thoughts focus on my future." I was frustrated at my answer, which barely scratched the surface of what I was feeling. Our conversation challenged me to consider where my thoughts lay. And more importantly, did I trust God with my past, present and future? It seemed it was a lesson I was continually learning.

"Why don't we pray," said Scott. "I want you to remember two things from tonight. First, God is in your past, present and future. And second, your outlook will change throughout your life, sometimes several times in one day." Was Scott saying that for my benefit or Paul and Kirsty's?

The following Monday, I had another meeting with Paul, only this time it was on the easier subject of interior design. Paul, Brian and Trish had agreed to the joint lease with the church café and now that the decision had been made, things were moving quickly.

After my uncertainties of last week, I was feeling more settled. As I'd read my Bible each morning, I'd prayed for wisdom about my past, present and future. So much of my confusion over the last few years centred on trying to decide my future, and I needed to figure that out. But maybe for now, it was okay to find contentment in the present rather than trying to analyse how all the pieces of my future would fit together. And today was the perfect day to live in the moment.

On Saturday, I had spent a glorious afternoon in creative planning. One perk of being a college student was having access to educational software packages. Before I started the college certificate, I had used free design software, but the access to the commercial offerings was a significant improvement. I created a computer generated mock-up of the new Smith Salon. From messages back and forward with the team, they had confirmed they wanted to keep the colour scheme we had used for the original salon. It was a great idea in terms of brand consistency, plus it reduced expenditure as we would reuse as much as possible. With the salon mock-up completed, I had turned my attention to the café. Although, I still wasn't sure what Tara wanted. So instead of creating mood boards, I collated a selection of design ideas that would drive our discussions. It was exciting to put the things I'd been learning into practice.

We sat around my breakfast bar, enjoying the bright March sunshine. Enveloped in the comforting aromas of fresh coffee and scones, we caught up on the latest thoughts and timing for the new venture. Tara pulled out a folder. "Before we go any further, I want to double check you have enough time to work on this, Jennifer. Be honest, is this a task too much between finishing your college certificate and the pregnancy?"

I shook my head. In my previous pregnancies, my second trimesters had been a breeze, the easy phase where morning sickness disappeared and vitality returned. But this time, my energy levels hadn't bounced back as much as I'd hoped. And it wasn't something I wanted to admit to anyone, especially with this exciting project to work on. I would just need to employ excellent time management and make sure I stuck to my decision to say no to everything else.

Before I could formulate my answer, Paul jumped in. "What if you project management it all and outsource the work? There might even be things we could take care of."

I smiled at Paul's suggestion. "That's a great idea. And I had been thinking of getting in some extra help for this one. Which we'll need anyway, as there are joinery, plumbing and electrical requirements." I opened up my laptop. "Let me show you what I've been thinking about. As we discussed, we'll give the new salon a similar look and feel to your current salon." I opened my design programme and pointed out the various jobs that would need to be tackled.

Paul couldn't keep his legs still as he studied my computer screen. "Looks great. Let me know what you need from me and when. Brian, Trish and I are all more than willing to help with any grafting. And Trish and I are happy to paint. We're not as good as you, but I'm confident we can meet the required standard."

"I'll hold you to that." I took a big bite of my fresh scone, slathered in raspberry jam. Food had taken on extra enjoyment since I'd moved beyond the morning sickness phase. "Okay, Tara, over to the café. I wasn't sure what kind of design you wanted, so I've got images with different looks and layouts and you can see which ones you like best."

Tara shrugged. "To be honest, I've not given much thought to the design. Hopefully, these will give me ideas, but I'm not much use at deciding colour schemes and layouts. When I think about the café, it's about how we'll serve the community, not what it will look like, which is why it's so important that you design the cafe for us. You're gifted at creating inviting spaces that attract people and make them want to stay." I smiled at Tara's self-awareness.

We all huddled round my laptop as I clicked through examples of café styles. I was confident the images would help her articulate what she wanted. As we progressed, she got enthusiastic about some features, quietly pointed to layouts that appealed and saw a few examples of styles she didn't like. As a result, I was getting a much clearer idea of what she wanted. I couldn't wait to start my design proposal.

"Let's talk about timing," I said, as I opened up my online calendar. "First, the salon." I looked over at Paul. "When are you hoping to open?"

Paul picked up his phone and scrolled through his calendar. "Ideally, early May."

My face scrunched up as I looked at my laptop. "That will be tight." I looked over at Paul. His shoulders slumped as my words registered. This was the horrible part of the job, managing people's expectations. "It's problematic to get trades people at short notice, but I'll start contacting people this afternoon and see who I can get lined up and for when. I'll let you know as soon as possible."

Paul fidgeted. I wasn't used to seeing his nervous tells. But I had to be honest with him about the timing concerns. I would do everything I could to reach his May target.

I turned round to Tara. "And what about the café? When are you hoping to open it?"

"We don't have a set date in mind. The salon is the priority. Maybe June?"

"Okay," I nodded, as I continued glancing down at my calendar. "I'll get things in place for the salon and ask everyone for their timings for the café."

Paul and Tara nodded their agreement. However, as Paul left, he struggled to smile. Determined to get his salon opened on time, I clicked on my contact list and started calling round the plumbers and joiners I knew. But determination to get the job done wouldn't make it happen. I prayed for cancellations that would open up availability for us. Loving God with all my mind meant that he was part of my business. How amazing to be able to pray for business decisions and clients.

KIRSTY

Sundays are my favourite day. Starting off with church gives me the peace and strength I need for the week ahead. Plus, it's the only whole day I get to spend with Paul.

As usual, Jo, Matt, Paul and myself sat together at church. I was looking forward to the service, but as the kids' church leaders got up to lead the all-age worship song, I didn't pay much attention. I confess I think of the all-together part of the service as just for the kids. However, the exuberance of the children gathered around the stage soon caught my attention. They were throwing themselves, some of them literally, into the actions. I looked at the screen with the words, 'nothing is impossible'. My eyes stayed fixed on the screen, taking in the rest of the words of the high-energy song. The words contained so much truth, truth that was reaching out to my insecurities.

I thought of the verse, *'Blessed are the peacemakers.'* Initially, I thought being a peacemaker was just about my family, but I was beginning to realise it was important for all my relationships. Like between me and Paul. Things were going really well for us, but I still had trouble finding peace in one area. Paul's past. How could I voice my concerns without sounding obsessive? The lyrics of the song told me nothing was impossible for God - did I believe that? Because if nothing was impossible for God, then I could trust him with my worries about Paul's past. Throughout the rest of the service, I kept glancing at Paul and thinking about God's promises.

Back at Paul and Matt's flat, we made up sandwiches and discussed what to do with our afternoon. Matt picked up the TV remote and surfed through the various streaming services. "Want to watch a movie?" We all nodded our agreement and settled down for a relaxing afternoon. We laughed and cheered at the tacky movie as the hero and heroine fought through a series of unrealistic misadventures and ended up in bed together. Jo reached over Matt for the remote and switched off the TV. "Ugh!"

I looked over at her. "What is it?"

"You know when you feel sick and every TV programme focuses on food?" I nodded. "Well, that's been my week as far as sex is concerned. Things I've seen on TV, chats with colleagues and even some of the stuff I've had to deal with at school. I thought I was okay with the whole waiting till we're married thing. But this week has made me feel like an absolute freak!" As Jo spoke, her hand gestures got bigger. She might be small, but when she gets excited, she needs a lot of space.

I swung my legs off the settee and turned round to face her. "It is hard. After all, with all the other stuff going on in the world, is it really that big a deal? It would be easy to talk ourselves round to a different perspective."

Matt brought us all cans of juice from the fridge before wading in with his thoughts. "And sometimes it can feel as if the Bible isn't totally clear on the subject. It was written thousands of years ago when people got married younger and tended to have more limited life spans. I guess back then, people left their parents' homes to join with their spouse. But that's not the case now. There's a verse in Hebrews that talks about keeping the marriage bed pure. I suppose you could argue around it and come to whatever conclusion you wanted."

Paul sat forward, ready to join the conversation. "I'm not as well versed in the Bible as you guys, and I'm probably approaching it from a different perspective. Obviously, it's not easy for me to wait, but I think it's the right decision. I've made no secret of the fact that by waiting till our wedding night, I'm showing that my life has changed. Do I still struggle? Of course I do. I know the pleasure that is waiting for me." At his words, my face immediately flamed red and I let my hair flop down over my cheeks. Paul noticed and grinned at me. "But what if I'm wrong? What if it doesn't matter because I have already committed to spending my life with Kirsty? Well, in that case, all I've done is deny myself a few extra months of pleasure. But if I'm right and wait, then I've honoured Kirsty. I've honoured Jesus. And what is yet to come is delayed gratification rather than taking what I want now."

"Excellent point, mate," said Matt. There was a pause in our conversation, everyone lost in their own thoughts. Paul's words made sense, but there was still one thing we needed to talk about. And maybe now was the right time. Hadn't God reminded me this morning that he is the God of miracles? And these conversations with our best friends were a safe place to talk about our worries. I cleared my voice. "Although I have one more worry that the rest of you don't need to deal with." I started playing with the cuff of my jumper, avoiding all eye contact. "Paul, you have experience that I don't. I've no idea what to expect with sex. Sitcoms and movies all make it seem perfect and amazing. But is it? What if I mess it up and I'm the worst person you've ever been with? I know this makes me sound naïve, but still…"

Paul pulled me into a hug and kissed the top of my head. "Hey, it's a new start for both of us. The experiences of my past mean nothing when it comes to you. Everyone is an individual and we get to discover each other." His words had me blushing once again. Stupid pale Scottish skin!

"Do you know what I've just realised?" he continued. "I'm in a new place in terms of relationships and friends. I've never had such deep conversations with friends before. All my life, I kept friendships on superficial levels. And I never stayed in a relationship long enough that I needed to understand or accommodate anyone else. So, Kirsty, I might have more experience in some parts of relationships, but you have more experience in other parts."

"Well, my past experiences don't exactly count!"

"Nope! You don't get to discount your past after raising concerns about mine. It's the same for both of us. We both have experience with previous partners, but none of those experiences were the real thing. This is. And it's unfamiliar territory for both of us."

"Aww, you guys," sighed Jo, clasping her hands in front of her. "You are so good for each other. And you've made my day so much better."

I leaned in and kissed Paul. Jo was right. We were good for each other. God had encouraged me to be a peacemaker today. And in doing so, my worries about Paul's past had been dealt with. Being a peacemaker wasn't just about taking peace to others, it was about experiencing it for yourself.

JENNIFER

A wonderful weekend of relaxing and celebration stretched before me. With their weddings only weeks apart, Jo and Kirsty had decided on a joint hen weekend at a country house hotel in Perthshire. The grouping comprised both of their mums, Paul's mum, their bridesmaids and me. Perthshire offered the most central location for a gathering of people coming from different parts of the country. And, as always, the drive from Glasgow to the heart of Scotland was beautiful, especially in the gathering strength of spring sunshine. Flecks of green peeked through on the roadside hedges and daffodils shared their joy. Lambs bounced about in the fields, playing their games of delight. It was a perfect spring afternoon.

On arrival at the hotel, we were ushered through to a large reception room fitted out with leather armchairs, settees and coffee tables. Old, stately windows showcased the beauty of the grounds: evergreen trees and rhododendron bushes ensured year round greenery; while stunning displays of daffodils added strokes of sunshine yellow. Beyond the gardens, the ancient Perthshire hills showed off their noble beauty. As soon as everyone was settled, a delicious afternoon tea was served. Over dainty sandwiches, cream scones and delicate tray bakes, we caught up on each other's news.

An afternoon of conversation and laughter filled the time between afternoon tea and our delicious dinner. After all the food and chat, I was exhausted and excused myself from the company, looking forward to an early night. However, the one thing I wasn't sure about this weekend was sharing a room with Kirsty's mum. From the moment we arrived, she had barely spoken to anyone. Kirsty kept glancing at her, trying to draw her into conversation. But Jean kept herself detached from the rest of us, her silence expressing disapproval. Was it all down to her annoyance at Kirsty's wedding dress search, or did it run deeper? Unfortunately, she followed my lead and also excused herself from the group. I didn't relish our time together. But this weekend wasn't about my enjoyment. I was here for Jo and Kirsty, and if that meant trying my best with Jean, then that's what I would do.

"I was planning on soaking in the bath for a while," I said to Kirsty's mum as we arrived at our room. "Would you like to use the bathroom first?" She nodded and grabbed her toiletry bag. The bathroom schedule leant itself to an easy first night together. By the time I came out, Jean was tucked up in bed and facing the wall. I was happy to let her keep to herself for tonight.

Over breakfast the following morning, Lynn asked for our attention as she glanced at her mobile phone. "Today we've all got spa treatments booked. Let me get the schedule pulled up. Jennifer, are you only getting a manicure and a pedicure? That seems boring."

I laughed at Lynn's blunt question. "It's called being pregnant. You need to be careful with treatments. I know I'm okay with getting my nails done, so I'll stick to that and the swimming pool."

"You're pregnant?" asked Jean.

Kirsty shot her mum a look of annoyance. "Mum, I told you Jennifer was pregnant."

"I can't keep track of all the people you know, Kirsty." Everyone suddenly became very interested in their plates. But at least in a mixed group, there was always someone who could jump in and deal with any social awkwardness.

Jo's mum looked over at me. "You must be so excited, Jennifer. When is the baby due again?"

With an almost collective sigh of relief, everyone resumed their breakfast. "The due date is the end of August. It was a surprise, and it's taken a bit of adjustment. But Scott and I are delighted and can't wait to meet this one." I rubbed my hands over my stomach.

"Do you know if you're having a girl or boy?"

"Not yet. We had the twelve week scan a few weeks ago. But we might find out at the next scan. I don't know if I want to know."

"So fun," continued Jo's mum. "And what are your girls saying about it?"

"The younger two are excited about having a baby in the house. And Chloe is very excited that she will no longer be the youngest."

"You'll be hoping for a boy," said Kirsty's mum. I'd already had a few people express the same sentiment. It was becoming old very quickly. I bit back all the sarcastic answers that fought to express themselves. Instead, I smiled at her. "I don't mind either way." I would need to be careful with my attitude to Jean this weekend. After all, I only knew her from Kirsty's stories. It was important to get to know her for myself.

I looked over at Jo and Kirsty. "So what are the brides-to-be getting done?"

"Rather than two smaller treatments, we've both opted for the full body massage," said Jo. "I can't wait. Lynn, what time are our massages?"

"The two of you are booked in at one o'clock." Lynn glanced down at her phone again. "Shall we just say that we're free for the rest of this morning until mid-afternoon, when we're all done with our treatments? And between times, you can use the pool, sauna and Jacuzzi."

Everyone agreed and those with the first appointments left the breakfast table. I went back to my room, grabbed my Bible and my book, and hid myself in the lounge with a coffee. Quiet reading time was a treat. In a rare place of solitude, away from my to-do lists, it was easy to remember to love the Lord with all my soul. I opened my Bible to the Psalms and smiled.

A few hours later, I exited the treatment area with shiny burgundy nail varnish. Susan came out at the same time, all relaxed from a shoulder massage. "Do you want to go for a cuppa?" she asked.

"That would be lovely." We walked through to the hotel bar and I noticed a sheltered outside area. "Would you be okay if we got our coats and sat outside for a bit?" Susan nodded. Cosied up in our coats, we ordered hot drinks and sat on the terrace. I lifted my face to the sun; a hint of warmth bringing the joy and hope of the new season. Birds were flitting between the tree branches and bushes, filling the air with song.

"We could be in a weekend break advert," joked Susan. "Sitting outside a beautiful stone building, sunglasses on, enjoying our coffees."

"It is beautiful, isn't it? I feel so relaxed and we've only been here for twenty-four hours."

"I can imagine it must be a lovely break for you. A bit of time to rest and relax from family and study responsibilities. We love our families, but it is nice to have some time for ourselves."

I nodded. "Yes, it's nice not being responsible for anyone for a few days. And it's good to get a break from my studies, although the only thing I have left for this year is the main assignment. And I've completed quite a bit of work towards it. It incorporates tasks we've been given throughout the year, bringing everything together as one project. Once that's handed in, I'm done and I can stop fretting about the pregnancy brain fog."

Our conversation was interrupted by the arrival of Jo's mum. "Can I join you ladies?"

"Of course," we replied. A waiter arrived as she sat down and took our order for another round of drinks.

"We were just talking about this lovely setting, and Jennifer getting the chance to relax," said Susan, bringing Jo's mum up to speed, before turning back to me. "What are your plans for interior design now?"

"I'm still trying to figure that out. As I said, I've almost completed my college certificate, so it's a nice point to take a break to have the baby. Then, I'll take the next academic year off and, depending on how I feel, I might go back to college a year in August or wait till the following year."

"Have you enjoyed the course?" asked Jo's mum, Elaine.

"It's been so good. It really has confirmed interior design is what I want to do. Although before I started the course, I assumed interior design was all about styling people's homes. But according to our lecturers, a lot of the work is in offices, hospitality and retail interiors. I'm not sure that's as appealing. But I'm still drawn to the profession."

"Well, you say that," said Susan. "But look at the wonderful job you did with Paul's salon. It looks amazing. You certainly transformed it into something special."

"That's very kind of you." I smiled at my coffee companions. "It's funny. Last year on our ski holiday I asked Paul, Jo and the others about their experiences of growing up with working mums. And now here I am talking to you about it. Before I started the course, I spent so much time wondering if the girls were old enough to cope with me going to college and now I'm stopping because of this one." I protectively circled my hands over my not-yet-there bump. "I feel like I'll never get to the point where I'm not juggling motherhood and career aspirations."

"I think it's a long-term issue," said Susan. "I constantly felt guilty about going out to work full-time and missing time with Paul and Lauren. But they don't seem to have any negative memories of my juggle. You need to work out the right balance for you."

"There can always be guilt," added Elaine. "It comes down to what works for you. And it's also about considering the present and the future. Life is a constant balancing act when the children are pre-high school. By the time they reach high school, they still need you, but in ways they can't always articulate and at the most random of times. As mums, we're always learning and adjusting." Elaine gave me a sympathetic smile. "It is confusing. And you'll always double guess what you think you should and shouldn't do. Think through what is best for you as a family and then don't listen to anyone else's advice." She laughed. "And, yes, I get the irony of me advising you to ignore advice!"

"Thanks, both of you. You've really helped."

Sitting in the spring sunshine, I turned my face to the sun. Talking with Elaine and Susan had been helpful. It was lovely to get the input of women who knew what they were talking about and could give me unbiased advice. I needed to figure out what worked for us as a family. But it was hard when every year held the same questions, albeit from a different perspective. Was it selfish to pursue a career? Or was it selfish to stay at home with the baby and my girls? As the guilt of motherhood threatened to overwhelm me, I took a deep breath and reminded myself to *'love the Lord with all my heart, mind and soul.' But Jesus, why am I always struggling with the same questions?*

KIRSTY

Things with Mum had partially thawed over the last twenty-four hours. But there was still a tension between us and that tension could only be dealt with if we spent time together. As we made our way to the dining room, I walked beside Mum and sat next to her at the table. While everyone was still settling down, a waiter took our drinks orders. I heard Mum tutting as several people ordered alcoholic drinks. I closed my eyes and counted to ten, hoping no one else had heard her.

"What did you do today, Mum?" I could do this. I could make things better between us. I would ignore her negative noises and comments and engage her in normal conversation.

"I sat in my room and watched some TV and had a nap." She fidgeted with the empty glass in front of her. I tried not to roll my eyes. Of course, she had kept to herself rather than engaging with the rest of the party. Why did she make everything so difficult? Or was I being unfair? After all everyone else already knew others in the group before this weekend. But then so did Mum. She'd met Susan and my friends before and she had as many prior connections as Elaine. I should probably stop comparing my mum to other mums. She always seemed to come up short. Was I judging her too harshly?

I needed to make more of an effort and include her in the weekend activities. It had been her decision not to get any spa treatments, but maybe I should have encouraged her to get a shoulder massage. Or maybe I should have had tea with her in the afternoon. Although, time with Mum always seemed to include guilt, but maybe this time it was deserved. Once again, my thoughts returned to the verse, *'Blessed are the peacemakers.'* I had no idea what that meant when it came to my family.

Picking up the menu, I skimmed over our choices for tonight's dinner. "What do you think you'll go for tonight, Mum?"

"It all looks so fancy; I just don't know."

Again, I fought the urge to roll my eyes. Why was this so difficult? I glanced through the menu, it was nice, but not that fancy. "Why don't you go for this fish dish?" I said, pointing to the menu, she usually enjoyed seafood. She made a non-committal reply and continued looking through the menu. Although when the waiter came to take our order, Mum went for the fish pie.

Elaine asked Mum some questions about the wedding planning and started comparing notes about how things were going with organising Jo and Matt's wedding. Jo and Matt are getting married in The Borders rather than in Glasgow, so we were both dealing with wedding preparations out with Glasgow.

As Elaine told Mum about the country hotel that Jo's wedding reception was going to be held in, Mum pointed her finger at me. "This one decided a marquee was appropriate for her wedding."

I joined in, determined to have a positive conversation with Mum about the wedding. Hopefully, having Elaine involved in the conversation would help. "It's going to be lovely, Mum. Just think, how many people have their wedding reception at a pretty harbour?"

"I suppose that's true," she conceded.

I took my cue and continued to discuss the wedding. "It's going to be beautiful. Everything's booked. We've confirmed the menu with the caterers. We've got a company doing the lights and the bar and the ceilidh band is booked too."

"It is amazing how many options the caterers gave us," added Mum. "I thought it would just be a basic buffet. But they're doing a three course meal."

I pulled out my phone and showed Mum and Elaine the pictures of marquees the lighting company had decorated. They both agreed it looked pretty.

By the time the waiters arrived with our main courses, Mum was engaged in conversation with Elaine and Susan. Finally! With Mum now including herself in the group, I let out a sigh and turned round to talk to Jennifer. I owed Jennifer big time for being the one stuck sharing a room with Mum. Although now that Mum, Elaine and Susan were talking, Lauren was left out on her own at the end of the table. Perhaps we could move seats for dessert. As the servers cleared away our dinner plates, Lauren asked for another vodka and coke. Mum turned round to stare at Lauren, "Don't you think you've had enough?"

I held my breath. How could Mum be so rude? Why, after ignoring my friends all weekend, did she express her displeasure at people's drink options? I tried to look round Mum to mouth an 'I'm sorry' to Lauren. Meanwhile, the rest of the group picked up on the tension. Jo took a sharp intake of breath as she watched, waiting to see how Lauren would react. To the other side of me, the conversation quietened as everyone's attention diverted to my mum.

Lauren merely smiled and replied, "I'm fine, Jean. You don't need to worry about me."

Silence.

'Blessed are the peacemakers.' I looked at the waiter Lauren had spoken to. "I'd love a diet coke. Does anyone else want another drink?" Several others asked for wine or soft drinks. The tension of Mum's accusation was dispelled. For now.

As we made our way through to the lounge, after dinner, I apologised to Lauren for Mum's comment. But she refused to let it be an issue. "Don't worry, it didn't bother me."

I couldn't believe how unfazed Lauren was by my mum's words. Maybe I should ask her for advice on how to deflect criticism.

We took up residence in our usual area of the lounge and ordered teas and coffees. "What will we do this evening?" asked Lynn. "Will we go into Perth?"

"I can't be bothered moving," I replied. "It's nice and quiet here. Why don't we sit around and chat for a bit and then decide?"

"I know," said Jo. "Why don't Jennifer, Jean, Susan and Mum tell us stories from their weddings?"

I kicked off my heels and pulled my legs up in front of me, ready to hear the stories of weddings past. "Why don't we start with the most recent? Susan, tell us a story from your wedding."

"Let me think…" she put her finger to her chin and considered her response. "Well, some of you know the story as our two brides-to-be and Lauren were there. It was a dark, wet December day. Not at all the type of day you want for your wedding. Paul was most upset with me because I insisted on wearing my raincoat over my wedding dress. But there was no way I was going to let the weather ruin my beautiful dress."

I laughed at Susan's storytelling. "Quite right. Your dress was beautiful. And, as for your son, he needs to deal with his issues with raincoats."

Susan laughed, then continued. "On a serious note. After the disaster of my first marriage, it was an amazing feeling to walk up the aisle and see Alex standing, waiting for me. I'm so grateful for this new start. But no matter how bad my first marriage was, it gave me Lauren and Paul. Enjoy your days, girls. Make the most of them. And know that you are both marrying good men. And yes, I know I'm slightly biased." Susan stood up and came over to hug both Jo and me. Happy tears sprung to my eyes.

"Your turn, Jennifer," said Jo.

"It was a beautiful, sunny June day." We laughed as Jennifer started her story in the same way as Susan. "However, the weather conditions of the day meant the pollen count was high. My dad suffers pretty badly from hay fever and by the time we arrived at the church, he was sneezing a lot. As we stood outside for our pre-wedding father and daughter photos, the breeze picked up. The wind must have gathered pollen as it blew over plants and bushes because all of a sudden my dad went in to a fit of non-stop sneezing. By the time we walked down the aisle, his eyes were streaming. Those who knew him knew it was his allergies, but most of the guests thought he was really emotional walking his daughter down the aisle. My poor dad. But it was so funny."

Jennifer wiped away the tears of laughter that were rolling down her cheeks. "But to be serious for a minute. I'd like to back up Susan's comments. It's beautiful to watch two relationships that are grounded in faith and love. Enjoy the build up to your weddings. And enjoy every minute of your special days." Following Susan's lead, Jennifer stood up and hugged Jo and me.

"Your turn, Mum," said Jo, as she looked over to her mum. A smile passed between them, suggesting this was a loved family tale, which had been shared many times before.

"Well, I got married on a beautiful, sunny spring day. And I was late for my wedding. But it wasn't because I intended to keep my groom waiting. The wedding taxi arrived to pick me up with plenty of time to spare, and I was ready for its arrival. We set off for the church, enjoying the warmth of the springtime sun streaming through the windows. My dad sat beside me, looking smart in his kilt. We were chatting about nothing in particular when the car came to a halt. We looked ahead of us to see the road was full of sheep!" There was a ripple of laughter round the group. "Three farm workers and a couple of sheep dogs were slowly guiding the sheep forward. They gave no indication of having seen us. So our driver beeped his horn. Clearly, he wasn't used to driving on country roads. Some of the sheep scattered at the sound of the horn and came running back, past the car. One of the farm workers gave us the sternest scowl and probably said a few choice words. We were then given a fabulous display of the skill and control of a shepherd with his dog. One dog was sent after the errant sheep and skilfully brought them back to the group. The driver, having learnt his lesson, left more space between us and the sheep and kept his hand far away from the horn."

"Oh my goodness," I said, laughing at the picture in my mind. "How late were you for your wedding?"

"I think I was about half an hour late. I'm not sure how nervous people were getting at the church. This was before everyone had a mobile phone. And you certainly wouldn't take one with you to your wedding. So there was no way to let people know why we were late. But it resulted in my dad coming up with a new speech on the spot so he could tell everyone about our journey to the wedding. At least everyone got a laugh from it."

"I guess you can't predict everything that can go wrong?" said Jo.

"No, you can't. You want everything to be perfect, but that's unlikely to happen. So you need to be prepared to roll with whatever the day brings and enjoy every moment. And, as Susan and Jennifer have already said, you're both marrying amazing men. And saying, 'I will' to them will be the most special part of your days." Elaine stood and hugged us both. I wiped away more tears. This was turning into quite the emotional experience.

"So what about you Mum?" I asked, praying that she would actually take part.

"I got married on a cloudy and still November day," began Mum. My shoulders relax and I exhaled a deep breath, as Mum, not only took part, but began her story in the same way the others had. "In our case, it was the calm after the storm. The day before had been one of the worst storms in living memory for folks in Lochcala. Gale force winds and torrential rain had battered the village for hours. So it was a pleasant surprise to wake up on the morning of my wedding to clear blue skies. But it didn't take long before word reached us about the damage." We all leaned in, eager to know what disaster had befallen Mum's wedding day. "A tree had fallen on top of the church, causing a gaping hole in the roof and the church was flooded with rainwater. We all trudged over to the church to inspect the damage. I was in my wellington boots and my hair in curlers." I smiled at the details she included. "What a state met us at the church. It was even worse than we'd feared. The wedding flowers, which had been delivered to the church the previous day, were obliterated. Water covered the floor and a wall and some pews had been damaged from the fallen tree. There was no way the wedding could take place at the church. We met with the minister, wondering what could be done. At his suggestion, we spoke to the manager of the hotel where we were having our reception and he agreed to us having the ceremony there. It was all hands on deck to get the hotel ready and we gave a local boy a few pounds to stand at the church to direct people to the hotel. So like Elaine, my wedding was late starting too."

"Oh my goodness, Mum! I had no idea." Mum merely shrugged her shoulders. I couldn't believe I had never heard this story before. Plus, it was unnerving how many of these wedding stories revolved around things going wrong.

"Aye, well, you just need to adapt to whatever happens."

I wondered what else Mum had adapted to in her life. Over the last few weeks, I'd seen glimpses of Mum that I'd never seen, or noticed, before. Maybe she'd experienced more disappointments in life than I realised. One weekend was never going to solve my issues with Mum but this weekend had caused me to reconsider our relationship. If I was to be a peacemaker, I needed to understand who Mum really was. I also needed to understand what it meant to be a peacemaker. When I first saw the verse in the manse study, I thought of a peacemaker as a cosy, twee thing. But I was beginning to realise it was something that could get messy and uncomfortable.

KIRSTY

Two weeks later, it was time for another party, only this time it was instigated by Lynn. Fed up with all the dating and wedding chat between Jo, Matt, Paul and myself, she had declared it was time for a wedding free, couple free night out. Tonight was about going out as a group of friends. Although we should have known better than to let Lynn plan it!

Lynn arrived at my flat with Carol and Jo. "We're having a '70s night at the roller disco," she announced as she took packages from her tote bag and handed them to each of us. I gasped when I saw my outfit for the evening. A glance round the others confirmed we all had matching white shiny shorts and yellow V-neck t-shirts. Knee-high rainbow coloured socks completed our looks. Jo couldn't stop laughing as she looked at the shorts and then at me.

"Lynn! What are you doing to us?"

"Giving you a fabulous night out. But don't worry, the boys' outfits are much worse than ours." Before I could ask what she meant, she connected her phone to my speaker and had a '70s playlist blaring out at us. "Come on, get into your '70s groove and clothing. The taxi will be here in half an hour."

I cringed, my face already flashing red. "I can't believe we're going to go out in public like this."

"At least it will be a night you'll never forget," teased Lynn, pulling on her knee-high socks.

When we reached Paul and Matt's flat, I was still at the embarrassed giggling stage. Thankfully, my raincoat hid my crazy clothing, although it couldn't hide the rainbow socks. There was a slight dampness in the air, so my raincoat was warranted, unlike my sunglasses. But if I had to go out in public, I needed to hide as much as possible.

Matt threw open the door and posed in his white flared trousers, red V-neck t-shirt and rainbow braces. We all giggled at his iconic '70s disco stance. "You're a lucky woman, Jo," I laughed as we walked into their flat. Paul was nowhere to be seen as we entered their living room, but a few minutes later, he joined us. How could he look so good in such a stupid outfit? He came over and kissed me on the cheek, "Love the raincoat." I giggled and snuggled into his hug.

"Is everyone ready to face dinner?" asked Lynn, as Paul and Matt put on their jackets. I groaned, mortified at the idea of walking through Glasgow city centre like this. Lynn looked at me and laughed. "Kirsty, stop looking so terrified. I was going to tell you once we were on our way, but I'll be nice and tell you now. We're having dinner at the roller disco. So you don't need to worry about people seeing you in these clothes."

I ran over and hugged her. "Thank you. Thank you. Thank you." I gushed. "That's the best news I've heard since you gave us these outfits."

The roller disco venue was huge. It looked straight out of the '70s with dark wood panelling on the walls and disco balls suspended from the ceiling. I glanced around, rubbing my arms. The room brought back memories of musty, old church halls. The décor looked tired, and the furniture was basic, with plastic chairs and Formica tables. This kind of venue required a crowd to inject atmosphere and warmth and so far, there was only a smattering of people standing about in small groups.

Our first challenge was swapping our nice safe shoes for the roller skates. We huddled together on a bench and laced up our skates. I have some hazy memories of skating when I was a kid, but most of them involved falling. "You can do this," whispered Paul, as he finished lacing up his roller skates and pecked my cheek. He tentatively stood and started moving forward. He wasn't gracious or smooth, but he was doing it. Matt was the next one up. He faced Jo and pushed himself towards her. I was scared to look in case it led to a collision. But when I looked back, they were still standing.

"Come on," said Carol, as she skated to me and held out her hand. I accepted her support and carefully rose. Carol had been my buddy on last year's ski holiday and had quietly and consistently cheered me on. I knew I could trust her. With a tremor of apprehension, I pushed myself up from the bench, holding Carol's hand. I was doing it! I was standing up in roller skates. "Now," said Carol, still keeping hold of my hand. "We're going to slowly make our way over to the rink. It's still nice and quiet, so it's the perfect time to get your balance and find your skating rhythm."

Slowly, we manoeuvred to the others. It wasn't pretty, but I did it without falling over. I took hope in my upright start. I clung to Carol's hand, building myself up to joining in the people circling the floor. Of course, Paul and Matt were already zooming about as if they'd been skating forever. And Jo and Lynn were practising skating forwards, then backwards. Why was I always the worst at physical activities?

"Come on," encouraged Carol. "Let's do this." Holding on tightly to Carol, I began my first circuit. Even though my legs were shaking, I remained upright. After another couple of laps, I was feeling more confident. "Okay, this time we're not going to hold hands, but I'll stay beside you," said Carol, as she let go of my hand. Initially, I reverted to my shaky legs, but after half a lap, my confidence returned. Maybe I could do this.

"You did it," enthused Carol, as I completed my first solo lap. I replied with a tentative smile. I wasn't ready to applaud my accomplishments yet. There was still plenty of time for mishaps.

Paul pulled up beside me and took my hand. "My turn," he said, as he pushed off and pulled me with him. Although his unexpected arrival nearly knocked me off balance, with just a few wobbles, I kept upright. Lynn skated up beside us. "Remember! This isn't a couples' night out. It's a friends' night out. No holding hands and being all smoochy."

Paul grinned at Lynn. A wave of panic came over me that he was about to commence some big public show of affection. Instead, he dropped my hand and skated over to Matt. He whispered something, then the two of them looked at us, smiled and skated off holding hands. My giggles returned. Lynn sighed but skated beside me for another couple of laps.

Jo and Carol joined us. "Great job, Kirsty. You've got this. Told you, you could do it," said Jo.

"Thanks. I just wish I wasn't always the one having to catch up with everyone else when it comes to activities."

"That's not true. Remember when we went wall climbing? You scampered up that wall before we'd even got off the first foot hold."

I laughed at the memory of our wall climbing expedition. "Yes, but then I twisted my ankle, falling over a helmet."

"I guess it just goes to show you can't be perfect at everything." As I laughed at Jo, my stomach rumbled and I declared it was time for food.

We collected hot dogs and drinks and took up residence at a table near the rink, looking forward to some people watching. A steady stream of people had arrived after us and the venue was warming up in temperature and atmosphere. Some people wore jeans and t-shirts but most had dressed for the occasion, in bright '70s fashion. The colours and outfits contributed to the growing party vibe. And there was a lot to be said for the upbeat disco music blasting through the hall's sound system.

The hot dogs and nachos were simple and bland, but it was cheap and cheerful. You came to places like this for the experience, not the food. All too quickly, our roller skating waiter cleared away our empty plates, and it was time to resume skating. Although first I needed to visit the little girl's room. In horror, I realised even a trip to the bathroom had to be done on wheels! This was definitely an occasion for a toilet buddy. "Hey, Jo, could you come to the toilet with me?" I whispered. She nodded, and we made our way to the ladies.

To begin with, it was all normal. As with any ladies' toilet, there was a queue. Jo went before me so I could watch how she navigated getting into the cubicle. It was a little tricky, but I managed it. But it turned out the challenge wasn't sitting down but standing back up. Every time I tried to put my weight on my feet, my skates shot out in front of me. I tried several times before I began to worry that I would spend the rest of the night sitting on the toilet. Should I take my skates off? And, as if trying to figure that out wasn't bad enough, I knew there was a queue for the facilities.

I shook my head. Took a deep breath and told myself I could do it. I put my feet out to the sides, bracing my legs against the cubicle walls. There was a slight gap between the door and the frame, which I estimated was wide enough for my fingers to fit through. Lunging forward, I gripped the door. Slowly I pushed myself up, all the while gripping the door and carefully sliding my hands upwards, pulling myself towards a standing position.

"Are you alright in there?" asked a woman. Somehow, I kept my mind on the task at hand and continued my upward momentum. "Fine, thanks." I couldn't believe my voice sounded so controlled. I was on the verge of giggles or tears, depending on how the next few seconds transpired.

In sheer relief, I stood upright and fixed myself. However, as I exited the stall, a line of women applauded my achievement. My face flushed red. Giggling followed, as well as looking at the floor. It was the most embarrassing hand wash ever. I couldn't wait to escape my crowd of well-wishers and hide with my friends.

When I returned to the hall, Paul was the only one still at the table. I stomped-skated my way over to him and sat down, dropping my head onto my arms. He reached over and lifted my head. "Hey, what happened?" I told him my sorry tale, tears threatening to come. Rather than reply with words, Paul leaned in and kissed me. A soft, slow kiss that deepened into a kiss of depth and promise. By the time he pulled back, I could no longer remember why I had been upset. He rubbed his thumbs across my cheeks, drying off the tiny trail of frustration tears.

"I wish you could see your bravery as clearly as you see your mishaps. You're doing something new. You're trying. That's way better than all these people who have skated before and have already figured out how to get up and down from a toilet." I burst out laughing at the sincere expression that accompanied Paul's silly words. Paul hadn't just kissed away my embarrassment, his laughter banished my insecurity.

And in my laughter, something else clicked into place. At our last pre-marriage course, Scott and Jennifer had talked about the present. Living in the now and not being defined by our past or always straining to get to the future. Once again, Lynn's crazy plans had been the right thing at the right time. I had been getting carried away with the wedding planning. Paul was full-on with all the changes to his business. We needed fun outings like tonight, we needed to guard our budding relationship.

"You are the perfect man for me, Paul Smith." I leaned in and kissed his warm lips. As I pulled away, I smiled at my gorgeous fiancé. "How would you like to go on a date with me tomorrow night?"

KIRSTY

On Friday afternoon, I boarded the bus to Lochcala, grateful for the accrued flexi-time that released me from work early. This was my last visit before the wedding. Paul should have been with me, but he was busy with the salon preparations. I know stereotypically wedding planning is the domain of the bride, but I wished Paul was more involved. So for this weekend, it would just be me and Mum. Since the hen weekend, things had been cordial between us. She didn't gush over things the way Paul's mum did, but she had softened ever so slightly. It made me wonder if she had any friends in Lochcala. She could talk at great length about several women in the village but seeing her with Paul's and Jo's mums had made me wonder if she had any genuine friends, or if she was merely acquainted with women who happened to live in the same village.

As the bus left the greyness of the city, I nestled into my seat, put my headphones on and gazed out the window. The spring sunshine was pushing against the dark of winter, the bright yellow flowers of the gorse bushes flourished on hillsides and trees were hinting at the promise of new leaves. The Argyll roads were getting busier as the year progressed, the Friday afternoon traffic taking people from the city for the weekend.

When the bus pulled into Lochcala, I smiled at the familiar setting. Something had shifted over the last few months, whether it was down to more visits home or making an effort with Mum, but I didn't disembark with the usual feeling of dread. However, as soon as I approached the family home all that changed. Raised voices carried on the breeze as I neared the kitchen door and as I entered, a tense atmosphere greeted me. James was standing next to the kitchen table, with Mum sitting in her chair.

I glanced between the two of them. "Is everything alright?"

James pushed past me and slammed the door as he thundered from the house. Mum merely got up to make us tea. "How was the journey?" she asked, pouring the boiling water into the teapot. Now I knew something was wrong. She never asks about my journey.

"Are you okay, Mum?"

"Yes, yes. I'm fine." She placed the teapot and a plate of biscuits on to the table between us. "Now, what are we working on this weekend?"

"Don't we need to talk about what just happened between you and James?"

"Nothing to discuss. It's time for wedding planning."

I wanted to push further. To find out what James' problem was. But when it comes to James, Mum will never say anything negative. Not even if he's just been shouting at her. My questions would need to wait until evening when I would see Craig. Maybe he knew what was going on. So instead, I pulled my wedding planner from my bag and flicked to the checklist.

With five weeks until the wedding, we were on to the final section. The wedding invitations had been posted a few weeks ago and replies were trickling in. Our first task was checking who had replied. So far, some old uncle on my dad's side was the only one to send a 'not coming'. I wasn't even sure if I'd ever met him. Why do weddings always include strange family members you don't know?

I cleared away our tea things, and we spread out a couple of sheets of A3 paper, ready to make up the seating plan. "Did Susan give you any indication of who needs to sit where?" asked Mum, as she looked through the list of Paul's guests.

"Not really. We can put her sister and brother-in-law at the same table as Aunt Joyce and Uncle Andy. And then Paul's cousins could probably be put with some of Paul's friends."

We spent half an hour working through the dynamics of our extended family, deciding who should sit with whom. I let Mum take the lead on the seating plan. It was one of the least exciting parts of all the planning.

To celebrate completing our task, pending final replies from guests, I made us another round of tea. As we sipped our tea, we checked through the invoices and confirmed all the payments were up to date. I leaned back and stretched, undoing the tension that had been building in my back and shoulders from being hunched over the table. "We covered a lot today, Mum. I think we're organised and running to plan."

Mum stood up and cleared away the teacups. "Oh but look at the time. I'll need to get dinner on for your dad and the boys." She made it sound as if neither of us required dinner.

"Why don't I pop down to the chippy and treat us to fish and chips?"

Mum nodded. "That would be lovely." I glanced at Mum as she sat down. She looked tired. Did the boys help around the house? Probably not. Although perhaps that was on her, too. She was too quick to run after them all. And now it was just the household habit.

"I'll go via Craig's," I said, as I grabbed my raincoat and purse. I was looking forward to seeing my favourite brother.

When I arrived at his flat, Craig scooped me into a hug. "It's good to have you back. You're much needed relief from the tension in that house."

"What is going on? When I arrived, James and Mum were in a shouting match. But he stormed out of the house as soon as I entered."

"I'm not entirely sure. I think it's something to do with a new girlfriend and some complications that have come up from when he lived with his last girlfriend."

I laughed at his waffled answer. "Oh well, I'm glad you're on it!" He shrugged and attempted a smile but he couldn't look me in the eye, a sure sign he knew more than he was telling. If that was how they wanted to play it, so be it. But someone would tell me James' secret before I returned to Glasgow.

The next morning I was woken by the sound of Mum and James arguing. Dad's deep, soft voice interjected, but I wasn't able to hear what was being said. If it wasn't for the creaky floorboards, I would tip toe to the top of the stairs to eavesdrop, but I knew the old house would give me away. James raised his voice, then the door slammed. I peeked out my window and saw him storming down the path. He jumped in his car and revved away.

I picked up my Bible from the bedside table. Best to give Mum and Dad a few minutes before I ventured downstairs. Once again, my search took me to the verse in Matthew. *'Blessed are the peacemakers, for they will be called children of God.'* I closed my eyes, scared about what the words might be telling me. It was one thing to be a peacemaker between Mum and myself. But was God now nudging me to be a peacemaker between Mum and James? Surely not. Maybe it was just a reminder to keep the peace between me and Mum.

When I joined Mum and Dad in the kitchen, they were sitting in silence, cups of lukewarm tea untouched in their hands. Had Mum been crying? Should I acknowledge the scene before me or pretend that nothing had happened? For as long as I could remember, the tension in the house always seemed to centre on me. I didn't know what to do when I was the onlooker.

Tea. Tea was always the icebreaker in such situations. "Can I freshen up your tea?" I asked, as I moved over to the sink to fill up the kettle. My question hung in the air. Neither Mum nor Dad seemed to even notice I'd entered the room. I gathered up their tea things and made a fresh pot and put some bread in the toaster. All I wanted to do was escape to Craig's flat, but I knew I was needed here. Despite wanting to keep well away from any fallout between my parents and James, I realised the timing of the wedding preparations meant I was here. And maybe I was here to be a peacemaker.

"What's going on?" I asked, as I sat down at the table and poured the tea. Mum continued staring in front of her and Dad briefly looked over at me. He almost looked surprised to see me in his kitchen. "It's nothing you need to worry about," he said, going back to stare at the mug in front of him.

It would be so easy to accept his remark. To keep my distance and let them fret over whatever had happened. But the verse from Matthew wouldn't let me go. Sometimes being a peacemaker meant asking the tough questions. "That's where you're wrong, Dad. I do worry. Because clearly something has you upset and it would appear it involves James. Now what is going on?"

Mum and Dad glanced at each other and sighed. Dad turned towards me. "We loaned him and Eileen money when they moved in together. We asked him to repay the money. But they frittered it away and Eileen is still in the house so they can't even return the deposit we paid on their flat."

I took a sip of tea. Giving myself time to think about Dad's words. I didn't doubt the frustration over the loan. But did it really warrant the ferocity of the arguments I had overheard this weekend? Had they loaned him that much money? Or was there something else they weren't telling me?

KIRSTY

All I could think about was James and the arguments between him and our parents. There had to be more to it. James wouldn't care about owing Mum and Dad money. I needed to find out what was going on, but before I could quiz Craig, there were wedding plans to take care of.

First up, Mum and I wrote out the name cards for the place settings. "Your writing is so much nicer than mine, Mum." I placed samples of our cards next to each other. "Look. Your writing has a lovely flow to it, whereas mine looks like a child has scrawled it." She smiled at the compliment.

Once the name cards were written, I opened my laptop, and we finalised the order of service. All we had to do was provide the running order, then the printers would present the words artistically on beautiful wedding stationery. Paul and I had each picked one hymn and Mum and Dad had picked the music for us to enter and leave the church.

We stopped for a quick lunch break before our visit to the florists. As Mum cleared up the lunch things, Dad nudged my arm. "Come out and see my vegetable patch." I knew our venture outside had nothing to do with admiring his vegetable patch, but I played along with his ruse and followed him to the garden. Once outside, he directed me to a bench out of view of the kitchen window. On either side of the bench, bright pansies spilled over planters. The rest of the garden still lay dormant from its winter rest and as for the vegetable patch, it had been cleared, but it certainly wasn't worthy of a trip outdoors. Dad cleared his throat and gazed to the end of the garden. "You're a good girl, Kirsty. You've made a real difference to your mum these past few months." I smiled and tried not to think about the fallout from my dress shopping. Dad picked up on my pause. "Don't worry about all that nonsense over your dress. She was hurt, but it's forgotten now. Not like the problems James is causing."

"What is going on, Dad? Surely it's not just down to money?"

"Before we say anything more about that. Let me finish telling you how much you've done for your mum. This wedding has taken her mind off James and his problems. She loves that new outfit she bought and keeps opening her wardrobe to look at it. She's had us all trying on our kilts, making sure everything is just so. And she's been telling anyone who'll listen, how much she's looking forward to the wedding and how proud she is of you."

"Really?" Dad's words were at odds with my experience of mum. It was good to know the wedding was bringing her joy, but I was frustrated she couldn't let herself experience it fully, or tell me herself. How was I supposed to navigate the role of peacemaker if people hid their true feelings?

"Yes. We're both proud of you, Kirsty. And I'm sorry we've not told you that enough. We would like to see you more. Your mum misses you more than she'll ever let on. And she would love you to move back here, but she realises that's not going to happen. I believe she's found a way to be happy for you and your life in Glasgow."

I smiled and pushed against Dad. "Thanks, Dad. I really appreciate you telling me all this." He smiled and made to stand up. But I wasn't willing to let him away that easily. "What's the thing with James?"

"That's a future conversation. It'll keep until after your wedding." Dad squeezed my hand and walked back to the house. Why would no one tell me what was going on? Their silence only made it seem more ominous. Were they trying to protect me, or themselves, by not discussing it until after the wedding?

Our visit to the florist confirmed everything was on track regarding my bouquet and the bridesmaids' posies. My bouquet was going to be a bunch of white roses, thistles and ivy. On a previous visit, the florist had shown me photos of bouquets she had crafted and had ordered the flowers for my bouquet and the bridesmaids. The bridesmaids' posies would be roses and thistles without the extra greenery. Mum ordered thistle buttonholes for the men in the bridal party. She also discussed ideas for her corsage. The florist suggested a white rose and thistle mix in keeping with the rest of the wedding party.

"Why don't we go for celebratory tea and cake?" I suggested. As we strolled to the Harbour Tearoom, the smirr of rain that had been hanging in the air all day finally lifted and a hint of sunshine broke through the clouds. I lifted my face to the sky. The weekend was going well. It was exciting to be dealing with the last minute wedding preparations.

We settled into a table by the window and enjoyed the view of the harbour. The zesty freshness of lemon lingered in the air, enticing us to order generous slices of lemon drizzle cake with our tea. As we enjoyed our afternoon treats, we reviewed everything we'd worked on over the weekend and what was left to do. "I can't believe the next time I come to Lochcala it will be for the wedding!"

"Are you still coming the Wednesday before the wedding?"

"Yes. We've hired a car for a few days to give us more flexibility. Hopefully, we'll arrive about lunch time or early afternoon. And our guests will arrive from the Thursday onwards. Although most will come on the Saturday."

"I take it everyone who wanted to stay found accommodation?" asked Mum, before taking another bite of her cake.

"As far as I know. Most people from Glasgow are making use of the wedding bus, it will be a long day for them. But I know the wedding party and Scott, Jennifer, Ben and Tara all found places here."

Mum reached over and rubbed the back of my hand. "You're a good girl, Kirsty." Weird that both Mum and Dad had said the same thing. This thing with James must have them rattled. "I'm looking forward to your wedding. It will be nice to have everyone together and celebrate."

After dinner, Craig, Andrew and myself went to the hotel bar for a drink. I hadn't seen much of Andrew during this visit as he'd been on night shift and had either been working or sleeping. As we entered the bar, Andrew and Craig nodded to several people and I smiled at the ones I recognised. Andrew made his way to the bar, while Craig and I claimed a table. "So, when did this start?" I asked, glancing over at the bar.

"When did what start?" asked Craig.

"Andrew coming out for drinks with us."

Craig smiled and started playing with one of the coasters on the table. "It's another result of the fall out with James." Craig glanced over to the bar, checking Andrew was still out of earshot. "I don't think the two of them have fallen out, but he's certainly not hanging out with James as much." Our conversation ended when Andrew arrived with our drinks. Andrew raised his glass. "Here's to our sister. The first to get married. Congratulations." I clinked Andrew's and Craig's glasses with mine. "Thank you, my wonderful ushers." We had asked each of my brothers to be ushers. Andrew and Craig had immediately said they would, whereas James hadn't said anything. Over our drinks, we chatted about the wedding and about Andrew's and Craig's plans for the summer. As someone entered the bar, Andrew looked up and nodded. I looked round to see who it was. It was James' ex-girlfriend, Eileen. I tried not to stare at the bump protruding from her. I whipped my gaze back round to Andrew and Craig. Andrew nodded. So there was a lot more to the arguments than money. Craig looked down at the table.

"Why did no one tell me?"

Craig continued to stare at the table, unsure of what to say. In contrast, Andrew held my gaze. "Mum didn't want it detracting from the wedding. She wants to pretend all is well with the family. I don't think she's ready to admit that James got Eileen pregnant, then left her."

"Is that why he left her?"

Andrew shrugged. "He'll never admit anything." He took a drink of his beer. "One thing's for sure. He's lost his place as Mum's favourite."

I sighed. Mum and Dad had never hidden the fact they had favourites. Andrew was Dad's favourite and James was Mum's. How much damage had been done in our family by that dynamic? Was there time to bring healing and peace to this generation before the next one arrived? "Has Eileen said anything to you about the baby?"

Andrew shook his head. But at this Craig stopped examining the table. "Well, that's not exactly true, is it?" Andrew looked at him, as Craig continued. "She has talked to you, Andrew. You're the only one in the family she'll talk to." Craig sighed and finally made eye contact with me. "I'm sorry I didn't tell you any of this. It's such a mess. She's spoken to Andrew and told him the baby is James' but that James stormed out as soon as he found out she was pregnant and said he wanted nothing to do with her or the baby."

"That's awful. Poor Eileen. Have you been able to talk to James about it, Andrew?"

"No. He's closed down on the subject and won't speak to anyone about it. Mum and Dad try every so often but it leads to arguments. I think he would move into his own place if he could. But he already owes Mum and Dad money and hasn't even tried to pay them back."

This was a lot to take in. However, the one thing I could be sure of was that James would never speak to me about it. All my life, he had needled me at every opportunity. And it wasn't good-natured sibling teasing. With James, there was always a hint of malice in his tone or in his comments. This would be the perfect opportunity to write him off and have nothing more to do with him. And yet... that wasn't an option.

PAUL

Life was moving at a crazy pace. The new salon and the wedding were only weeks away, and I wasn't prepared for either.

I had no idea how Jennifer did it, but she found contractors to remove the old shop fittings and erect the partition walls between the café and the salon. With her managing the work schedule, I was confident we would meet our target date, but that didn't mean I wasn't worried.

As I worked through my full Saturday schedule, I constantly repeated, *'be joyful in hope, patient in affliction, faithful in prayer'*. I loved being a hairdresser, it was the job I was born to do. But with this unexpected move, I was having to fight through the sludge of frustration, desperately seeking joy. It was a struggle to be patient but I could definitely work at being more faithful in prayer. Jennifer had prayed, and the contractors had been able to fit us in around delays in their other jobs. I had to pray too. But what did that look like in a salon full of clients? As I was still trying to figure that out,

Carol arrived for her appointment. "What can I do for you today, Carol?"

She blew her fringe away from her eyes. "Trim the fringe and take away all my dead-ends, please."

"No problem. Follow me and I'll get your hair washed." As I led Carol over to the sink, a thought popped into my head. What if I used hair washing time to pray? As I washed and conditioned Carol's hair, I prayed for the final few days at our current location. As I massaged her scalp, I prayed for the new salon and the work to be completed there.

By the time I led Carol over to my workstation, I felt a lightness. The joy of hope was bouncing inside. For the first time in weeks, conversation with my client didn't feel forced. We laughed about the roller disco and chatted about the wedding. It would be easy to attribute the change in attitude to Carol. But when my next client, Rachel, arrived I did the same thing. In the midst of a busy salon, with the incense of coconut hair products and the sound of hairdryers, I prayed. The lightness stayed with me. The joking conversation continued with Rachel. As we chatted and made eye contact via the mirror, I noticed the faint beginnings of a rainbow above the rooftops of the South Side. Rainbows – beauty and promise combined. *Be joyful in hope, patient in affliction, faithful in prayer.*

At the end of the day, I offered to take Brian and Trish out for dinner. An offer they snapped up. We went to an American-style diner that had recently opened and placed our orders. Sitting in the booth, Brian let out a sigh. "What a busy day. It was great, but I'm exhausted."

I smiled across at Brian and Trish, the two of them fighting yawns. "Hate to tell you, but your workday isn't over yet. I brought you here under false pretences. We need to discuss the work on the salon."

Brian laughed. "Maybe let me get some food inside me first."

When our plates were empty, we turned our attention to work. I checked my phone. "Jennifer has sent me a text to let me know the partition walls and plumbing have been completed." We high-fived each other at the good news. "I think she has painters lined up for the beginning of the week."

Trish frowned. "No, she messaged me earlier to let me know the painters have been delayed on their current job. But she said it would be okay because she'll do it instead."

"What? She agreed to stick with project managing, rather than doing physical work." I should have known Jennifer would end up taking on more of the work than we had agreed.

"I tried to talk her out of it," said Trish. "I even told her pregnant women aren't supposed to paint, something about the fumes. But she cut me down with just one text."

I laughed as I imagined that conversation. "Yep, that sounds about right for Jennifer. Do you know when she is planning to paint?"

"No. She was quite vague about it. But the flooring guys are coming on Wednesday. So I'm guessing Monday or Tuesday."

"I'll ask her at church tomorrow." It was just like Jennifer to put herself out for others. She wasn't good at following her own advice, despite being the first to tell others to slow down.

We ordered dessert and discussed what needed to happen between now and opening the new salon. Hopefully, we would only be closed for a few days for the transition. "Have you guys had any more thoughts about doing something special for the opening?" I asked, before stuffing another spoonful of chocolate fudge cake into my mouth.

Trish played with her ice cream sundae. "I think we should keep the opening low-key. For one thing, we don't know if we'll make our target date. It's one thing to shift appointments with regular clients, it's another thing to risk changing appointments with new clients." Brian and I nodded in agreement. "And there is a certain wedding coming up soon.

You've got enough party planning going on without a salon party."

I laughed at Trish's comments. "Did Kirsty tell you to say that?"

Trish put her hand on her heart and flashed a shocked expression. "I can't believe you would think that. We girls look out for each other, that's all." I loved that Kirsty and Trish had a great rapport.

Brian pushed his empty dessert bowl away. "I know! Why don't we get Elsie to organise a summer themed party? It will give us time to settle in and it gives you time to focus on your wedding and the time off for your honeymoon. Then the party can be a launch celebration for us and the cafe."

"That's a great idea, mate." I scooped up the last of my cake and sat back with a satisfied sigh. Decent food and good conversation completed my day. There was joy in the business again. So many things were still unknown but being able to pray about it and work through the details with these colleagues brought peace and joy.

JENNIFER

My mind was in overdrive. I sat at my breakfast bar, chugging down a mug of coffee and fretting over all the things I needed to do this week. I had an appointment with my midwife on Thursday. Tuesday and Wednesday were college, including the finishing touches to my graded unit. But my main task for today was to do at least one coat of paint in the salon. Paul had tried to talk me out of it, as had Trish. But I was having none of it. I might need a few breaks, but I could still paint a wall. Although I had taken them up on their offer to help.

As soon as I finished my coffee, my mug went into the dishwasher and I switched it on. Next up, I grabbed the laundry basket from the utility room and walked upstairs to collect washing from the girls' rooms. With spring sunshine warming the upstairs of the house, I opened all the bedroom windows. Time to blow away the winter gloom with the spring freshness. Walking along the hallway, I noticed the door into the hall cupboard was open. Which reminded me, I had a pack of paint rollers that would be handy for today. I searched through the clutter, but the rollers were nowhere to be seen. I glanced at my watch, I had an hour and a half before I was due to meet Paul and Trish. Surely in that time I would be able to source the rollers, and if not, it was a good excuse to start clearing out this space in preparation for the nursery.

The laundry collection all forgotten, I set about my new task. I moved the bigger items cluttering the floor out to the hall. Just as I turned my attention to the shelves, the door slammed shut. I jumped at the sound but continued with my shelf-clearing task. A few minutes later, I tried to open the door to put another box out into the hall, but the doorknob wouldn't budge. I struggled with it for several minutes before realising I was stuck. So much for all that good fresh air, more like evil door-slamming-drafts. Inhaling some big, deep breaths, I fought against the rising panic. I look around, searching for something to aid my escape. There was nothing obvious and of course the box with the screwdrivers had been one of the first boxes I'd put out in the hall. All that remained were boxes of baby toys and children's clothing, nothing useful there. I patted my pockets, looking for my phone. Nothing. I was sure I had it in my pocket.

Panic was once again threatening. And with it, the horrible feeling of nausea. I was trapped. I tried to calm down with more deep breaths, but this time my body refused the calming influence and resorted to tears. Big, fat, ugly sobbing tears pouring out of my face. I slid down to the floor and gave in to all my emotions. As the tears subsided, the hiccups took their place. Oh great!

"Get a grip!" I shouted to myself. This was ridiculous. *'Father, please help me calm down and show me the solution to get out of here.'*

A few more deep breaths and calm returned. I looked around the cupboard, still not seeing anything that would help me out of my predicament. And then I heard a high-pitched trill. The noise made me laugh and shout at myself for being so silly! I moved the boxes on the floor and uncovered my phone, seeing a new text message from Kirsty. It must have fallen out of my pocket while I was moving things. I grabbed the phone and called Scott. Unfortunately, it went straight to his voicemail. Great. He would be in a meeting with clients. I tried the office number. Janice, his personal assistant, answered and confirmed he was in a meeting. "Do you know how much longer he'll be?"

"I'm not sure. Let me check his schedule." There was a slight pause, followed by the noise of typing. "His current meeting is scheduled to last for another half hour and then he's straight into a meeting with his next client. Would you like me to get him to call you back?"

By this stage, I wasn't sure whether to laugh or cry. "The thing is, Janice. I'm shut in a cupboard and I can't get out. I need Scott to come home and rescue me." What must she think of me? But by now, I didn't care, I just wanted out.

"Janice? Janice?" The line wasn't dead, but nor was there any reply. What was going on? Should I hang up? I looked at my phone waiting for the answer. "Janice? Janice, are you there?"

I was about to hang up when Scott's breathless voice came over the phone. "Jennifer? Are you there?"

"Hi, I'm here."

"Where are you?"

"I'm trapped in the upstairs cupboard. I was looking for something and the door banged shut and I can't turn the handle."

"Didn't you see the post-it note on the door to say to leave it open because the knob needed replaced?" I shook my head. Not that it conveyed anything. We were on a phone call, not a video call. "I'm leaving now. I'll be there as quickly as I can." The line went dead. In the post-call silence, I tried to determine how annoyed he would be with me. And now, he was letting clients down to come and rescue me. My imagination went into overdrive and tears once again rolled down my face.

I swiped my tears away and scrolled through the music on my phone, selecting my current worship playlist. The music brought calm to the little room. I leaned against the shelves and enjoyed the hope and peace of several songs. Next, I opened the Bible app on my phone and opened up to Matthew. *'Love the Lord your God with all your heart and with all your soul and with all your mind'*. I took some deep breaths. Breathing in the words, letting them penetrate, bringing me peace, helping me think about Jesus, instead of being caught up in my own thoughts. I closed my eyes and returned my focus to the worship music playing on my phone.

I'm not sure if I was sleeping when Scott arrived, or just very close to it. "Jennifer," he shouted, as he worked the door handle from his side. "I'm here. I'll get you out as quickly as I can."

I shouted back to let him know I was okay. Hopefully, it wouldn't take him long. Pregnancy has a way of affecting bladders and I was getting desperate for the toilet. Plus, my left leg was spiking with 'pins and needles' because of the way I'd been sitting. I couldn't wait to be free.

I've no idea how Scott eventually got the door open. But it involved a lot of banging and a can of lubricant. Eventually, the door opened and Scott rushed in and helped me to my feet. "Bathroom!" I yelled, as he guided me out to the hall.

Ten minutes later, we were sitting in the kitchen enjoying mugs of coffee and slices of toast. "Don't you need to get back to work?" I asked. Since he'd arrived home, Scott seemed completely focussed on me. Yet now the panic was over, would his focus return to work and his missed meeting? There were too many emotions vying for my attention today.

"No, it's fine. I got one of the other partners to step in to cover my meetings."

"You did?"

"Of course. You're more important than a client meeting." He winked at me. I suppressed the giggle that was rising within, instead letting a smile play on my lips. He leaned over and kissed me. "Plus, can you imagine the ribbing I would get if I let my pregnant wife stay cooped up in a cupboard all day?" Now the giggles gushed out.

"So now that I'm home. Let's talk about what happened. Why were you tackling that cupboard on your own?" He had me there. I blushed as I filled him in on my morning. Refilling our coffees, he sighed. "So your response to having too much on was to add something else to the mix." I squirmed under his questions - he was right.

"How about we break this down and work out your priorities for the next few months? First, ignore that hall cupboard. The baby will be in our room for a while, so there's no need to tackle that now." I was about to object when he held up his hand. "No. You've to leave it for now. I know you love the challenge of a new design project, but that one can wait." I blew a strand of hair away from my face and sat back. There was no arguing with such logic.

"Next up, your graded unit for college. What do you still need to do?"

As I summarised the areas that still needed work, he tapped on his phone and broke it into a bullet-point list. For each point we discussed timing. Scott was taking my unwieldy to-do list and breaking it down into manageable tasks.

"And finally, the design project for Paul and Tara. What is realistic for you to do and how much should other people do?"

"There are several things it's easy for me to do. For one thing, I can..." I slapped my hand across my mouth. "Oh my goodness, Scott!" I checked my watch. "I'm supposed to be meeting Paul and Trish in ten minutes to paint the salon."

Scott didn't say anything. Instead, he picked up his phone and selected a contact. "Paul? I believe Jennifer arranged to meet you to paint the salon?" I heard the tone of Paul's voice but couldn't hear the words. "She's had a bit of an incident this morning. Would you and Trish be okay to take care of the painting today?" Back to a muffled response from Paul. "No, no. She's fine. Just a bit of a mishap. But I'm making her rest this afternoon." He glanced over at me as Paul replied. "Thanks. Speak soon."

"Scott, I'm fine." Although, my words were more of an automatic response than heartfelt conviction.

"You need to look after yourself and our baby. So it's an afternoon of rest for you."

Sometimes in the day to day of life, it's easy to take each other for granted. But sitting across from Scott, coffee mugs and toast crumbs between us, I was reminded of the many forms love takes. Today, love came home from work to rescue his pregnant wife from a cupboard.

I leaned over and kissed Scott's cheek. "Thank you."

A mischievous smile spread across his face. "I've told the office I'm working from home for the rest of the day. So if you need to have some bed rest this afternoon, I'm more than happy to keep you company."

I laughed as I stood up from the breakfast bar. "Well… It's not the worst idea."

KIRSTY

Saturday morning was our final dress fitting at South Veil Bridal! We all trooped in, excited to try on our dresses. As the bride, I went first. I'd also brought my shoes, to ensure the dress was fitted to the perfect length. They were gorgeous white satin court shoes with slim ankle straps decorated with tiny diamantes.

I walked through to the viewing area and smiled at the gasps of my wonderful friends. Standing on the platform, I looked into the mirrors surrounding me, taking in every reflection. Running my hands over the delicate lace, I smiled. I loved this dress. The apricot colour of the satin, the delicate pattern of the lace, the shape, the style – it was all perfect.

While I continued admiring my dress, Jo, Lynn and Carol went to get changed into their bridesmaid dresses. I clapped my hands when the three of them returned. "You're all so beautiful. The dresses work really well together and the colour mix is gorgeous."

Samantha offered to take a picture of the four of us. She handed my phone back to me and I scanned through the photos. "It's such a shame Lauren couldn't be with us to complete the line-up." Samantha disappeared and came back with Lauren's dress. "I'll put Lauren's dress on a mannequin, and then you can see the impact of the dresses together." South Veil Bridal hadn't just provided me with my perfect dress, but also the perfect shop owner. Every time I come here, Samantha knows exactly what I need and makes it happen. I sent a couple of the photos to Lauren with a 'wish you were here' message. "I don't want to take my dress off," I said, as I stood in the middle of my bridesmaids.

When we were finally back in our regular clothes, Samantha joined us. "When would you like to take your dresses? They should be ready for collection by next weekend."

"I'll pick them up on the twenty-fourth, the day I'm going to Lochcala. Is that okay?"

"Yes. That's all fine. And, of course, we'd love to see some of your wedding photos. It's always lovely to see our brides on their special day."

"Absolutely," I said, as I hugged my favourite shop owner.

When we booked our dress fittings for today, we had declared it a girls' day out. So once we were finished at the bridal shop, we made our way into the city centre for window shopping, then dinner. Although the rest of the group groaned when I insisted on a salad bar for dinner. But good friends that they are, they complied. And they even commented on how tasty the salads were, although that might have been down to the amount of dressing they added. However, on route to my flat, Carol stopped at a dessert shop and bought four big helpings of cookie dough.

Settled on my couches, sweet desserts in hand, we binge watched wedding movies. We laughed at the changing wedding fashions of the decades. "I bet they all thought they looked amazing at the time," said Carol. "We love our dresses and they look so elegant. I can't imagine them ever looking dated."

"I know what you mean," replied Jo.

"Bridesmaid dresses have definitely improved," said Lynn. "Have you seen some of the funny photo reels of bridesmaid dresses from the 1970s?" I shook my head. "No one ever looks happy in them. Probably because even by the fashion standards of the '70s they were awful. Let me look them up." Lynn cast her phone to my TV, and we all laughed at the photos.

"Now I'm even more grateful for our gorgeous dresses," sighed Carol, as Lynn switched off her phone.

Lynn cleared her throat. "So, will any eligible guys be at your wedding?"

"I guess." I thought through the guest list. "Paul has some single friends coming. But whether they are eligible is a different matter."

Lynn hesitated and looked at her fingers. "And is Andrew bringing anyone to the wedding?"

"Eww!!!" I'd been aware of her focus on Andrew at the engagement party, but I didn't think there was anything to it. "Please don't even think about it, Lynn. When it comes to my family, my advice is stay clear."

Lynn sighed and scowled. I hoped it was in resignation but I have a horrible feeling it was annoyance at my response. "Trust me, Lynn. Andrew is not someone to pursue."

"We'll see," she said, as she walked through to the kitchen. "Anyone else for another drink?"

What was it with my brothers? Even when I was miles away from them, they still seemed to cause friction. How could I be a peacemaker in this one?

After I waved my friends off, I grabbed my phone, hopeful for a video chat with Paul. We wouldn't be seeing much of each other this weekend, as he was busy with the salon and the move. Paul's tired face appeared on my screen. Seeing him made me miss him more. I checked my watch. I was tempted to phone for a taxi to take me to him, but Saturday nights are notoriously difficult to get taxis and I didn't want to impose when he had so much going on.

"Hey, you. How was your last day in The Smith Salon, mark one?"

He attempted to smile through his tiredness. "It was good, and it was sad. I'm getting excited about the new place, but there's a tug of emotions at saying goodbye to where it started."

"Are you getting all soppy on me?"

"Ha! You wish! Don't worry. I'll be back to my usual cold-hearted self the next time you see me."

"No one could ever accuse you of being cold-hearted." My words moved our conversation from flippant to pensive. Did Paul sense it too? We were only a few weeks away from our wedding and yet it was still out of reach. I wanted to be with Paul now. To feel his arms around me and to stay there forever.

"Hey, how did the dress fittings go?"

"So good. Can you believe the next time I go to South Veil it will be with you and we'll be collecting my dress and the bridesmaid dresses?"

He beamed a heart-stopping smile at me. "I can't wait." Neither could I. Our call returned to silence. I was lost in thoughts of our wedding and I suspected Paul was just too tired to speak. But when he did speak, it was to end our call. "Sorry, I need to go now. I'm beat and we've got a tonne of stuff to get done tomorrow."

"Sure. No worries. I'll see you tomorrow at church."

"Thanks." He sent me one more tired smile. "Dream of me. I'll be dreaming of you."

I continued to stare at the blank screen. My thoughts brimming with my beautiful dress and my handsome fiancé. I smiled as I lay down to sleep, hoping my dreams would match my reality.

PAUL

I entered the salon for the final time. It was time to say goodbye to the place where the adventure of being a small business owner began.

Over the last few days, there had been a flurry of activity as the sinks and fixtures had been removed and now it was nothing more than a featureless shell. All that remained were a few boxes filled with the contents of our kitchen cupboards. I said a prayer of thanks for what had been established here and for what was yet to come. I had been confused and anxious when I got the letter telling me the lease was ending. For several weeks, life had been fraught and uncertain. However, now that the move was here, the overriding emotion was excitement.

When Brian and Trish arrived, we had one last walk round, grabbed the boxes, and locked the door of our first salon. We exchanged half-smiles as we took our first tentative steps away, but as soon as we rounded the corner to Kilmarnock Road, we picked up pace. Unlocking the door to the next phase in our dream, we grinned at one another. Trish put on her party playlist and we busied around the salon, setting up our workstations and making sure the flow of the area worked for us. Renovation smells of wood and paint would soon be replaced with the familiar smells of hair products. After all the hassle and frustration of having to move premises, excitement and hope bubbled through me.

With everything in place, we surveyed our new salon. "It looks great," I said, smiling as I took it all in. "Now it feels like ours." I still loved the navy and cream décor. The large mirrors and lighting features that Jennifer had sourced for our previous location looked even better in their new home. We walked through to the kitchen. It was still under construction. Even though Jennifer had told us this area wouldn't be completed until next month, I was disappointed to see how unfinished it was. Similarly, the toilets still needed work. Temporary plywood doors were in place and the walls had still to be plastered and painted.

A few hours later, a knock on the window signalled the arrival of my friends for their tour of the new premises and celebratory pizza. It was excitement and hugs all round. Jennifer took everyone through to the café and explained how things would be laid out. While the others occupied the café area, I led Kirsty back to the salon. "So, what do you think?"

She gave a little squeal of excitement and hugged me. "I love it, Paul. This is a great location for you. The Smith Salon will soar to new heights here."

I smiled at my beautiful fiancée. Cupping her face in my hands, I leaned in and kissed her. In a few weeks, there would be more to look forward to than mere kisses.

"Ugh! Kissing alert!" said Lynn, as the group returned to the salon. Kirsty laughed and wiped her lipstick from my lips.

"I heard a rumour that you were supplying pizza," said Matt.

I grinned at my flatmate. "I know that's the only reason you came. But don't worry, it's time for food. There's a great pizza place just a few doors down. Let me know what you want and I'll get our order." Everyone shouted out toppings, and then Kirsty and I walked out of the salon hand-in-hand to get dinner.

"I'm so proud of you," she said, as we walked along the street in the warmth of the spring sunshine.

"Well, that goes both ways. And, again, I'm sorry that the timing of all this conflicted with the wedding planning."

Kirsty leaned in and kissed me on the cheek. "It's fine. It was just one of those things. Plus, your business is now my business. So all this work you're doing is for our future."

"You really are amazing, Kirsty Price. I used to think being in a long term relationship was boring. But I just keep falling more and more in love with you." I was rewarded with a beautiful, radiant smile.

The mouth-watering aromas of Italian herbs and pizza toppings teased my grumbling stomach as we entered the restaurant. While we waited for our pizzas, we chatted about the final wedding preparations. As Kirsty spoke, I listened and nodded, all the while playing with her engagement ring. I loved to hear the animation in her voice when she spoke about our wedding. But then she became silent for a few seconds. When she spoke, it was in a hushed whisper. "I just wish I could do something about the situation with James."

"But what can you do? You're down here and they are in Lochcala and they haven't exactly invited you into the situation."

"I guess." She fidgeted with her hair and looked at the floor. "Don't laugh at what I'm about to tell you. But over the last couple of months, I keep coming back to the Bible verse that says *'blessed are the peacemakers'*. And whenever I think about that verse, I think about my parents and brothers. It's changed my attitude to Mum, and, as a result, we've been able to talk a bit more. Our relationship hasn't been transformed, but it's better. But when it comes to James, can I make a difference?"

I squeezed her hand and grinned. "Have I told you recently how amazing you are?" Her giggles returned. "Why don't we pray about it?" She nodded. We prayed for peace for Kirsty's family. And for wisdom in our dealings with James.

Fifteen minutes later, we were back in the salon. Everyone grabbing a space on the floor and settling down to enjoy pizza. Even Jennifer was easing herself down to the floor. "Jennifer, what are you doing? There are chairs you could use."

She flashed a defiant glance. "I am not sitting on a chair while everyone else is on the floor. That's not good for conversation."

"I guess not." I lifted my can of juice. "Well, here's to all of you. Thank you for practical help and for friendship. It makes a huge difference for us to open this salon, knowing you guys are cheering us on."

Everyone raised their drinks and cheered. "Here's to the fabulous new location for The Smith Salon," said Jennifer.

"I can't wait to get a decent coffee now when I get my hair cut," said Kirsty.

I looked at her with open mouth and raised eyebrows. "Are you trying to say I've not been providing you with quality coffee?" Kirsty laughed and winked at me.

"I'm excited about this combination. What a treat to have a haircut and tea and cake," said Carol. Everyone grinned at Carol's enthusiasm.

"What did you decide in terms of an opening event or offers?" said Matt.

Brian jumped in to answer. "Elsie is going to organise a joint party for the salon and the café." He beamed at Elsie, who had also joined us for tonight's celebration. I suspect Brian is quite attracted to Elsie. "And she'll do a great job promoting the salon, just like she did with our last location." Elsie laughed at the compliment and brushed it off with some comment about it providing practical experience for her event management course.

"And thanks for the social media posts this week too," I said to Elsie. Explaining to the group that she had been coming along most days to record video clips of the moving process to put out on our social media.

And then, as often happens in our friendship grouping, the conversation turned to the weddings. Trish and Brian were going to be doing the wedding hairstyles for Kirsty and the bridesmaids. And they took the opportunity to finalise their plans. "I've got to say," said Kirsty. "I am loving having our own team of personal hairstylists on hand. It's something I could get stressed about if I didn't know you guys."

"Plus you know we'll see you right or we'd have Paul to answer to," laughed Trish.

Kirsty joined in the joking. "And which one of you has drawn the short straw of doing Paul's wedding haircut?"

"We've been taking it in turns to cut his hair so he can decide who is worthy of performing such an important task," said Brian.

"You know what he's like," continued Trish. "You could produce the perfect cut, but he will fixate on that one little hair that escaped the scissors."

I jumped in before anyone else could assault my character. "Don't listen to them, Kirsty. They are the evil ones. You know I'm easy going and wouldn't give these guys a hard time about anything."

"Well... Normally I would believe you. But you can be a bit particular when it comes to your hair."

Everyone laughed. "She's got you there, mate," said Matt. "I would stop before you make it worse for yourself."

I might be the brunt of the current joke, but I loved this group of people. I looked around the room. Each person here made my life better. The last couple of years had been an adventure and there was so much more to come. Tomorrow, we would open our new salon. Next month, I would marry the woman of my dreams. And it was all covered in the hope of faith. *Be joyful in hope, patient in affliction, faithful in prayer.*

JENNIFER

I took a deep breath and entered the college atrium. The last thing I had to do for this academic year was hand in my assignment. As far as assignments go, this one had been an absolute joy to work on. But even though I'd enjoyed our task of designing a home office, I was still nervous. What if I'd gone off topic or made some catastrophic mistake? The lecturers had gone over all the aspects of the assignment and I was sure I had followed all their rules. But what if the pregnancy brain fog had clouded my judgement or caused me to forget some vital piece of information?

The corridors, normally bustling with students and noise, were quiet, with classes finished for the academic year and students working on their final assignments. In my worry about what my lecturer would say, my journey to the classroom alternated between a march and a crawl. But for all my current nerves, I would miss this place. Once again, I felt the little tug of despair that I was giving this up for now. I rubbed my hand over my stomach and whispered, "Sorry, baby."

When I entered the classroom, my lecturer was sitting with another student. I walked to the back of the room and looked at posters I'd gazed at a thousand times throughout the year. As I waited, I thought about the topics we had covered this year. I had learned so much. My planning and thought processes had been sharpened. My approach to projects streamlined. And my awareness of colour and texture and their compliments and contrasts honed. Plus, it confirmed this was the profession I wanted to pursue.

"Jennifer how are you?" asked Jim. I hadn't even noticed the other student leaving.

"Doing fine, thanks. I've brought my assignment."

"Great. You're the first one to hand it in. Let's go over the basic checklist to ensure you've included everything."

He motioned for us to sit at one of the desks. Without saying anything, he flicked through my work. "Perfect. You've got everything included here." And that was it. That was all the feedback I got. I knew he wasn't allowed to change anything, but I had hoped for some indication of my grade.

"Have you decided what you're going to do next?"

"The baby is due in August, so I won't be back next year. I don't know yet if I'll take one year out or two. Assuming I'm able to progress to the next level of the course."

"Obviously, we'll need to wait and see how your assignment scores. But you've passed all your modules and I can't see any issues with your assignment. We'll confirm next month, but I'm sure we'll be offering you a place whenever you want to resume your studies."

I left the classroom with a lightness in my step. Well, as much of a lightness as you can manage when you're nearly five months pregnant. I appreciated my lecturer's comments. He had given me as much reassurance as he could. For today, I could celebrate the completion of my first year as an interior design student. It had been fun to be a student again and use my brain. *Love the Lord with all your mind.*

And now it was time for lunch, then shopping with Tara. In the warmth of the May sunshine, we opted for a city centre restaurant that offered outside tables. Sitting in silence for a few moments, we took in the sights and sounds of people rushing up and down Buchanan Street. It felt very luxurious to relax in the sun, sunglasses shielding us from the glare of the city centre, and sip on iced drinks. I filled Tara in on my meeting with my lecturer. "That all sounds very encouraging. You must be so proud and relieved."

"I am, and it's a great relief to hand in my assignment." The waiter brought our salads and as we munched our way through them, we discussed which shops we would visit in our search for wedding outfits. The shopping started smoothly enough. First, we went to one of the few remaining department stores in the city centre. Tara opted for a beautiful mix'n'match selection, that provided a perfect combination of outfits to see her through a few weddings. As the co-pastor of the church, she was constantly being invited to weddings.

However, by the time Tara paid for her outfits, I had lost the will to shop. We meandered through several stores but I was no longer excited about our shopping trip. Buying clothes when you're pregnant is always tricky. What fits you one week might not fit you the next. And you never know when your bump will suddenly expand. Absent-mindedly, I flicked through rails of maternity clothes, completely uninspired. Tara gave me a reassuring smile. "You know, for this to work, you have to try on some outfits."

I glanced round at my friend and sighed. "Actually, for this to work, I think you might have to choose for me. I'm just not feeling the shopping vibes today."

"How about this one, then?" Tara held up a dress.

I shrugged my shoulders. "I know this will sound silly. But it looks really mumsy, and I don't want to look like that for a wedding."

"It doesn't sound silly, and I know exactly what you mean." I appreciated Tara's gentle reply, especially as I felt I was having a complete childish strop.

"I think what you need now is more sustenance. That salad didn't contain enough energy for you. Let's visit the café next door for coffee and cake, and then we'll try again." Tara knows me too well. The idea of coffee and cake was much more appealing than clothes shopping. By the time I had devoured the tangy lemon curd muffin, I felt re-energised and ready to shop.

Once again, Tara took the lead as we entered a store. "Why don't you go to the changing rooms and I'll bring you a selection of dresses. Try them on and see what you feel comfortable in."

"I'll give it a go. But I'm still not sure I'll like anything I try on today."

"Well, let's just try, anyway."

The first couple of dresses confirmed my suspicion. Today was just one of those days when shopping was not the answer.

By the third dress, I was ready to call the whole thing off. The light colouring and unflattering cut made me feel like a beached whale. With my previous pregnancies, I had a cute baby bump by this stage. But here I was, five months into the pregnancy and still looking overweight rather than pregnant. Where was my cute baby bump? Gazing into the mirror, I stroked my hands over my expanding girth. Hopefully by the wedding it would be obvious I was carrying a baby rather than several donuts too many.

I came out of the changing room to show Tara. Her frown confirmed she viewed this dress with the same disdain I did. "This just isn't working. Maybe I'll have a look online when I get home and see if I'm inspired by images of glowing pregnant models."

Tara placed her hands on her hips and looked at me. "That dress is not for you. I'll admit that. But I refuse to give up yet. Get back in that changing room. You've got two more dresses to try on."

Deflated, I returned to the changing room and tugged off the offending dress. I ran my hand over the next dress. The material was soft and flowy. Maybe this dress could work. I pulled it down over my head and smoothed it out. Looking in the mirror, I actually smiled. The navy blue background had a beautiful slimming effect and the midnight blossom print lifted the impact of the dress. I couldn't wait to show Tara. This time, I almost skipped out of the changing room.

She beamed at me. "Yes! That's the one. Do you like it?"

I returned her smile. "I do. It feels lovely. And the print is beautiful. Thank you." I hugged my friend and returned to the changing room. Before removing the dress, I looked in the mirror one more time, already planning on buying strappy silver sandals and a silver bag. I smiled at the reflection in front of me. This morning I had handed in my final assignment for the year and now I was ready to transition from student to pregnant mummy. I might even have let out a little squeal of excitement.

KIRSTY

I giggled with excitement as I ran around my flat, giving it a final clean before Paul arrived. I had to stop calling it my flat. In three days, it would be 'our' flat. It was a small flat for one person, and I wasn't sure where Paul's things would go. But as a newly married couple, it would be romantic to squeeze together. Once again, I checked my bags, making sure I had everything I needed. We had booked a nice hotel room in Inveraray for our wedding night. The day after our wedding would involve a quick stop off at my flat (our flat!) to drop off our wedding things and pick up our honeymoon suitcases before heading to Glasgow airport.

The doorbell buzzed, then a few seconds later Paul bounded into the flat and pulled me into a big hug, turning me round and round in circles. He set me down and immediately leant in for a kiss. It started off as a quick peck, but as soon as his lips left mine, they returned. This time more gently. He ran his hands through my hair and I was putty in those hands. Eventually, he broke away from me and grinned. "Are you ready?" I simply nodded. His kiss had silenced my ability to talk.

He grabbed my bags, and we went outside. I started laughing when I saw the hire car. It was a beautiful silver convertible. "Really?"

"Don't make out it's some guy thing. You're insured on it too. I bet you won't say no to driving this beauty." He had me there. What a great way to start our wedding adventure.

First, Paul drove to South Veil Bridal to pick up my dress and the bridesmaid dresses. Samantha hugged us and wished us well for our wedding. Paul carefully laid the dress carriers over his kilt in the boot. He jumped into the driver's seat and pushed the button for our convertible fun to begin. With sunglasses on, we left Glasgow, basking in the May sunshine. Excited for the wonders that lay ahead.

May has always been one of the best months weather wise in Scotland and this year was no exception. But of course, as my weather checks had gone from the long-range forecast to the short-range forecast, it was looking increasingly likely our wedding day was going to be overcast, with rain coming in during the day. But, as the saying goes, you can't do anything about the weather.

After an hour, Paul pulled into a picnic area at Loch Lomond. He took a cool bag from the back seat of the car and led me to a table at the side of the loch. While he laid out the food he'd purchased from the deli round from my flat, I looked to the iconic shape of Ben Lomond. "It's so beautiful here."

Paul stopped laying out our picnic and followed my gaze to the hills. "It is. And I'm grateful we get this moment. I'm sure when we arrive at Lochcala, everything will be full on."

"Exactly. I don't think we'll get much time alone with all the guest-welcoming and last-minute arrangements. At least it's only for a few days."

A grin spread up his face. "And then you're all mine!"

My face flushed, and I scrambled to divert the conversation. "So, is this the longest you've taken off work?"

"Yep. I'm not into holidays. I'm not sure why. Maybe I don't feel the need for time off because I love my work. Or maybe it's because I've never had someone to escape with."

I leaned over and kissed him. "You do say the nicest things." I took a sip of juice and looked out to the Loch. "Are you worried about being away from the salon?"

"No. Brian and Trish have got everything covered. There were a few teething problems, but now it's back to business as usual." Paul took a massive bite from his sandwich. I glanced over at him. He hadn't mentioned any problems before. Would he need to deal with salon issues on the run-up to our wedding, or worse yet, while we were on honeymoon? Paul reached over and rubbed my shoulder. "And before you go down warrens of worry, stop." I tried to smile at his tease. "It was only a few minor problems. That's why I never mentioned anything. Some clients turned up at our old salon, not realising we'd moved. The lock on the salon door had to be changed. An electrician came on the wrong day to work in the café and we lost all power."

I tried to push my niggling worries away. "And everything is okay now?"

"Yes. And even if anything does happen, Brian and Trish are more than capable of dealing with it. Plus, there are loads of positives with our new location. Being on a main road has already brought new clients. And our part of the unit is bigger than I realised, so we have space for two more workstations. Plus, the joiners are booked in to work at the café for the next two weeks. So it's perfect timing. And, even if it wasn't, I don't care. Because in three days I'm marrying the most breath-taking woman I know."

I laughed and threw a grape at him.

Paul handed me the keys as he cleared away our lunch wrappings. I squealed with delight as I settled down behind the steering wheel, enjoying the comfort of the soft leather. Driving along the twisting loch-side roads, we enjoyed the full experience of our convertible. All around us, nature was blossoming in spring beauty, the fresh green of the grass and trees, glimpses of bluebells amongst the trees and the vivid blooms of rhododendrons. By the time we drove into Lochcala, we were singing along to our favourite tunes. I don't think I've ever felt so relaxed arriving at the family home.

"Mum? We're here," I sang, as I walked through the back door. She sleepily rose from her chair. "Oops, sorry. I didn't mean to wake you up."

"It's fine," she said. "I wasn't sleeping. I was just resting my eyes."

I smiled at Mum's attempt to ease any worries I had about disturbing her. "Come to the window and see the car Paul hired for us?" She barely glanced out the window or acknowledged the stylish car. I had to remind myself we had come a long way in the last few months, but that didn't mean we got excited about the same things.

Mum turned round and made towards the Aga. "Are you wanting a cup of tea?"

"No thanks. We're going to take the dresses upstairs, and then we're going out for a walk. Do you want anything while we're out?" She shook her head and went back to her chair. It made me question again what kind of life Mum had, she seemed to spend a lot time in that chair.

Out in the beautiful Lochcala sunshine, Paul and I climbed to the castle ruin. Sitting on the grass, we watched the little ferry sail to the marina on the other side of the loch. The May sunshine warmed our bare arms and a gentle breeze blew up from the sea. Nests, hidden in the crevices of the castle ruins, sheltered baby birds as their parents flew back and forward with food. The little baby bird chirps echoed around the old stone walls. Paul put his arm around me and I snuggled in beside him.

"Thank you," I whispered.

"What for?"

"For taking me away from all this. But also reminding me how beautiful it is."

"I think I know what you mean. But those two sentences seem at odds with each other."

I nudged him and smiled. "I know I had already moved to Glasgow when we met, but you are my reason to stay there. And your romantic proposal reminded me how beautiful it is here. Lochcala is my childhood home, the place where my dysfunctional family lives, and the place of painful teenage memories. And yet, despite all that, it is a place of beauty. Just look at this view. How many people can say they grew up with a view of a castle from their bedroom window?"

Paul squeezed me in tighter. "You really are amazing. If only you could see how wonderful you are. Your family loves you, even if they seem incapable of showing it most of the time. For years they underestimated you, told you what you could and couldn't do, told you how to think and feel. But you were brave and walked away from that when you moved to Glasgow. You dealt with the unwanted advances of your manager. And I suspect it's not the first time you had to deal with sexual harassment." He put his finger under my chin and brought my gaze to his. "Kirsty, you are beautiful and you are stronger than you realise. You have nothing to thank me for. I'm the one who gains most from this relationship." He leaned in and kissed me. A toe-tingling, romantic kiss that confirmed all his words of affirmation. Was I really on the verge of marrying this incredible man?

As we rested in each other's arms in the afternoon sun, the sound of seabirds and distant voices drifted on the breeze. "Just imagine how stunning our wedding photographs will be. We'll have the choice of castle backdrop or sea backdrop for our photos." Thoughts of Paul, looking rugged and handsome in his kilt, standing against the castle, filled my imagination with wonderful daydreams. "You'll look like a clansman of old standing up here in your kilt."

Paul laughed. "Who cares about that? Have you seen how hot the bride is?"

I laughed and pushed him away. "You're so corny!"

"And you're stuck with me." He grabbed me and started tickling me. I screamed with laughter and jumped up, running away from him. He chased after me, but I think it took him longer than he expected to catch me. When he did, he twirled me around and kissed me.

This afternoon was a perfect moment. We both knew there wouldn't be much time to be alone before the wedding. But neither of us realised that our peace was about to be shattered.

PAUL

We sauntered down from the castle, caught up in our own little bubble of bliss. But as we approached Kirsty's house, we could hear James shouting.

Kirsty stopped and looked at me. Her beautiful eyes reflecting the turmoil of her family. "Oh no!" She ran into the house.

My eyes adjusted to the darkness in the kitchen, the brightness and joy of our afternoon left at the door. Kirsty's mum sat in her chair, holding her head in her hands, the sound of gentle sobs coming from her. Kirsty knelt beside her mum, her arm round her shoulders. Her dad stood across the table from James, the object giving them space to throw accusations at each other without it coming to physical blows.

I'd never heard Kirsty's dad raise his voice before, but the deep bellow emitting from the big man was intimidating. "James, the girl is pregnant. Stop running away from your responsibilities."

"She doesn't want me. And I don't want her."

"And what about the baby?"

"It's nothing to do with me," spat James, in sheer defiance.

Kirsty stood up and walked over to stand beside her dad. Even in the dimness, I glimpsed the fire in her eyes. And yet, somehow, her words came out in softness and peace. "What happened, James?"

"It's none of your business, miss goody-goody. Don't think you can come here and pass judgement on me."

"I wouldn't do that, James. But I will stick up for my niece or nephew. That poor baby doesn't deserve all this animosity. You can rage all you like, but Eileen is pregnant, and it's time to think about her and the baby."

I was proud of the way she stood up to James, especially because I knew it wasn't easy for her. However, based on the way James was glaring at Kirsty, he certainly didn't share my opinion.

And that's when I realised, I was witnessing a change in Kirsty's family. While James stood up straight and puffed out his chest, he had lost his power, or at least part of his power, to intimidate Kirsty. With the realisation that she was called to be a peacemaker, she stood her ground and looked James in the eye. The puffed up stance remained, but the sound level dropped when he replied. "It must be nice to stand on your pedestal and cast judgement on the rest of us."

"That's not what I'm doing, and you know it. Since you moved back in, you've been argumentative and demanding. Playing the victim, blaming everyone else."

"You don't know what you're talking about."

"Well, either tell someone what's going on or don't. The choice is yours."

James looked as if he was about to say something else but stopped himself. Instead, he picked up a rucksack that lay at his feet and hoisted it on to his shoulders. Without thinking, I stood between him and the door. He stopped in front of me. Staring me up and down. The gleam in his eye gave away his intentions. Before his fist swung towards me, I was ready for him and ducked to the side. Instead of hitting me, he punched the side of his mum's chair.

Everything stopped, maybe even time, as we all stared at each other. Nobody knew what to do next.

James glared at each of us and moved towards the door. In a movement much quicker than his bulk suggested possible, Kirsty's dad was beside James, his hand covering James' hand on the door handle. "Son, before you leave, you owe everyone an apology."

"What for?"

Mr Price removed his hand from his son's and shook his head. "When you're able to work that out and apologise, you're welcome to come home. But until then, it's best you stay away."

"Like I'd want to be anywhere near you." He slammed the door behind him, making sure he escaped with the last word.

Kirsty rushed to my side. "Paul! I'm so sorry he took a swing at you."

I took her hands in mine. "You don't need to apologize. And it wasn't as if he was all that subtle. I could see his punch coming a mile off. There was plenty of time to get out of the way."

Mr Price patted me on the shoulder. "All the same, son, I'm sorry one of my boys tried to punch you in my house."

We left Kirsty's mum and dad to themselves and went to Craig's flat to drop off my bags. Craig stood with his mouth gaping as we told him about James. "I'm no fan of my brother," he said, shaking his head. "But this is a new low, even for him."

"Do you think he'll be okay?" said Kirsty.

"Really? After everything that's happened, you're still worrying about him! James will be fine. He'll land on his feet somewhere. Meanwhile, he's left his usual path of destruction behind him. How were Mum and Dad when you left them?"

"Not great. But we wanted to give them time to talk about it."

"Probably for the best." Craig glanced at his watch. "What do you want to do about dinner?"

Kirsty looked around his flat. "Why don't I make a big pot of pasta and we can invite Mum and Dad round when it's ready?"

My stomach rumbled as the aroma of bacon and onions wafted through from the kitchen. While Kirsty cooked, I stashed my kilt and bag in Craig's bedroom and we tidied his living room for everyone else coming. Andrew and Mr and Mrs Price arrived by the time dinner was ready. And judging by the silence that accompanied them, Andrew had been filled in on what happened.

"What are your plans for the next two days?" asked Craig, doing his part to lift the mood over dinner.

"Our friends Jo and Matt arrive tomorrow evening. Then more family and friends on Friday. So we'll be showing them round Lochcala."

"Well, I'm excited for the first family wedding in years," said Andrew, between forkfuls of pasta. "Hey, Kirsty, remember when you were a flower girl for Mum's cousin's wedding? Didn't you refuse to walk down the aisle?"

I looked at Kirsty in pretend shock. "Really? You never told me this. I hope you're not going to refuse to walk down the aisle on Saturday?"

Kirsty blushed at the attention. "Can I just say I was three years old at the time? And I don't remember anything about that wedding. I wonder if that actually happened, or if it's a family tale that has become larger than life."

By the time the pasta bowls were cleared, everyone was in a lighter mood. Andrew looked out the window and pointed to the street. "Is that your hire car out there?"

"I take it you're referring to the sporty wee convertible. It's amazing."

"You realise you can't bring a car like that here and not take us out for a spin?"

Kirsty grabbed the keys and led us down to the car. As Andrew and Craig drooled over the convertible, Mr and Mrs Price excused themselves. Kirsty dangled the keys. "Shall we go for a drive along the coast?" Before she could say anything more, her brothers jumped into the back seat. A warm breeze whipped round us as we drove away from Lochcala. Andrew took on the role of DJ and connected his phone to the car's Bluetooth, putting on familiar tracks for us to sing along to. As we drove, they all shouted out landmarks. Pointing to places they played as children and letting me know when a particularly beautiful view was about to appear. We were five songs into Andrew's playlist when Kirsty pulled over and we jumped out. "Skimming beach," shouted Craig, as he ran ahead of us. Andrew and Kirsty laughed and ran after their brother. We selected smooth, flat stones from the edge of the beach before we raced across the sand to the water's edge. The three of them stood in a line and counted down from five, then skimmed their stones across the water. I watched for a couple of rounds before I joined in. Each time, Kirsty achieved one or two more skims than her brothers. The flying stones formed ripples where they kissed the water. Once we'd exhausted our supply of stones, we sat together on the fine, golden sand looking out to the islands of the Inner Hebrides.

After all the James drama, Kirsty, Andrew and Craig needed this time together. Tonight was proving to be a time of nostalgic memories for the three of them, a time of healing. Looking out at the lowering sun, we sat in silence, enjoying the beauty of our surroundings. Each person lost in their own thoughts. I wrapped my arm around Kirsty and pulled her close. Kirsty, my fiancée, the peacemaker. As the sun continued to set, my eyes were drawn to the colours playing across the sky. Sitting on the sand with Kirsty and her brothers, I prayed for the Price family and that this wedding would be a time of love, joy and peace. That regardless of what happened next with James the wedding would be a celebration.

I also said a prayer of thanks that I had avoided his punch. It wouldn't look good to have a black eye for my wedding!

PAUL

Kirsty arrived at the hotel in her raincoat and heels. I raised my eyebrow at her coat. "What?" She giggled. "Don't you like my shoes?"

"The shoes are great. You know it's about the raincoat."

"Well, unfortunately, Mr Fiancé, there is a horrible drizzle in the air, and I need my raincoat to protect my lovely new dress."

Maybe I should go easy on the raincoat teasing. After all, no one wants rain for their wedding day and after a beautiful May, it looked as if it that's what we would be getting.

"Why don't I take that coat for you and hang it up?"

"That would be lovely, thank you," said Kirsty, as she began unbuttoning her raincoat. But then she stopped and stared at me. "Just to check – you mean you're going to hang it up. Not throw it away?"

I gave her my best mock-hurt expression. "I can't believe you would think so little of me." Her giggles returned as I hung up her coat.

Kirsty looked stunning in the fitted dress and high heels that showed off her height and figure to full effect. It was the night before our wedding, and we were having a celebratory dinner with our closest friends and family at the Harbour Hotel. As we entered the small function room, Kirsty immediately walked over to Lauren and Jo. It meant a lot that my sister and bride-to-be were developing a deep friendship. In contrast, Kirsty's mum and dad stood alone to the side of the room. The frown on Jean's face probably keeping everyone at a distance. Beside me, Craig nudged me with his elbow, bringing my attention back to the grouping I was in. "Ignore them. Mum and Dad have never been good at parties."

"Why is that?"

"To be honest, I don't know. We got so used to it growing up that we don't even question it anymore. It's just who they are." I sighed and looked at the silent couple. Hopefully, at some point tonight, they would be drawn into the festivities. In contrast, Andrew was fully engaged in the evening. Without James dragging him down, he was good company. Wednesday night had definitely been a watershed moment for Andrew and Kirsty. An unspoken truce was developing between them. Kirsty was bringing peace to her family.

One of the waitresses appeared and informed us they were ready to serve dinner. Everyone shuffled to the long table. Kirsty and I sat in the middle, and Matt and the bridesmaids sat around us. Thankfully, Scott, Jennifer, Mum and Alex sat with Kirsty's mum and dad. If anyone could get that pair talking, it would be Mum and Jennifer. Tonight was a time to party and thank those who had already arrived for tomorrow's wedding.

The Scottish fayre of prawns, followed by Balmoral chicken and ending with cranachan, was well suited to the setting. With exposed stone walls, tartan carpet and deer antler chandeliers, you could be excused for thinking you were in a movie set or a tourist advert.

As soon as the meal was finished, Kirsty's mum and dad excused themselves. With their departure, there was an audible sigh of relief and everyone felt free to socialise. But the most interesting thing to observe was Andrew. Kirsty had told me all about her brother and his constant procession of girlfriends. I recognised that lifestyle. So when I saw him approach Lauren, I felt a burst of brotherly protection. Although whatever Lauren said to him kept him at arm's length. He didn't immediately retreat, but she was keeping a distance and involving other people in the grouping. And Lynn was happy to be part of that grouping, laughing at Andrew's comments just a bit too much. What was it about weddings that had people on the lookout for a potential partner?

As the party fizzled out, I pulled Kirsty into a hug. "Hey, how are you doing almost-Mrs Smith?"

I was rewarded with a gleaming smile. "I'm doing great, thanks."

"How would you feel about sneaking away from our party?" The smile that lit her face told me she agreed. "We could sneak up to the castle and enjoy some alone time before the craziness of tomorrow?"

"Give me five minutes to change into leggings and a hoodie."

Fifteen minutes later, we were on our way to the castle. We walked past the harbour, looking down on the recently erected marquee. I couldn't wait to see the marquee all lit up and filled with our friends and family. When we walked into that venue tomorrow we would be married. Leaving the harbour behind, we navigated our way up the stone steps, trying not to slip on the damp path. Now was not the time for a sprained or broken ankle.

We ran across the grass to the ruin, trying to get as much shelter as possible from the rain. Kirsty pulled her raincoat up higher in her fight against the weather. When we reached the ruin, we snuggled into each other. "I can't wait to become your wife tomorrow."

"Don't tell anyone. But I'm excited about that too. I can't believe how much my life has changed since I first met you." I traced her cheekbones with my finger, then leaned in and kissed her soft, beautiful lips. Ahead of me was a lifetime of kissing those lips. I was the luckiest man alive.

We sat in silence for a few moments. Enjoying the steady rhythm of the light rainfall from our sheltered spot. It wasn't cold, but Kirsty gave a shiver and snuggled closer into my side. I planted a kiss on her hair. "Did you enjoy yourself tonight?"

"I did, thanks. It was so nice spending the evening with our friends and family. Although I owe you an apology." What could Kirsty need to apologise for? Other than constantly wearing her raincoat! "I'm sorry that Andrew seemed to be hitting on your sister."

"Yes, I noticed. Thankfully, Lauren can take care of herself. But it looked like Lynn was showing a bit of interest in him."

"Ugh!" Kirsty's shoulders slumped. "She asked me about Andrew a few weeks ago. I told her not to go anywhere near him. But when does Lynn ever take my advice?"

"I guess attraction outweighs wisdom."

Kirsty laughed. "Oh well, hopefully, it doesn't go anywhere."

"Do you think your mum and dad enjoyed tonight?"

"I don't know." Kirsty gazed out over the harbour. "I swing back and forwards so much with Mum. I think we're making progress, then it's back to normal. Am I making a difference?"

"Yes. You are. Just think about this week. You were there for your mum and dad when James was shouting at them. And think about Wednesday night with Andrew."

"I guess. I know things have changed in my relationship with my parents. But then tonight happens and they withdraw into some weird place."

I kissed her cheek. "I'm sorry."

"Me too. But then I figure God has prompted me to be a peacemaker with my family. But that also means being a peacemaker with myself. It's not all on me. I need to trust God and do what I can, even though I don't know what will happen. And maybe it will never be the perfect thing I'm hoping for. But is my idea of perfect the right one? And when do we ever get to that 'perfect place' anyway?"

In the dim evening light I wasn't sure if I could make out the crinkle in her forehead or just knew it would be there. Increasingly, I was catching myself in these moments of understanding what it meant to love someone, noticing the little things and anticipating how they would react. I swallowed the lump in my throat and reached over to smooth the frown from her forehead. "Did I ever tell you I think you're amazing?"

Kirsty replied with a kiss. A kiss that deepened. A kiss that made us forget about the rain and the damp grass. However, not even that kiss could compete against a bright flash of lightning followed by an almost immediate clash of thunder. After another round of thunder and lightning, the clouds exploded, the rain coming down so hard it bounced back up from the ground. Kirsty squealed and tried to pull her raincoat higher. "Let's get you home," I said, jumping up and helping her up. "This way," shouted Kirsty, as she pulled me in the opposite direction to take us down the track rather than risking the old stone steps.

By the time we reached her parents' house, we were soaked. Standing under the small porch at the back door, we caught our breath. I pulled Kirsty into my arms and kissed her. I only meant to give her a quick kiss goodnight, but those lips cried out for more and our kiss deepened. The waiting was almost over. Soon, we would enjoy more than mere kisses. I stepped back, smiled, and walked down the path. When I reached the pavement, I looked back and shouted, "Goodnight, Kirsty Price. I love you and can't wait to marry you tomorrow." I heard her laughter as she let herself into the house.

Back at Craig's flat, I eased onto the sofa bed and settled down to sleep. Tonight would be my last night sleeping alone.

For many, our choice to not sleep together until we were married must seem old fashioned and unnecessary. But I was grateful for the strength to wait. It let me know my womanising addiction was broken. It proved I was starting over with Kirsty. She was the love of my life. The only woman for me.

JENNIFER

Driving through Argyll in May is one of life's pleasures. Stunning views of lochs and waterfalls. Hillsides waking from their winter slumber or thriving with forestry plantations. It was an ever changing journey. And, of course, a journey on a bank holiday weekend had to include a stop at Inveraray for ice cream. The girls were desperate for a break by the time we reached the picturesque, white-walled town. Plus, I'm not going to lie. I needed some tangy raspberry ripple ice cream too. One bonus of pregnancy clothing is scoffing ice cream and other treats without worrying if your dress will still fit.

An hour after our ice cream stop we drove into Lochcala. The quiet little town came to life around the harbour. The shops, tourists and boats bringing colour and vitality to the place. Scott followed the satnav's instructions to get to our holiday house, just a few minutes' walk from the harbour. The girls bolted from the car and raced round the house and gardens, desperate to run off their pent up energy. Downstairs there was a good sized living room and kitchen and two double bedrooms. Upstairs, a large attic bedroom was perfect for the girls. "Now remember, girls, Ben and Tara will be sharing the house with us for a few nights, so don't take over." Half an hour later, we were sitting in the garden, car unpacked and bedrooms allocated. The garden opened onto fields, the sounds of bleating lambs completing the idyllic setting.

In the evening, we walked down to the hotel for Paul and Kirsty's pre-wedding dinner. Chloe was pulling my hand, desperate to see the harbour and the boats. I guess when you grow up in the city, fields and harbours capture your imagination. Unfortunately, the blue skies of earlier had been replaced with layers of clouds and a smirr of heaviness hung in the air. But at least in the hotel, there was brightness and celebration. Although, as soon as we arrived, Kirsty raced over and pulled me aside. "Jennifer, I'm so sorry to ask you this again, but could you and Scott please sit with my mum and dad?"

I nodded, happy to oblige. "But will they be okay with the girls' noise and energy?" Even as I spoke, Chloe was throwing herself at Paul.

Kirsty grimaced. "Hopefully, it will be a welcome distraction. We've had some more family issues since I arrived. I'll fill you in another time."

I reached out and hugged Kirsty. "You enjoy your night and don't worry about your parents." She smiled and mouthed her 'thank you' as we wandered over to join in the conversation with her bridesmaids.

As for Kirsty's mum and dad, we ended up having a pleasant time. Thankfully, the girls behaved well, even Chloe. Between courses, they disappeared to the corner of the room and watched TV programmes we had downloaded onto their tablet. Scott's not a fan of small talk, but he was happy to chat with Kirsty's dad about the duties of a police officer in rural Argyll. Their in-depth conversation removed all awkwardness and ensured there were no long silences. At various points, I directed wedding related questions to Kirsty's mum. She responded politely but didn't seem bothered about engaging in conversation. And I didn't feel the need to push. If she wanted more conversation, she could instigate it, too. Thankfully, Susan and Alex were beside me, and they were easy dinner companions.

By the time I finished my meal, I was feeling uncomfortable. I pushed back from the table and rubbed my sides. I wasn't sure if it was wishful thinking, or if I had a bump now rather than just looking overweight. Even in mid-conversation, Scott picked up on my discomfort and, still looking at Kirsty's dad, put his arm round my shoulders. When they got to a natural break in their conversation, he looked round to me. "How are you doing? Do you want to go back to the holiday house?"

I continued rubbing my strained sides and nodded. "Yes, please."

As soon as we were back at the house, I changed into my comfy pjs and downed a cool glass of water. Scott settled the girls in bed, then returned to the living room. He handed me a cup of tea, then proceeded to rub my feet. I leaned back on the settee. "Oh Scott. That is the best feeling ever. Thank you."

"Really? Me rubbing your feet is the best feeling ever?"

I laughed at his raised eyebrow. "Okay. Let me rephrase that. It's the best feeling today."

"That's better," he replied, as he continued to massage my tired feet. "Do you think you'll be okay for tomorrow?"

"Of course. I'm just pregnant. It's not as if there's anything wrong with me."

"I know. I was more thinking in terms of your energy levels."

"I'll be fine. And I can always come back here if I get tired."

"Maybe we could come back between the service and reception. The time between will be spent taking pictures. It's not like we'll miss anything."

"That could be a good idea. We'll see how things go." I took a drink of tea. "You did really well talking to Kirsty's dad tonight."

"It was easy. He's a nice guy, and it was interesting to hear stories about a different lifestyle and career." Scott always loved hearing people's stories. Even when we were at university, he would talk with people into the wee hours of the night, listening to their hopes and dreams.

I stretched my legs and yawned. "I think that's enough excitement for you for one day," said Scott, as he stood up and took my hand. "Let's get to bed. You need a good sleep before tomorrow."

I happily followed Scott through to the bedroom. The king size bed was calling me with its big puffy duvet and fluffy pillows. I flopped onto the bed and sighed. This was my happy place. But after just a few hours of sleep, pregnancy bladder capacity meant I needed to get up. The sound of rain from outside probably wasn't helping. I threw on a cardigan and tiptoed through to the bathroom. After my visit to the bathroom, I continued to the kitchen to make myself a cup of tea. With mug in hand, I opened the back door of the house to enjoy the evening air. The light at the back door lit up the falling rain, causing a beautiful display of illuminated crystals. The tin porch magnified its rhythmic sound and the happy scent of summer rain played with my senses. If I was in a musical, I'd be out dancing in the garden. But this was no movie, and I was content to enjoy the scene from the dryness of the porch. I grabbed a chair and enjoyed the rain's symphony.

Little flutterings in my womb let me know that someone else was awake with me. "Hey, baby," I whispered to my bump as I ran my hands over it. "Do you think you'll enjoy playing in the rain? It will bring you puddles to jump and splash in. You wouldn't think it now, but Amy loved jumping in puddles when she was little. But look at her now, a high school pupil, too cool to play in puddles." I looked back down at my bump. "Maybe with you I'll remember to treasure each moment. Not as a memory, but as it happens. And I don't want to just do it with you. I want to love each moment as it happens with all four of you. Hopefully, I'm learning to find love, joy and peace in the present. I don't want to romanticise the past or strive for something in the future. I want to live in the present." More flutterings let me know the baby was engaging with the conversation. I smiled as I gazed out at the rain, content in the moment.

THE WEDDING

KIRSTY

A gentle knock on my bedroom door woke me from the final fragments of sleep. "Good morning," chorused Mum and Dad as they entered my room. Dad opened the curtains while Mum sat a breakfast tray on the bed. It was just tea and toast, but the single white rose on the tray let me know she had planned this. As I fingered the delicate petals, Dad cleared his throat. "I'm afraid we've got bad news."

Mum glared at him. "You could at least let the girl finish her breakfast first."

"It's okay," I said, trying to give a reassuring smile. "I know it rained a lot last night and that it's still raining."

Dad exchanged a glance with Mum and sighed. "It's not just that it's been raining and still is. There's been a landslide at The Rest and be Thankful. The road is impassable." I sat bolt upright in bed.

"But most of our guests are travelling that way. What are we going to do?" I tried to hold back the tears. "It's going to take them over an hour longer to get here. What are we going to do?"

Dad shuffled where he stood, unable to cope with my emotions. "Andrew is downstairs. Why don't you come down and we'll talk about it?"

My uneaten breakfast remained on the bed as I followed Dad down to the kitchen, I felt as if I was watching someone else walk through the house. In my anxiousness, my senses could not process anything. What did this all mean for my wedding? Was the whole thing now in jeopardy?

I walked into the silent kitchen. No one had anything to offer, only hopes that people would hear about the landslide and change their plans. Residents of Argyll are used to the frequent landslides and the resulting sixty mile diversion, but why today? It would have a major impact on guests' arrival times, maybe even put some people off coming. Dad shuffled about, my tears pushing him way out of his comfort zone. I looked at Dad, Mum and Andrew. None of them knew what to say. I stood up and made for the door. "I need to see Paul."

"But you're not supposed to see each other before the wedding," blurted out Mum.

"Oh Mum! That's superstitious nonsense. I need to see him." I grabbed my old wellington boots that still sat by the back door. It had been years since I'd last ran in wellies, but the wibbly noise of flapping boots brought a strange comfort and chased away further tears. When I arrived at Craig's flat, I threw myself into Paul's arms and took deep, comforting breaths. "The road? What are we going to do?" I asked, as I nestled into him.

Craig silently walked into his living room and gave me a mug of coffee. "Start by sitting down and thinking through the options."

"What are our options?"

"We've been talking about that," said Paul, as he led me over to the settee and sat down beside me. Before he could say anything more, Mum, Dad and Andrew arrived. Craig brought them mugs of coffee too, and then we sat down to discuss the latest dilemma. "First, we need to contact the bus company to find out their revised arrival time," said Paul, as he checked his watch. "They should know about the diversion by now. And then we need to get in touch with Ben and Tara, I think they were planning on driving up quite early, anyway. And then we need to talk to the minister and discuss pushing back the wedding."

I sat silently, not knowing what to say. In the grand scheme of things, delaying our wedding by an hour wasn't a disaster, but I couldn't believe it was something we had to deal with. Paul draped his arm around my shoulders and prayed for peace and wisdom as we worked out our next steps. I echoed his 'amen'. He squeezed my hand, bringing my focus back to him. "Why don't we make the most of it?"

I gave him a questioning look. "I'm struggling to see what we can make the most of."

"Let's start by getting my mum and Alex and Jo, Lynn, Carol and Lauren here. We can split the list of people we need to contact between us. And then once we've contacted everyone, we can celebrate with brunch."

I forced a smile. "How on earth are you able to turn this round from being a disaster to being a party?"

"I guess with everything that's happened with the salon, God's been teaching me about finding joy in change. Things might look as if they've gone off-track, but God's still in control." He winked at me and smiled.

He was right. Yes, things were not going to plan, but in a few hours, I would marry this wonderful man. And that was what today was really all about. I leaned in and kissed my amazing almost-husband.

I looked over at my parents. "Mum and Dad, could you speak to the minister?" They nodded their agreement and left the flat. "Right, boys, will we start making calls?" Although now that the panic was over, I suddenly realised the state of my appearance. My face was makeup free, and I hadn't even brushed my hair. I was wearing tatty short pyjamas with my old high school hoody. And my wellies completed the sophisticated ensemble. I giggled. Nothing was going to plan, but where there had been worry, now love, joy and peace were nudging in.

PAUL

Kirsty sat beside me on Craig's living room floor. She leaned her head against the wall and sighed. "How are you?" I whispered, as I reached for her hand.

"I'm okay now. It was a tough start, and I don't think I reacted very well when Dad told me about the landslide, but Mum, Dad and Andrew followed me here to see how they could help. With the way the rain is still coming down, I doubt we'll be able to get the photos I wanted at the castle and we'll lose at least an hour of our wedding, but I'm happy. And we've even been gifted this bonus time right here."

I grinned at her positive outlook. Throughout the engagement, Kirsty had put plan after plan in place to ensure our day would run smoothly and yet here we are firefighting the last-minute changes to our wedding. Similarly, I had tried my hardest to make the salon a success. But I couldn't have predicted our lease being cut short. This year was showing us that no matter how thoroughly we plan, there will always be unknowns. Some of these unexpected things will lead to better places, some to worse. We'll never be able to plan for every scenario, but we can choose how we react. Kirsty thinks she's weak, but today was just another example of her resilience. I lifted her left hand to my lips and kissed her ring finger. Today, we would commit to each other for the rest of our lives. I couldn't wait.

Laughter and music now filled Craig's flat. Our amazing wedding party had rallied round and taken on the various tasks of our unexpected to-do list. Within half an hour, we had contacted the caterers, the bus company and as many of the guests as we could. And now we were enjoying our well-deserved wedding brunch. Mum, Alex and Lauren had come to Craig's flat via the grocery store and brought juice, fruit and pastries. While we were eating, Brian and Trish arrived. Trish almost screamed when she saw Kirsty's unruly hair.

"Time for work," announced Trish, as if we'd been sitting about all morning. "Kirsty, let's get to your house and start work on your hair."

Kirsty jumped up, then turned round to pull me up beside her. "I'll see you at the altar, husband." There was no stopping the grin spreading across my face.

I followed them outside and watched as they walked away. Alone on the pavement, there was a stillness. I could still hear the sounds of music and laughter from Craig's flat, but it was as if I was in a bubble of silence. I walked down to the harbour and sat on a wet bench. Even in adverse weather, Lochcala cast its charm. Boats bobbed about on the water. Puddles rippled with the constant drops of rain. A few seagulls cried out and locals and tourists were beginning to venture outside.

I closed my eyes and lifted my face to the rain. *'Be joyful in hope, patient in affliction, faithful in prayer.'* The verse had carried me through a lot these last few months. *'Thank you, Father. Thank you that you are faithful. Thank you that you offer us joy and hope. Be the centre of today. Be the centre of my marriage to Kirsty. Let our marriage be built on you. Amen.'*

JENNIFER

This morning was not going to plan. After enjoying the storm last night, it had taken me a while to get back to sleep, and today my energy levels were paying the price for my midnight storm watching. I woke up groggy and grumpy. Scott took his cue and ushered the girls out the door for a walk around the harbour. By the time they returned I felt slightly more human, I'm sure the two mugs of coffee helped. And the sight of the crusty bread and salad for lunch brought a smile to my lips. Just as we set the table, Ben and Tara arrived, looking as frazzled as I had felt earlier.

"What a journey," said Ben, as he devoured his sandwich. "That's quite the diversion. I can imagine a few guests will miss the ceremony."

"Have you heard from the worship team?" I asked.

"Paul phoned them earlier, they are on their way and will be here in plenty of time." Ben checked his watch. "I know we've still got a few hours until the wedding but I'd like to go to the church now and get settled and prepared."

"Can we do anything to help?" asked Scott.

"You already have," said Tara. "Lunch and coffee was exactly what we needed."

As we waved them off, Amy suggested watching a movie together. "Why don't we pull out the bed settee?" I suggested. "Girls, get your duvets and pillows. Scott, can you open up the bed settee? And while you all do that, I'll quickly clean up the kitchen." Amongst whoops of excitement from the girls, we all set about our tasks and within minutes we snuggled down for our afternoon movie. Amy pushed in to get beside me and I wrapped my arm around her as we pulled our duvets up. Part way through the movie, I drifted off to sleep. When I woke up, it was the final scene of the film. Amy and Emma were sleeping on either side of me and Scott was sitting on the floor next to Chloe, helping her complete a jigsaw.

If I'd learned anything from the last few years, it was that life was always changing. What was that saying? The only certainty is change. And the only constant is Jesus, the same yesterday, today and forever. And, when I focussed on loving him with all my heart, soul and mind, it didn't matter what changed round about me. Last night had been a precious gift, sitting on my own watching the rain. And this moment was a precious one too, surrounded by my family. I ran my hand over my bump and said a prayer of thanksgiving for Scott and our children as I felt the flutter of kicks below my hand.

But a glance at my watch soon had me jumping up. The wedding would be starting in half an hour and none of us were ready!

KIRSTY

"Am I doing your hair first?" asked Trish.

Jo jumped in and answered before I could reply. "Yes, start with Kirsty." She turned round to address Brian. "Who are you starting with?"

"I'll go alphabetically. Carol, you're up first, then Lauren, then Lynn."

As the small living room transformed into a makeshift hair salon, Dad escaped to Craig's flat to get changed. Trish, who had previously practised my wedding style, quickly got to work with tongs and hair spray and clips.

"It was so stressful driving up this morning," said Trish, as she began curling my hair. "When we saw the diversion signs, we panicked when we realised how much it added to our journey."

"It's terrible," I replied. "That road's always been prone to mudslides, but it's getting worse. And that's with some controls in place. I don't know what the solution is. As you said, the diversion is long."

"How stressful was it for you guys this morning, changing plans and getting in touch with everyone?"

"It was okay. There were enough people to help. So it didn't take long to contact everyone."

Jo turned up the music on her portable speaker and handed out glasses of fresh orange. "Today feels like a daylong party, between our impromptu brunch and now hanging out together for hairstyling. I'm loving these connections you've brought into our lives, Kirsty. It's quite decadent to have such talented friends to call on."

The stress of the morning was fading away. Jo was right. There was a party atmosphere. Maybe for the first time ever in this house. It took a lot of persuasion, but we even talked Mum into letting Trish style her hair. I shared a secret smile with Jo. As Trish started work on Mum's hair, I disappeared to my room. Sitting at my window, I looked out over the familiar view, except now a marquee was pitched at the harbour. The rain was still coming down and judging by the clouds, it looked as if it was here to stay. Of course, no one wants rain on their wedding day, but somehow it added something extra to the day – I couldn't quite define what.

I looked around my bedroom. Now that I was getting married, Mum was finally ready to admit that I wouldn't be moving back to Lochcala. This was the last time I would be in my bedroom. But already, it looked and felt different with my wedding dress and the bridesmaid dresses hanging up. While we had been making phone calls this morning, Mum had returned to unpack our dresses. I ran my hands over the chiffon, silk and lace. The colour of the bridesmaid dresses all different, but together a beautiful palette of colours. I picked up my Bible from the bedside table and flicked to the gospel of Matthew. *'Blessed are the peacemakers, for they will be called children of God.'*

Picking up my phone, I scrolled through to my worship playlist and returned to my seat by the window. I closed my eyes and drank in the peace. Softly, I sang along. Surprising myself at how peaceful I felt, considering all that had gone wrong this morning. *'Thank you, Father, for your gift of peace.'* Although, at that precise moment, my peace was shattered by the sound of bridesmaids thundering up the stairs. I laughed as they burst through the door.

Jo led the group. "Time to get our party dresses on!" She grabbed my hands and pulled me up. Lauren took my phone and switched it off. She then scrolled through her phone. "I've created a wedding playlist for us." I laughed as 'Here Comes the Bride' erupted from her phone. Thankfully, she had also added some floor filling tunes to the playlist for us to dance and sing along to. Jo and Lauren helped me into my dress before getting their own dresses on. "I wish we had a bigger room to get ready in," I said, as we shuffled round each other. "I would love to be in a big, bright airy room with enormous mirrors so I could get a proper look at us together."

"Where would the fun be in that?" said Jo as she fastened my necklace. "This is what we're used to. Getting ready in your wee flat for our nights out in Glasgow."

I giggled. "Good point."

The jewellery, hair accessories and shoes were all added, and then we went down to the living room. Lynn, the selfie-queen, had been taking lots of photos. They would make a lovely record of our day. And now that we were all ready, Lynn got us to pose with funny faces just as the official photographer and Dad arrived.

With the rain still coming down outside, the pre-wedding photographs were all taken in the cramped cottage. Photographs of me and Dad, looking very handsome in his kilt. Photos of me with Mum, looking lovely in her dress. Then photos of me and the bridesmaids.

As the photographer finished our pre-church shots, he confirmed our wedding photos would all be taken in the church or in the marquee due to the rain. I was disappointed at not getting my castle wedding photographs, but there was still fun to be had. Before he packed his equipment, Jo stepped in front of the photographer. We exchanged looks and laughed. "Actually," she said. "Kirsty and I have props for some additional photographs, if you don't mind?"

"No problem," he replied.

I turned to my bridesmaids to fill them in on my plan while Jo retrieved the suitcase she had snuck into the house.

PAUL

"Come on, we're late," I shouted to my best man and ushers. I couldn't be late for my own wedding! Our footsteps echoed as we ran up the hill to the church. Although, to call our movement running was generous. Fighting against the rain, battling with golf umbrellas and encumbered with ghillie brogues, it was more of a jog-walk-shuffle than a run. The kilt might be the iconic apparel for weddings, especially in a setting like Lochcala, but there are a lot of time sapping parts to it. It had taken us longer than expected to deal with the intricacies of the ruche ties, the kilt buckles, the flashes for our socks and the lace up brogues.

When we reached the church, a lone bagpiper played. I didn't know a piper had been booked for the wedding. Matt took his phone out of his sporran and shot a video of the four of us with the piper. Then, with a nod to the piper, we sought shelter in the church. Standing in the doorway, various guests shook our hands and wished me well and then the bus arrived with our Glasgow guests. A fresh wave of well-wishers – family members, men from the bible study group, guys from the gym and friends from church drifted in. I laughed as Mum and Alex joined us at the back of the church with carrier bags filled with small cartons of juice and biscuits for our weary travellers. They certainly looked grateful for the provisions after their longer than expected journey.

Ben came up beside us. "Okay, gentlemen, time to get you to the front. Your bride will be approaching any minute." I checked my watch and was about to follow Ben when Jennifer, Scott and the girls came rushing in. This couple have supported me through so much over the last few years – faith, business, relationships. And if it wasn't for their love and guidance, I wouldn't be standing here today. As we exchanged quick hugs, I swallowed the lump in my throat. After a morning of problem solving, I wasn't prepared for emotions. I took a deep breath and looked out over Lochcala, composing myself before I entered the sanctuary. Walking towards the front, there were more handshakes and good wishes from those sitting at the ends of the aisles. The little church was full of friends and family celebrating our special day.

The worship team, who had been playing quiet instrumental music, now went into the song that signalled Kirsty was outside. I shuffled about, too excited to stand still.

The music changed again and Kirsty entered the church. She hadn't told me anything about her dress, but I knew she would be stunning in whatever she wore. More beautiful than she realises and stronger than she knows. I took a deep breath and looked around to see my stunning bride.

The one reaction I hadn't expected was laugher. But at the sight of my bride, I burst out laughing and ripples of laughter spread around the church. Kirsty walked down the aisle in her raincoat and wedding dress. Followed by four bridesmaids in their raincoats and bridesmaid dresses.

Life with Kirsty would never be boring.

KIRSTY

Amidst the laughter of our friends and family, I glided to Paul. The church was full, but the only person I saw was Paul. Seeing him in his kilt filled me with pride and wonder that I was getting to marry this man. I didn't care that it was raining. I didn't care that we had to start the wedding later than planned. All I cared about was this man standing beside me.

Paul took my hand and whispered, "I always did like you in raincoats and sunglasses."

I giggled. "That's not how I remember it. I seem to remember a certain hairdresser having a big problem with all the women going about Glasgow in boring raincoats and sunglasses."

Paul shrugged. "Well, if that's how you choose to remember it."

As the laughter subsided, I removed my raincoat and handed it to Jo. My bridesmaids also removed their raincoats. When I turned back round to face Paul, his eyebrows rose, and he mouthed 'wow'. I dipped my head and smiled and nestled into his side. And then we turned to face Ben. It was time for our wedding to begin. Our amazing, beautiful wedding.

As Dad said his 'I do' to giving me away, he leaned in and kissed me on the cheek. I pulled him in to a hug and whispered, "Thank you, Dad." And I was thankful for him. We are not a perfect family, but he has always been there for me. Even though he imposed rules I thought weren't fair, he thought they were. And I could see that now.

A cosy blanket of peace nestled over me. Today was a day of love, joy and peace. Today was a day for being thankful. We started by singing the hymn, The Lord Is My Shepherd. It might not be the most obvious wedding hymn, but it's familiar for most people, whether they attend church or not.

When the congregation sat down, Ben opened his Bible. "I asked God what Bible verses he wanted me to share for Paul and Kirsty's wedding. And the verse that kept coming to mind was from the book of Galatians, found in the New Testament, chapter five, verses twenty-two and twenty-three. 'But the fruit of the Spirit is love, joy, peace, patience, kindness, goodness, faithfulness, gentleness and self-control. Against such things there is no law.'"

I smiled as Ben preached from one of my favourite verses. Love, joy and peace. Over the last few years, each element had been a major part of my story. Foundations that had deepened my faith and given me confidence to be me. As Ben continued his talk, I said a prayer of thanksgiving.

And then it was time for our vows. Jo took my flowers, and Paul and I turned to face each other. He took my hands in his and smoothed his thumb over the back of my hand. As I gazed into his eyes, he winked at me. His smile melted my heart and drove away the flutter of nerves that appeared anytime I had to speak in front of a crowd. As Ben began our vows, our friends and family disappeared and it was only the three of us. I know the vows are a public declaration, but as far as I was concerned, they were just for me and Paul. When we had discussed the service with Ben, we decided to go with the traditional vows, which we now repeated. And I meant every one of them. I chose to love and honour Paul in sickness and in health, for richer for poorer, till death do us part. With our vows promised, we exchanged our wedding rings, and Ben declared we were husband and wife. As soon as the rings were on our fingers, Paul pulled me into his arms and kissed me to the cheers of the congregation. My first kiss with my husband.

Ben laughed and then informed everyone that while we went to the vestry to sign the register, the worship band would play one of our selected tunes. When we reached the vestry, Jo wrapped me up in a big hug. "Congratulations!" she squealed. I returned the hug, thanking God for this special friend. "Thank you," I whispered. The rest of the grouping said their congratulations too. Ben had said to us during our wedding rehearsal that signing the register would give us a minute to catch our breath, and he was right. It was time to take a few deep breaths after the formal ceremony.

We returned to the church, and the service finished with one more hymn. Rather than leaving for the marquee, we stayed in the church for the official photographs. Thankfully, the Lochcala church is beautiful, with its stone walls and arches. And now that the service was over and my nerves abated, I could take in the beauty of the wedding decorations. Stunning flower arrangements comprising white roses, gladioli, daisies, gypsophila and thistles with tartan tulle cascading from the stands stood at the front of the church. Further waves of tartan tulle hung round the sides of the church, and corsages of white roses and thistles were attached to the ends of the pews. I had made my peace with the rain, but I still felt the tinge of sadness that our wedding photos wouldn't be showcasing the stunning views of Lochcala. However, the wedding photographer proved himself more enterprising than I had given him credit for and took several photographs at the church entrance, capturing the striking backdrop of the harbour.

JENNIFER

Tears filled my eyes as Paul and Kirsty exchanged their vows. I could pretend it was pregnancy hormones causing the tears, but who was I kidding? And anyway, what did it matter? They were happy tears. It was a beautiful thing to witness two friends commit to each other forever. I thought back to the first time I met Kirsty. She was uncertain of her faith, overwhelmed by life in Glasgow, and boyfriend troubles seemed to be a constant feature of her life. But now she was maturing into a confident woman. And as for Paul. What a change in him over the last few years. Paul combined good looks and an outgoing personality. It was a privilege to walk beside him, as he chose time after time to keep his focus on Jesus. They were an easy couple to cheer on. And today was the perfect occasion to celebrate them both. They had endured a shaky start to their day, but they had seen beyond the problems and understood today was about more than the weather or perfect timing. Today was about their love.

I leaned my head on Scott's shoulder and sighed. Today wasn't the end of anything. It was the continuation of Paul and Kirsty's journey together. But somehow today brought closure. Maybe it was closure to their past as they stepped into their future. At their final pre-marriage meeting, we had talked about the future and how they would navigate it as a married couple. I was excited for them.

As I let out a muffled yawn, Scott whispered, "Let's go back to the holiday house for an hour so you can rest before the reception."

"That is a wonderful idea. And do you think someone might make me a lovely mug of coffee while I'm resting?"

"I'm sure that could be arranged." After fifteen years of marriage, Scott still knew how to make me smile. Today was a day to celebrate love. And I had a lot to celebrate.

PAUL

Kirsty was radiant. She glowed in happiness as she posed for photo after photo. It seemed surreal that we were married. That I was married. Being faithful to one woman had been an alien concept until a few years ago. Before knowing Jesus, I had no intention of settling down. Committing to one woman sounded boring and old. But how wrong I'd been. Of course, we'd had fallouts and misunderstandings, but the treasure far outweighed any negatives.

I laughed as Kirsty and the bridesmaids put their raincoats on for some photographs. After the photographer nodded his head, happy that he had the right shot. Kirsty shouted me over. "Come on, Paul. You need to be in at least one Raincoat photo." For the next few minutes, I posed with Kirsty and her bridesmaids. Then Lauren threw her raincoat over my shoulders and I heard the click and saw the flash of more photos being taken. Kirsty laughed. "Now we have official proof of you in a raincoat."

"There's nothing wrong with raincoats," I said, pulling Kirsty into my arms and kissing her. Which, of course, led to more photos.

Kirsty pulled away and play punched me on the arm. "Ha! Have I finally changed your attitude to raincoats?"

I kissed her again. "I wouldn't go that far. Especially as that dress is far too sexy to be hidden beneath a boring old raincoat."

By the time we arrived at the marquee, a great atmosphere was building. The sound of talking and laughter rose above the background music. Someone had brought the flower displays from the church. A balloon arch in blues and greens stood behind the top table, and fairy lights hung all around the sides. Even though I was the one who suggested a marquee, I had no idea it would look this good.

While Kirsty went to talk to her work colleagues, I looked over the sea of smiling faces. My attention was quickly brought to one little guest when Chloe came rushing towards me and threw herself into my side. "Paul! Paul! Did you not see me waving to you in the church?"

"Sorry, I missed that. It must have been all those enormous hats in the way." There was no way I could let my little friend down by telling her I only had eyes for my beautiful bride.

"Sorry, Paul," said Jennifer, as she reached me and pulled Chloe off my side. "You need to be careful, Chloe. There are lots of people and they don't want you pushing into them."

"It's okay, Mum. I was really careful. And Paul doesn't mind. Do you, Paul?" I smiled at Chloe as Jennifer shot me an apologetic glance. Jennifer quickly moved the conversation on. "So, how are you both now that the wedding is underway?"

"We're good." I glanced around the room, looking for Kirsty. She was still with her work colleagues, laughing and chatting. "Kirsty's been amazing. I can't believe how well she coped with all the bad news this morning."

Jennifer followed my gaze to Kirsty. "She's more resilient than she realises. I've seen it in her for years. You're seeing it more, too. She'll be the last one to realise how strong she really is, but she has come a long way since meeting you. You're good for each other, which makes today even more special."

I grinned. "We owe you and Scott so much. Thank you." Jennifer squeezed my hand and went off in search of her family and I went to my bride. Just as I reached Kirsty's side, Ben announced it was time for everyone to take their seats for the meal. The piper, who had been playing at the entrance of the marquee, performed his last duty of the day - piping me and Kirsty to the top table. We all applauded as he walked out of the tent, playing all the way.

Next, Ben stood up and introduced the speeches. I was grateful we had opted to get them over and done with before dinner. As the groom, all I had to say was, 'On behalf of my wife and I,' and I got a cheer. It was a positive way to start. The next essential of the groom's speech was to say how beautiful the bride looks. Easy. Then finish by thanking a host of people. I only hoped I could remember all the people I needed to thank. I took out my phone and looked at my Notes app to check. I finished up by presenting hampers to the parents. Then sat down to polite applause. Next up was Matt, with the best man's speech. He had been making lots of comments about how much I should bribe him to keep all my secrets. But Matt was a good guy, right?

Matt stood and grinned at me. "You'll be glad to know I'm going to keep this short. We're all hungry and we don't want to keep the catering staff waiting." A ripple of laughter circled the marquee. "This speech has been a nightmare to write. As many of you know, Paul and I are flatmates, so I have a lot of embarrassing stories about him. However, I'm getting married in six weeks and Paul is going to be my best man, so I need to be kind to him or he'll get his revenge. So, all I'm going to say is Paul is an amazing guy and Kirsty is a lucky girl. Shall we toast to that?" People glanced at each other as they cautiously rose for the toast. Matt brought his hands down, indicating for people to sit back down. "Or is he?" Everyone laughed as they sat back down.

"Last year, a group of us went on a ski holiday and it was the worst week of our lives. Not just because I had a terrible fall and tore a tendon in my leg and our friend Jennifer sprained her wrist. But because of these two. The attraction between them was obvious to everyone except them. And we were all desperate for them to kiss so we could enjoy our holiday." Everyone laughed. I glanced at Kirsty, who was wiping away tears of laughter. "But somehow the two of them missed the perfect opportunity to get together. So when did they start dating? When they were back in Glasgow and Kirsty was bunged up with a cold!" Kirsty blushed as our guests laughed. "These two never do life the easy way. And those of us privileged to call them friends know life will never be boring with Paul and Kirsty around."

Matt lifted his glass. "Paul, Kirsty, we love you and we're thankful you finally worked out you were made for each other. To Paul and Kirsty. The Bride and Groom." Everyone stood up and joined in the toast. I would thank Matt later. But for now, it was another excuse to kiss my hot bride.

KIRSTY

I was still wiping away my tears from Matt's speech when Ben stood up to say grace. As soon as the 'amen' left his lips, the head waiter gave a nod and the waiting staff sprang into action, delivering plates with melon and raspberry coulee to all the guests. I hadn't realised how hungry I was until I took my first bite of melon. The tangy combination woke up my taste buds and had me desperate for the next course. I hoped the catering staff would be super-efficient. Not only to quell my appetite, but we had a lot of time to make up and I wanted to dance. The starter plates were whisked away and, with very little gap, plates of chicken, roast potatoes and vegetables were placed in front of us. If Paul had been hoping for any leftovers from me, he was disappointed. I cleared every smear of gravy from my plate. Again there was a good efficient turnaround, and we were soon enjoying our profiteroles. The wedding cake would be served at our mid-dance break, so for now, it was time to clear the tables and let the ceilidh band get set up.

"Come with me," said Paul as he took my hand and led me outside. The rain had finally stopped and rays of sunlight were fighting through the gloom. Clouds were breaking and lifting, forming grand shapes instead of the earlier mass of greyness that filled the sky. Lochcala really was a beautiful place. I leaned against my husband and sighed. Jo and Matt joined us. "Let's get some outside photographs," suggested Jo. "I'll get Craig and the rest of the bridal party."

Craig soon appeared and positioned us with the harbour as our backdrop. Paul put his arm around me, and Jo, Matt, Lauren, Lynn and Carol positioned themselves around us. "We need to get you and Andrew in the photo too," I said to Craig. He shouted to someone in the tent and Dad came out to take the pictures. Craig and Andrew joined our grouping. I noticed Andrew made sure he was next to Lauren. More people came outside as they realised the rain had stopped. There were so many phones pointed in our direction. After a few minutes, most people meandered back inside. But just before I entered the marquee, I looked back at the harbour and up to the castle. I still felt a pang of regret that these views weren't in our official photos. As I continued to gaze at the castle, Paul leaned in to kiss me, a soft, tender kiss. A kiss that was annoyingly brought to an abrupt end as Craig pushed in between us.

"Check this out," he said, holding his camera so we could see the display. I gasped, "Wow! Craig! They are amazing." He had captured a couple of candid photos of us. One caught me looking out to the harbour, while Paul looked at me. And the second was the kiss he'd interrupted. But the amazing thing in both photographs was the sun beam glistening in the background between us. These photos would be getting framed.

A shout from the marquee let us know the band was ready to start. Rather than beginning with a traditional waltz, we had requested to get right into the ceilidh dances with a St Bernard's Waltz. The band started up the first tune, and the caller reached for the microphone. "Ladies and Gentlemen please welcome your bride and groom to the dance floor." We walked out to the flash of cameras and phones and the sound of cheers and whistles. My fabulous wedding dress was about to get tested. Hopefully the button securing my train would hold.

Could it handle a ceilidh? Paul twirled me twice, then pulled me in and held me tightly, ready to begin our first dance. I held his right hand and placed my left arm round his waist. I loved the feeling of his tweed jacket against my arm. The scent of his aftershave pulled me closer. I was looking forward to my first dance with my husband. We flowed round the dance floor twice and then the caller invited the rest of the wedding party to join us. I looked around as my best friends and close family all joined in the St Bernard's Waltz. As the music ended, Paul leaned me back in his arms, then brought me up to kiss me. I put my arms round his neck and laughed.

Next up, I danced with my dad. "I'm so proud of you," he said, as we circled round the floor to the tune of the Canadian Barn Dance.

"Thanks, Dad."

"You've done wonders for your mum over the last few months. She's been much easier to live with. It's been good for her to have the wedding to focus on." Dancing with my dad at my wedding wasn't the right time to discuss family dynamics, but once again, I felt a pang of pity for Mum. Maybe I should invite her to Glasgow more often. Maybe even get both of them down for a weekend of city living. Before I could get lost in my thoughts, Dad spun me round extra fast and had me laughing and enjoying the fun of dancing with him.

Outside, the sunbeams were beating back the clouds and brightening the evening sky. The rivulets of water that had been running down the plastic windows had now dried up and the summer evening light lit up the harbour and beyond, to the silhouette of the castle.

The dance floor was getting busier and busier with each dance. All around me were smiling faces, glowing in the evening sun and in the exertion of the dancing. The ceilidh band wasn't the most charismatic band ever, but it didn't matter. Everyone was here to party. It was another reminder that you don't need perfection to experience perfection.

PAUL

Despite the joy of the wedding, there were two irritants which were detracting from the day. First, there was the background worry about whether James would turn up. And second, every time I saw Lauren, Andrew was right beside her. He'd even switched places with Craig so he could be the one next to her at the meal. And there he was again, sitting next to her. I glared at Andrew. Did I need to intervene? I didn't want to fall out with him over my sister. But if he kept pushing it, I would.

After a few more dances, I decided I needed to act. Just as I approached them, the caller announced the last dance before the break would be a Dashing White Sergeant. "Great," cried Lauren, as I approached her and Andrew. "We already have our three people for the dance." She grabbed my hand and Andrew's and led us to the dance floor.

Kirsty, Jo and Matt ran over to join us and took their positions across from us. This would be a fun set if I wasn't so annoyed at Andrew. The dance started and our set took off for a count of eight. Going faster and faster with each count, my annoyance at Andrew was momentarily replaced by the energy and excitement of the dance. As we progressed round to meet our new set, we had to slow down as this line of three comprised older people. With the slower speed, Lauren spoke to me as we danced together. "What are you doing?" she hissed.

"What do you mean?"

"You know exactly what I mean. You've got your big brother's face on. Back off. I don't need you to step in." Before I could respond, she turned round to dance with Andrew. During our next spin, she continued with, "I know Andrew's type and I know how to look after myself." She skipped over to spin with Andrew. Back to me. "Don't you think I've learned how to take care of myself?" Then she was back to Andrew. And as the three of us came back into line, she finished with, "I'm fine. You don't need to protect me." And then she smiled.

"But thank you for caring." And with our next progression, we were back to a younger set and faster dancing. Lauren had reassured me and put me in my place with amazing efficiency. Sometimes I forget how capable and strong she is. Much like Mum.

When the band brought the dance to its conclusion, we were near the marquee entrance. Andrew broke off first and marched towards the doorway. I couldn't understand why he was storming off until I looked over and saw James staggering at the entrance. Lauren and I followed. By the time we reached them, Andrew had already placed his hand on James' chest to stop him from coming any further inside. "Out," he growled to his brother. James was no match for his older brother and had no choice but to retreat.

"What are you doing here?" Andrew asked once we were outside.

"It's my baby sister's wedding. I was invited. So here I am."

"You're too late," continued Andrew. "And you're drunk. Why don't you go back home and sleep it off?"

"No, I want to see Kirsty."

I stood silently to the side, not sure what to do. I didn't want to intervene and make matters worse, but I wasn't willing to walk away in case things escalated and James managed to get anywhere near Kirsty. Lauren darted back into the marquee and returned with Kirsty's dad and Craig.

Mr Price silently walked over to James and took hold of his arm. "Come on, son. We'll take you home." Before the Price men could leave the harbour, Kirsty came rushing out from the tent. "What's going on?" she asked, taking in the scene before her.

James broke away from Andrew's hold. "Kirsty! It's your wedding day and I wanted to come and see you."

As James approached Kirsty, I was ready to step in his way, but she cast me a sideways glance and held her hand out to me. I took it and stood beside her. She turned her full attention back to James. "It's not a good idea for you to be here, James. Hopefully the next time we're in Lochcala we'll see you." Her quietly spoken words stopped him in his tracks. The look of defiance slipped and his shoulders slumped. Andrew and Craig came either side of him and guiding him away before anything more could be said.

"We'll take him home," said Kirsty's dad, looking over at us. "You go back inside. We'll be back in a few minutes."

Lauren returned to the marquee and Kirsty put her arm around my waist as we watched her dad and brothers walk away, an overwhelming sense of peace settling over us. Misguided romantic notions would say I should have confronted James and defended my bride. But the situation had played out perfectly with Kirsty and her dad dealing with James.

I placed my finger on her chin and turned her gaze to me. "Are you okay?"

"Surprisingly, yes. I can't believe how at peace I feel. Being a peacemaker isn't always easy but then you experience moments like this."

I hugged her to my side and placed a kiss on her hair. As we turned to go back into the marquee, I paused, my eyes drawn to the castle. Looking at those ancient ruins a plan formed in my mind. I may not have been the person to deal with James, but maybe there was something else I could do for my bride. Back in the marquee I went in search of Matt.

JENNIFER

During the first half of the evening, I had enjoyed a few of the less energetic dances. And the girls had a great time dancing with their dad and Ben. Now the supper break had been called, my family regrouped around our table. Rolls and sausage were laid out on a serving table, as well as slices of cake. Rather than consume a whole roll each, I selected three and cut them up for us to share and selected five pieces of cake. The cake was a traditional wedding fruit cake, but thankfully it was moist and delicious. The food was plentiful and tasty; whereas the catering size cups didn't offer nearly enough tea and I required several refills.

Scott glanced over at me as I rubbed my sides and tried to hide the yawn that was building, a concerned frown shadowing his face. Before I could reassure him I was fine, Jo came bounding over to me. "Hey, I hope you're doing okay, Jennifer?" I nodded my reply. "Would you two be willing to be part of a surprise for Kirsty?"

"What did you have in mind?"

"Well, the rain has finally stopped. And, as the reception needs to finish early because of the landslide diversion. Paul suggested a group of us get together up at the castle later."

"That sounds like a lovely idea." I glanced over at Scott and nodded. "We'd love to be part of that. I'll see if Ben and Tara can take the girls back to the holiday house."

The thought of the extra surprise for Kirsty and the supper gave me renewed energy. I didn't want to miss out on any part of this special day due to baby tiredness. I rubbed my bump as I finished my tea.

KIRSTY

The day was disappearing too quickly! I danced every dance. Spoke to as many people as I could. And posed for countless photos and selfies. By the time I scoffed a slice of wedding cake, I was ready for the second half of our ceilidh. Andrew, Craig and Dad entered the marquee just as the caller announced we would resume our dancing with another Dashing White Sergeant. I ran over to them and grabbed Andrew and Craig, pulling them on to the dance floor. As we twirled and skipped our way through the reel, we laughed and joked together. When the dance ended, Andrew and Craig linked their arms and twirled me round and round. Once again, my thoughts returned to the canvas in the church manse. It was only a few months since I read the words, 'blessed are the peacemakers, for they will be called children of God.' And now look at us. Things with Mum, Dad and Andrew weren't perfect, but it was definitely better. Was it due to a lack of faith that I hadn't believed change was possible, or was it because I'd held on to past hurts? Whatever the reason, the last few months had taught me change was possible. I hugged my brothers and was just about to get a drink when one of my uncles asked me to dance. After the Canadian Barn Dance, a progressive dance, so I got to dance with lots of male guests, I went in search of my husband. But I couldn't see him anywhere, or Matt, Andrew or Craig. Where were they all? Before I could give it any more thought, Brian asked me to dance.

A couple of dances later, I spotted the four of them walking into the marquee. Where had they been and what were they up to? As soon as the current Virginia Reel came to its end, I rushed over to my husband. I still giggled every time I called him that. "Where have you lot been?"

Paul put his arms around me and pulled me in close. "We were just enjoying the evening air, although the midges are biting now the rain has cleared."

It wasn't the most convincing of answers, but I was intent on dancing with him rather than quizzing him. The caller announced a waltz, and we took to the dance floor. I guess if you know how to waltz, they might be enjoyable, but they are so boring compared to other dances. Although, when you're locked in the arms of your husband, they can be very romantic. As we danced, Paul nuzzled into my neck and complimented my choice of wedding dress. He drew his fingers over my bare back and I melted against him, looking forward to a lifetime of dances with my groom.

After three more dances, the caller announced the last dance of our reception. "Take your partners for your final dance of the evening. At the Bride's request we're finishing with the Orcadian Strip The Willow." Paul and I walked on to the dance floor hand-in-hand. I loved we were ending our wedding with my favourite dance. As the bride and groom, we got the prime first-couple position. The music started, and we spun together as fast as we could for a count of sixteen, and then we were off, I skipped out to each man in the line, while Paul spun with the next woman in the line and then we met in the middle. We twirled, spun and laughed our way along, both of us gasping for breath by the time we reached the end.

Today had been brilliant. But it had flown by. I couldn't believe it was the last dance already. Thankfully, several people had been capturing video clips throughout the day, mementos of the people who were here and the fun we shared. But now wasn't a time to get sad. There were still minutes remaining and I wanted to enjoy every one of them.

Paul

The Orcadian Strip the Willow finished just as Matt and Jo completed their turn. The four of us stood together out of breath and cheeks glowing from the exertion of the fast paced dance. As the final notes played out, the caller spoke into the microphone. "Ladies and Gentlemen, please gather round your bride and groom for Auld Lang Syne." I took Kirsty's hand and led her into the middle of the circle that linked around us. Tiny little tears of joy sprang up in the corners of her eyes. As we sang the last verse, our guests came rushing into the middle where we stood. I wrapped Kirsty in my arms. From Auld Lang Syne, the band went into 'Loch Lomond'. We were joined in the middle by our parents and the bridal party. I kept my arms around Kirsty and gazed into her eyes as we slow danced while all our friends and family jumped and shouted around us. This time, as the song came to its conclusion, I took advantage of another opportunity to kiss my beautiful bride.

Eventually, I pulled away and those around us cheered. Even now, Kirsty blushed with the attention. I ran my thumb over her reddened cheeks and winked at her. She smiled back and laughed.

A group hug ensued, as our Glasgow friends all said their farewells and boarded the bus. As soon as they left, Craig, Andrew and Matt strode up to us. Matt coughed for attention. "Ladies and Gentlemen, your bride and groom are now leaving." To the cheers and applause of the remaining guests, we were shuffled outside. With the broken clouds, the tiniest hint of light played in the sky. I kept a tight hold of Kirsty's hand and led her to Andrew's Land Rover. She hesitated. "I don't understand. Where is our car?"

"We have something lined up, but it's a surprise, so you'll just need to trust us." She glanced between me, Andrew and Craig and then climbed into the back of Andrew's 4x4. Andrew slowly pulled away from the harbour as our guests all waved and cheered. He crawled along the quiet streets of Lochcala before eventually ascending to the castle ruin and parking next to our hire car. As soon as Andrew turned off the engine, Jo opened Kirsty's door and handed her raincoat and trainers. "You need to put these on or your shoes will get ruined." Kirsty gave a nervous laugh as she took the items. When she was ready, I helped her from the car and led her towards the castle. I walked slowly, letting the others get into position. As we turned the corner, Kirsty gasped. We had set up the area the way it had been for our engagement. Poles held up a canopy of fairy lights, shining against the darkening shades of twilight. Travel rugs lay scattered underneath the lights. And standing next to it all were Jo, Matt, Lynn, Carol, Lauren, Andrew, Craig, Scott and Jennifer.

"Who did this?" whispered Kirsty. "Is this why you guys disappeared earlier?"

I leaned over and kissed her cheek. "We wanted you to have your castle reception."

"You guys, this is amazing! Thank you all so much."

Craig had his camera ready and took several photographs of us at the castle before we sat down on the rugs, huddling in together, the lights twinkled above us. And beyond them, several stars were now adding their far-off sparkle. The rain of the last twenty-four hours had stirred up the scents of summer, from the smell of the ground to the nearby pine trees and the wildflowers that brightened the grass. Lauren sat her phone in the middle of the circle and put on her cheesy wedding playlist.

But the best thing was sitting with my arm around my wife. I laughed at the thought of Kirsty wearing a raincoat with her wedding dress, simply because she knew it was unexpected and a tease. Don't tell her, but I am warming to raincoats, or maybe it's just the woman inside this pink raincoat. The first time I saw Kirsty, she was in a raincoat and big sunglasses, hiding behind whatever mask she could find. But now look at her. Next to me was a woman who was learning confidence. A woman who was teaching me the wonder of faith and love, joy and peace. My wife.

Kirsty

My wedding day hadn't gone to plan, but it had been perfect. As with the stories at my hen weekend, the things that had gone wrong today would be our funny stories in the future.

I shivered as the cool night air blew around us. "Time to go?" whispered Paul. I nodded my agreement. He stood up and pulled me up beside him and everyone else stood. Jennifer rubbed her sides. She looked tired. We walked over and hugged Jennifer and Scott. "Thank you for everything," I said. "For teaching us and showing us what it means to love God with our heart, mind and soul." Jennifer brushed away a tear and smiled.

The rest of the group formed an archway for us to run through, their arms held high. Andrew and Craig, my brothers, who had worked so hard to ensure I had the best day possible.

Lynn and Carol, my stable, supportive friends. Lauren, my new sister, someone who would teach me how to be more self-assured. Jo and Matt our best friends. Our forever friends.

Paul and I laughed as we ran through their archway to our car. We turned round and waved. As I started the engine, I looked round at Paul. "So, husband, are you ready to begin married life?"

His kiss told me he was more than ready!

THE END

Acknowledgements

Thank you so much to everyone who has helped in bringing this book to print. Your input and encouragement is truly valued.

Innes, Calum, Cameron and Cara. Thank you so much my fab wee family for being part of this journey. And thank you for always cheering me on.

Thanks to the Raincoats & Wedding Dresses 'first responders' team. To Lorna, Joy, Fiona, Joan, Stacy and Innes. Your insight and feedback challenged me, inspired me and encouraged me.

Thanks to Tanya Rochat. Once again, you have produced a stunning cover.

And thank you to you, the reader, for buying this book and encouraging an aspiring author. Enjoy

xxx

A couple of notes about Raincoats & Wedding Dresses:

Jennifer listens to a song called 'She's Fearless' in her house. It's by Scott Nicol, a good friend of mine and a fab singer – check out his website www.scottnicol.us

And, just in case any of you try to find Lochcala on a map, I'm afraid to tell you it's made up! But it is inspired by some of the beautiful harbour villages of Argyll.

Keep In Touch

Check out my website for further information and my online shop. Why not sign up to receive regular newsletters?

www.carolinejohnston.co.uk

Follow me on social media for updates and news:

www.facebook.com/carolinejohnstonauthor

www.twitter.com/author_caroline

www.instagram.com/carolinej_author